CARAMEL PECAN ROLL MURDER

"Here we go!" Mike said, jumping to Sonny's boat. "You can let go now, Hannah."

Norman cut his speed and got behind Sonny's boat. Hannah watched as Mike moved between the seats and reached Sonny, who was still slumped over the wheel in exactly the same position.

Neither Hannah nor Norman said a word as they watched Mike leaning over Sonny. Both men seemed frozen in their positions for a moment, and then Mike cut the motor on Sonny's fishing boat.

Hannah's cell phone began to ring, and she answered quickly. "Mike, is everything okay?"

"No. I need you and Norman to go back to the Inn and get Doc. And if Doc's got a patient, you can tell him that there's no need to hurry."

"Does that mean Sonny is . . ."

"Yes. You can tell Doc I'm calling the crime scene boys and I'd like him to get out to establish the time of death before they arrive."

"Then Sonny was . . . murdered?"

"Sure looks like it to me . . ."

Books by Joanne Fluke

Hannah Swensen Mysteries
CHOCOLATE CHIP COOKIE MURDER
STRAWBERRY SHORTCAKE MURDER
BLUEBERRY MUFFIN MURDER
LEMON MERINGUE PIE MURDER
FUDGE CUPCAKE MURDER
SUGAR COOKIE MURDER
PEACH COBBLER MURDER
CHERRY CHEESECAKE MURDER
KEY LIME PIE MURDER
CANDY CANE MURDER
CARROT CAKE MURDER
CREAM PUFF MURDER
PLUM PUDDING MURDER
APPLE TURNOVER MURDER
DEVIL'S FOOD CAKE MURDER
GINGERBREAD COOKIE MURDER
CINNAMON ROLL MURDER
RED VELVET CUPCAKE MURDER
BLACKBERRY PIE MURDER
DOUBLE FUDGE BROWNIE MURDER
WEDDING CAKE MURDER
CHRISTMAS CARAMEL MURDER
BANANA CREAM PIE MURDER
RASPBERRY DANISH MURDER
CHRISTMAS CAKE MURDER
CHOCOLATE CREAM PIE MURDER
CHRISTMAS SWEETS
COCONUT LAYER CAKE MURDER
CHRISTMAS CUPCAKE MURDER
TRIPLE CHOCOLATE CHEESECAKE MURDER
CARAMEL PECAN ROLL MURDER
PINK LEMONADE CAKE MURDER
JOANNE FLUKE'S LAKE EDEN COOKBOOK

Suspense Novels
VIDEO KILL
WINTER CHILL
DEAD GIVEAWAY
THE OTHER CHILD
COLD JUDGMENT
FATAL IDENTITY
FINAL APPEAL
VENGEANCE IS MINE
EYES
WICKED
DEADLY MEMORIES
THE STEPCHILD

Published by Kensington Publishing Corp.

CARAMEL PECAN ROLL MURDER

JOANNE FLUKE

Kensington Publishing Corp.
www.kensingtonbooks.com

This book is dedicated to my friend,
Linda Raphael Jessup.
We miss you, Lyn!

Acknowledgments

Grateful thanks to my extended family for putting up with me while I was writing this book.

Hugs to Trudi Nash and her husband, David, for being brave enough to taste several of my recipes and even try them out on their kids. And to Trudi, who came up with the Special Boursin Cheese-Filled Mushrooms recipe.

Thank you to my friends and neighbors: Mel & Kurt, Gina, Dee Appleton, Jay, Richard Jordan, Laura Levine, the real Nancy and Heiti, Dan, Mark & Mandy at Faux Library, Daryl and her staff at Groves Accountancy, Gene and Ron at SDSA, and my friends at HomeStreet Bank.

Hugs to my Minnesota friends: Lois Meister, Bev & Jim, Val, RuthAnn, Dorothy & Sister Sue, and Mary & Jim.

Big hugs to my editor, John Scognamiglio. His patience seems endless and his suggestions are insightful and incredibly helpful.

Hugs for Meg Ruley and the staff at the Jane Rotrosen Agency for their constant support and sage advice.

Thanks to all the wonderful people at Kensington Publishing who keep Hannah sleuthing and baking yummy goodies.

Thank you to Robin in Production, and Larissa in Publicity.
Both of you go above and beyond to support the Hannah books.
Thanks to Hiro Kimura for his delicious caramel pecan rolls on the cover.
I wish mine looked exactly like that!

Thank you to Lou Malcangi at Kensington for designing all of Hannah's gorgeous book covers. They're deliciously wonderful.

Thanks to John at *Placed4Success* for Hannah's movie and TV placements, his presence on Hannah's social media, and for being my son.

Thanks to Tami Chase for designing and managing my website at **www.JoanneFluke.com** and for giving support to all of Hannah's social media.

Thank you to Kathy Allen for making the recipes and giving them their final test.

A big hug to JQ for helping Hannah and me for so many happy years.

Kudos to Beth and her phalanx of sewing machines for her gorgeous embroidery on Hannah's hats, visors, aprons, and tote bags.

Thank you to food stylist, friend, and media guide Lois Brown for her expertise with the launch parties at Poisoned Pen in Scottsdale, AZ, and baking for the TV food segments at KPNX in Phoenix.

Thanks also to Destry, the lovely, totally unflappable producer and host of *Arizona Midday*.

Hugs to Debbie R. for expert help with social media and thank you to everyone who's joined Team Swensen.

Thank you to Dr. Rahhal, Dr. Umali, Dr. and Cathy Line, Dr. Levy, Dr. Koslowski, and Drs. Ashley and Lee for answering my book-related medical and dental questions.

Hugs to all the Hannah fans who read the books, share their family recipes, post on my Facebook page, **Joanne Fluke Author**, and watch the Hannah movies.

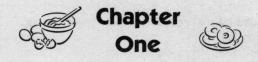

Chapter One

Hannah Swensen took the last pan of Butterscotch Delight Cookies out of her industrial oven and placed them on shelves in the bakers rack. She was almost through with the baking she did every morning for her customers at The Cookie Jar, her bakery and coffee shop. One glance at the clock on the kitchen wall told Hannah that she had plenty of time for a bracing cup of coffee from the kitchen pot before she had to bake the final batches of sweet treats she needed for the day.

As she was pouring her coffee, the phone on the kitchen wall rang. Rather than wait for her partner, Lisa Herman Beeseman, or Lisa's Aunt Nancy to answer it, Hannah decided to do it. "The Cookie Jar," she answered. "This is Hannah."

"Hannah!" The man's voice on the other end of the line sounded slightly breathless. "Did Earl come in for coffee this morning?"

"Hold on, Mike. I'll check," Hannah said, recognizing the voice of her friend, Winnetka County Detective Mike Kingston. "Is something wrong?"

"I'll say! I've got a mess out here on the highway and I need Earl to come out with the tow truck."

"A wreck?"

"More than one. Some idiot with a fishing boat jack-knifed it coming out of the Corner Tavern. Somebody from Iowa was going too fast and hit him, another driver rear-ended the guy from Iowa, and there's going to be more if Lonnie and I don't get this cleaned up fast."

"Hold on. Let me see if Earl's here." Hannah hurried to the swinging restaurant-style door that led from the kitchen to the coffee shop and pushed it open. Earl Flensburg and his wife, Carrie, were sitting at a table in the back having coffee and several of Hannah's freshly baked confections. She motioned to Earl, and when he came into the kitchen, she handed him the phone. "It's Mike. Trouble on the highway."

"What's going on?" Earl asked, taking the phone from Hannah. He listened for a moment and then he gave a little nod. "Okay, I got it," he said. "Carrie's here and we're coming."

Earl handed the phone back to Hannah. "Mike wanted to know if Digger's here. When I said he was, Mike said to tell him he needs Digger too."

Hannah shivered. The chill she felt had nothing to do with the temperature of the kitchen. "Somebody died?"

Earl shook his head. "No. Mike just wants Digger to get out there with the hearse to slow down the traffic that's coming from Minneapolis."

Hannah understood immediately. Digger Gibson was the local undertaker and there was something about a big black hearse on the road that brought home the fact that people were not immortal. The sight of Digger's hearse caused traffic to slow down and drive more carefully. The Minnesota Highway Patrol called Digger every year when fishing season opened, and Digger drove the stretch from Minneapolis to Lake Eden multiple times on opening day to slow the traffic and prevent accidents. This year Digger would do double duty, patrolling the highway on the official opening of the fishing season, and now it seemed that Digger would have to go out one week early for the first day of the Walleye Fishing Tournament that was being held at the Lake Eden Inn.

"Will you ask Lisa to put on another big pot of coffee?" Hannah asked Earl. "I'll pack up some cookies back here, and you and Carrie can take them out there."

"Will do," Earl said, going back out the door to the coffee shop.

As Hannah packed up the cookies, she thought about the fishing tournament. It wasn't due to start until tomorrow, but it seemed that some contestants were arriving early. This was a slow time of year at the Lake Eden Inn, and Hannah knew that the owners, Sally and Dick Laughlin, were grateful to Wally Wallace for choosing to hold his fishing tournament at their hotel.

Wally was practically a Minnesota legend. When he'd taken over the boat-building business from his father-in-law he had turned it into a huge success. Wallace Watercraft was a money-making enterprise and Wally Boats were popular fishing crafts all over the country. Once Wally had achieved success with his fishing boats, he had opened a chain of sporting goods stores that were popular nationwide. When tourists from other states came to Minnesota, one of the attractions that they wanted to visit was Wally's flagship sporting goods store.

Wally Wallace took his popularity seriously. He understood that being a business tycoon came with a certain responsibility. Wally funded charities, established college scholarships, provided entry-level jobs for countless Minnesota teenagers, and sponsored sports events. When the local high school football team, the Jordan High Gulls, had needed new uniforms and equipment, all it had taken was a letter to Wally and the uniforms were designed and delivered. Of course the uniforms had the Wally's Sporting Goods logo on the back, but that was fine with everyone concerned.

Because of Wally's generosity, everyone in Minnesota was willing to bend the rules a bit for him. If Wally asked for a favor, it was very likely to be granted. Just recently, Wally had managed to obtain early fishing licenses for everyone who had signed up for his Walleye Fishing Tournament. The early, temporary fishing licenses were only good for the duration of the competition and were limited to fishing on Eden Lake.

Of course Wally's tournament had been well advertised, and the last Hannah had heard, Sally and Dick were close to running out of rooms.

When Hannah had finished packaging cookies, she took them out to Lisa and Aunt Nancy. Then she got back to work to complete the day's baking.

It didn't take long to thaw the puff pastry dough she planned to use for her Danish. Once she'd rolled out the dough and cut it into the required-size pieces, she placed them on a baking sheet and began to make the Lemon Curd. Today's special treat would be Lemon Danish and she could hardly wait to sample them.

Hannah flipped her loose-leaf recipe book to her Great-Grandmother Elsa's recipe, got out a saucepan, and followed the directions her great-grandmother had written. She would fill the Danish with Lemon Curd and once they were baked, she'd drizzle a bit of powdered sugar frosting over the tops.

The Lemon Curd turned out to be easy to make, and Hannah had just pulled it off the stovetop and was giving it a final stir when there was a knock on her back kitchen door.

"Norman," she said aloud, smiling as she recognized the knock. She pulled open the door without bothering to look through the peephole that Mike and Lonnie had insisted on installing, and said, "Come in and have a seat."

"I can only stay for a couple of minutes," Norman said, hanging his jacket on a hook by the back door and walking to the work station to take his favorite stool.

"Do you have time for coffee?"

"Just one cup. I need to pick up some cookies to take to Mike."

"You have time, then. I already sent the cookies out to Mike with Earl and Carrie."

"Mike knew that, but he just called me to ask me to bring out more. Another four cars couldn't stop in time. It's turning into a big accident scene, Hannah."

"Oh, dear!" Hannah poured a cup of coffee for Norman and walked over to the bakers rack to see what she could send with him. "Is anyone badly injured?"

"Mike said it wasn't that bad yet. He was just worried that the situation might escalate."

"That's always a possibility." Hannah removed several trays of cookies and began to package them. "Does Mike want more coffee?"

"He said it couldn't hurt. I'll go tell Lisa."

"Okay." Hannah finished packaging the cookies for

Mike and packed up a half-dozen for Norman. As she turned, she glanced out the kitchen window and began to frown.

"What's wrong?" Norman asked, coming back in from the coffee shop.

"It looks like rain outside."

"I know."

"Let's just hope it blows over."

"That's exactly what Mike said. Rain is the last thing we need at the scene of an accident." Norman walked back to his stool at the work station and picked up his coffee cup. "It's lonely in the mornings without you, Hannah. I guess I'm getting too used to having you stay with me."

Warning bells went off in Hannah's head and she refrained from saying anything at all. It was cozy and comfortable staying with Norman, and she loved the fireplace in the master bedroom. Still, it was temporary and she missed living at her condo. Having Norman move to the guest bedroom made her feel guilty. If only the bad memories would fade for her and for Moishe, she could go back to her own place.

"Did you feed the cats?" she asked, taking a plate of cookies to the work station and setting them down on the stainless steel surface.

"Of course I did. Moishe wouldn't let me forget to feed him! And come to think about it, neither would Cuddles. I think she's learned a trick or two from Moishe, because she's not happy unless she gets her breakfast on time."

Hannah began to smile. Her cat, twenty-three-pound Moishe, demanded his breakfast and howled about it if he didn't get it soon enough. He also demanded his treats when they got home from work, his bedtime snack of fish-shaped, salmon-flavored kitty cookies, and his daily ration of tuna. "I think we've raised two spoiled cats."

"I think you're right." Norman reached out for a cookie. "What are these, Hannah?"

"Butterscotch Delight Cookies."

"They're pretty with that drizzle of icing on top." Norman bit into his cookie and began to smile. "And they're really good! Do you mind if I take the rest of these with me, Hannah?"

"I don't mind at all. Just save some for you and don't let Mike eat them all."

"I won't. I'll go get the coffee from Lisa and head out to the highway, then. Do you want me to pick you up from work tonight?"

"Sure. Come over when you're through for the day."

"Dinner at home? Or out?"

Hannah came close to frowning. That sounded a bit too domestic for her. She'd been staying at Norman's house for three weeks now and perhaps it was time to make a change.

"I could use a hamburger," Norman said. "How about one of Rose's patty melts?"

"That sounds good to me," Hannah said quickly.

"Thanks, Hannah. See you later, then." Norman grabbed his jacket, put it on, and opened the back door. "I'll be here by four."

"That's good for me," Hannah told him.

After Norman left, Hannah went back to her baking. The Lemon Curd had cooled enough for her to use it. She'd already spooned on the cream cheese mixture and now it was time for the Lemon Curd. Once each Danish had its Lemon Curd in place, she folded over the corners of the puff pastry, brushed on the egg wash, and sprinkled sugar on top. It didn't take long at all to bake them, and less than a half hour later, she was through baking. She should probably bake another couple of batches of cookies since she'd sent so many out to the accident scene, but she needed a cup of coffee first. Once she'd poured it, she walked back to the work station, sat down on her favorite stool, and gave a long sigh. She hadn't slept well last night and she was tired. Perhaps she'd rest her eyes for a moment and then she'd decide which cookies to make next.

BUTTERSCOTCH DELIGHT COOKIES

DO NOT preheat oven—This cookie dough must chill before baking.

Ingredients:

8 ounces *(2 sticks, ½ pound)* salted butter

⅔ cup white *(granulated)* sugar

⅔ cup brown sugar *(pack it down in the cup when you measure it)*

1 teaspoon salt

2 teaspoons vanilla extract

½ teaspoon baking soda

1 teaspoon baking powder

2 large eggs, beaten *(just whip them up in a glass with a fork)*

3 cups all-purpose flour *(pack it down in the cup when you measure it)*

2 cups butterscotch chips *(I used Nestlé)*

Directions:

Hannah's 1st Note: You can mix these cookies up by hand, but it's easiest with an electric mixer.

Prepare your cookie sheets by spraying them with Pam or another nonstick cooking spray.

Alternatively, you can line your cookie sheets with parchment paper.

Melt the butter in a microwave-safe bowl on HIGH for 1 minute *(60 seconds)*.

Let the melted butter sit in the microwave for an additional minute. If it's not completely melted, microwave it in 20-second increments with 20-second standing times until it is melted.

Set the melted butter on the kitchen counter to let it cool a bit.

Put the white sugar in the bowl of an electric mixer.

Sprinkle the brown sugar on top of the white sugar.

Add the teaspoon of salt.

Turn the mixer on LOW and mix until the sugars and salt are well blended.

With the mixer still running on LOW speed, add the 2 teaspoons of vanilla extract, then mix it in.

With the mixer still running on LOW speed, add the baking soda and the baking powder. Mix thoroughly.

Add the eggs, mixing after each addition.

Shut off the mixer and scrape down the inside of the mixing bowl.

Turn the mixer back on LOW speed again and add the melted butter.

Mix the melted butter in thoroughly.

Measure out the flour and add it to your mixing bowl in half-cup increments, mixing thoroughly after each addition.

Turn off the mixer, scrape down the sides of the bowl, and take the bowl out of the mixer.

Use a mixing spoon to mix in the 2 cups of butterscotch chips *(that's one 12-ounce package)*. Give the cookie dough a final stir by hand.

Cover the dough with a piece of plastic wrap and set it in the refrigerator to chill.

Let the cookie dough chill for at least 45 minutes. *(Overnight is fine too.)*

When you're ready to bake your cookies, preheat your oven to 375 degrees F., rack in the middle position. Leave your cookie dough in the refrigerator until your oven has come up to baking temperature.

Take your cookie dough out of the refrigerator and use a spoon or a 2-teaspoon scooper to transfer balls of dough to your prepared cookie sheets, 12 cookies to a standard-sized cookie sheet.

Bake your Butterscotch Delight Cookies at 375 degrees F. for 10 to 14 minutes. (*Mine took 12 minutes.*)

When your cookies are done, take them out of the oven and place them on cold stovetop burners or wire racks. Let them cool on the cookie sheets for at least 3 minutes and then remove them to wire racks to complete cooling.

Yield: 2 and ½ to 3 dozen soft, butterscotchy cookies that everyone will love.

Hannah's 2nd Note: These cookies are good just the way they are, but if you want to decorate them a bit, mix up the Powdered Sugar Drizzle recipe and drizzle a bit over each cookie. The Powdered Sugar Drizzle recipe is given on the following page.

POWDERED SUGAR DRIZZLE

Ingredients:

> 1 cup powdered sugar *(pack it down in the cup when you measure it)*
> 1 teaspoon vanilla extract
> 2 to 4 Tablespoons of milk *(if needed for consistency)*

Directions:

Place the sugar and vanilla in a bowl.

Starting with 2 Tablespoons of milk, mix everything together until it's of the proper consistency. If it's too thick, add more milk until it's the consistency of a drizzle. If it's too thin, add more powdered sugar.

Use a spoon from your silverware drawer to drizzle the mixture over your cooled cookies. You can also use a pastry bag, or you can squeeze it out through the nozzle of a squeeze bottle.

Hannah's Note: If you're old enough, you may remember the refillable squeeze bottles lunch counters and diners used to use for mus-

tard and ketchup. You can buy clean, fresh squeeze bottles like that at places like Smart and Final or any cooking supply store. Then all you have to do is take off the top and cut off the tip of the nozzle to use it to drizzle the frosting over your cookies.

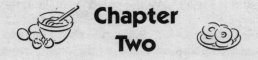

Chapter Two

It was a movie of the past few months of her life and Hannah didn't want to watch it. And even though she was more than reticent, she took a seat in the empty theater and sat down. Her favorite song was playing on the soundtrack, the song she'd thought of as their song. Tears began to form in her eyes, but not enough to shed them.

They stood there on the balcony of a Las Vegas hotel, and she shivered slightly even though his arms were warm around her. It was quiet, the early silence that comes before dawn. The sunrise was coming, but the sky was dark and inky black, the black of loss, the black of supreme tragedy.

And slowly enough to be almost imperceptible, a faint hint of colors began to appear on the horizon. The sun was preparing to rise and with it would come the sorrows of the day, the day that she had promised to go to the airport with him to say goodbye.

"I love to watch the sunrise," he said softly. "It's like a resurrection for me. I can forget the mistakes I made in the past because everything is fresh and new again. And if I try, I have the power to make it the best day of my life."

Hannah didn't say anything. She didn't have to. She simply turned and kissed him as the music came to a crescendo and the screen shifted to the next scene.

One more kiss and he was walking away through the checkpoint, leaving her with tears in her eyes that threatened to spill down her cheeks. She stood there, unable to force her legs to move for several minutes, and then, finally, she turned away. He was gone and she felt bereft.

Hannah sighed. She'd never felt so alone. She knew he was coming back in a week, but that didn't really help right now. Ross was gone and she felt desolate.

"Excuse me, miss." One of the TSA agents, the one Ross had talked to while he was waiting for his shoes and carry-on, approached her. "Please come with me."

"Come with you . . . where?"

"To the scanner."

"But . . . I'm not flying anywhere. I just came here to see someone . . ." Hannah paused as she spotted Ross on the other side of the scanner. "There he is, the man I brought to the airport. What's happening?"

"It'll be fine," the agent said, smiling at her. "Just follow me, please."

Ross was beckoning to her. If he wanted her to follow the TSA agent, she would. The agent led her to the scanner, and he motioned for Ross to come through. "You'd better ask her in a hurry," he said to Ross. "Your flight leaves in ten minutes."

Ross hurried through the scanner and folded his arms around Hannah. "I couldn't leave without asking you," he told her.

"Without asking me what?"

Ross took both of her hands in his and dropped

to one knee. "Hannah Louise Swensen . . . will you marry me?"

"Oh!" Hannah gasped. Suddenly, her knees began to shake and then she was kneeling on the floor by Ross. His arms closed around her, his lips met hers, and Hannah knew she'd never felt so happy in her whole life.

The kiss seemed to last for eons, but then they heard the sound of applause. Hannah and Ross looked up to see a circle of TSA agents surrounding them and clapping.

The refrain of their song gained volume, and Hannah did her best to swallow the lump in her throat as the scene changed again. It was her wedding day and she was in the back of a garbage truck, stuck in the dumpster where she'd hidden from the killer who'd attempted to make her his next victim. No time to dress in her wedding gown, no time for Michelle and Andrea to do her hair, no time to pack for the Mexican Riviera cruise she'd been awarded for winning the Dessert Chef Contest.

Of course Mike had come through. He'd stopped the garbage truck, he and the driver had extricated her from the depths of the dumpster, and she'd run down the aisle of the church, decorated with butter wrappers, spaghetti sauce, and various unidentified food items clinging to her jeans and sweatshirt.

She still remembered Grandma Knudson's comment. "That's our Hannah," she'd said. The congregation had laughed, Grandma Knudson had taken them down to the church basement for coffee and cookies, and Andrea, Michelle, and their mother had taken Hannah off to the parsonage to get cleaned up and ready to become Ross's bride.

Their honeymoon had been wonderful. There were

new things to see, places to visit, food to eat, and long nights of love to enjoy. Hannah remembered thinking that she'd never been so happy. But it hadn't lasted, at least not that long.

Less than a month later, Hannah had come home from work to find Ross gone. No note, no message on her answer phone, just his missing suitcases and most of his clothes. She'd been panic-stricken. What had happened to him? Mike and Norman had calmed her down and promised to find out what had happened to Ross.

Mike, and his detectives, had done exactly that. Hannah felt tears roll down her cheeks as she remembered that awful night when Mike had told her that Ross was married, but it wasn't to her. That Ross had gone back to his legal wife and Hannah's wedding was a fake.

And then, an even harder blow had struck. Ross had come back, several weeks later, and he'd threatened to kill her if she didn't do exactly what he wanted.

Hannah had believed the hard edge in his voice and the icy coldness in his eyes. She had no doubt that he would have killed her if he had the chance. But Hannah and her friends hadn't given him the chance, and Ross had ended up dead on the carpet in her condo.

Did she still love Ross? There were times when Hannah thought she did, that love couldn't be extinguished that rapidly. Inversely, there were other times when she despised him for duping her, for making her fall in love with him. She had loved him completely, accepting everything he'd told her as truth. He had duped her, betrayed her trust, and Hannah wasn't sure if she could ever love anyone unconditionally again.

"Hannah? What's wrong, Hannah?"

A female voice roused her from her unhappy dream,

and Hannah sat up so fast, she almost tipped over her mug of coffee. "Sally?" she asked, staring at the woman who had come into the kitchen.

"What's wrong, Hannah?" Sally repeated. "You were crying in your sleep. Was it a nightmare?"

Hannah thought fast. She was almost sure that Sally would keep her confidence, but she didn't want to admit she'd been crying over her failed marriage.

"Nothing's wrong," she said quickly. "I fell asleep and I must have had a nightmare."

"Well, I'm glad I came in to wake you up. It must have been a doozy of a dream."

"Oh, it was," Hannah said, thinking fast. "I was dreaming that I ran out of chocolate."

"Good heavens!" Sally began to laugh. "That's awful, Hannah! What would we do without chocolate?"

"We'd all sink into a morass of depression," Hannah replied, regaining her equilibrium and managing a smile. "Did you come to pick up your order of cookies, Sally?"

"I did. Lisa and Aunt Nancy already loaded them into my car. I already had a cup of coffee with them in the coffee shop, but I'd love to have another with you now. I have something I need to talk to you about."

Hannah hurried to the kitchen coffeepot. She refilled her cup for herself and poured fresh coffee for Sally. "Would you like to taste one of my new Lemon Danish?"

"I'd *love* to! I was so busy this morning, I forgot all about breakfast. You know how it is the day before a big event, don't you?"

"Not really. I've never been so busy that I forgot about breakfast."

"Well . . . I had a lot on my mind this morning. It's not going well, Hannah."

"The fishing tournament?"

"That's part of it. I thought I had everything covered. I called in more waitstaff, an extra bartender and bar back for Dick, and two additions to the housekeeping staff."

"It sounds like you're all set."

Sally gave a rueful laugh. "That's what *I* thought. Of course I didn't plan on losing my dessert chef for the entire week of the contest."

"Good heavens!" Hannah was clearly shocked. "That's terrible, Sally! Did he quit?"

"No, he's totally reliable. But neither one of us planned on his mother getting really sick. Dick took him to the airport last night and he flew out to Cleveland. He called me this morning and told me that his mother had emergency surgery."

"I hope she'll be all right."

"He said the doctors told him she came through the surgery just fine, but she'll be hospitalized for most of the week. His sister's coming to take care of her when she gets out of the hospital, but that means I'll be without him for at least a week."

"What are you going to do?"

Sally gave a little shrug. "What *can* I do? I can manage the baking, but I'm going to need someone to help me. That's the reason I sat down and talked to Lisa and Aunt Nancy. I was hoping to hire Aunt Nancy or Marge to help me."

"That makes sense. We can get along just fine here. This is a slow time of year for us."

"That's what Lisa told me, right before she said that they could handle everything here."

"Then you're going to try to hire Marge?"

Sally shook her head. "Not unless there's no other

choice. Marge is a great baker, but she's not used to my kitchen."

"Neither is Lisa or Aunt Nancy."

"I know. That's probably why they suggested that I hire you."

"Me?" Hannah's eyebrows shot up in surprise. "But I do the morning baking here."

"I know, but Aunt Nancy said she'd take over your job and Marge and Jack could help Lisa in the coffee shop. It's only for a half day, Hannah. You'd be free to go right after the noon buffet. Lisa said you don't need to come back here for the afternoon and that they could handle everything at The Cookie Jar. I know Norman's entered as a contestant. You could go out with him in his fishing boat in the afternoons." Sally stopped speaking and gave a little sigh. "What do you say, Hannah? Will you help me out?"

Hannah took a moment to think about it. She could use a change of scenery. Maybe Andrea could come along to help her. She was certain that Andrea would like to meet Wally Wallace and Sonny Bowman, the star of Wally's televised fishing show. Andrea was becoming a big help in the kitchen, assembling ingredients for the recipes, using the industrial mixer, and taking baked goods out of the oven.

"Hannah?"

"Just let me consider it for a minute while I get a Lemon Danish for us."

Hannah walked over to the bakers rack and a few seconds later, she was back. "Try my new Danish, Sally. I want to know if you like it."

Sally took a bite of her Danish and smiled. "It's wonderful, Hannah. I want you to bake these on the first morning, if it's not too much work." Sally stopped speaking and she gave a little sigh. "You will help me out, won't you, Hannah? I can't really handle this all by myself."

Sally was clearly nervous about her answer, and Hannah took pity on her. Sally was a good friend and she was really in a bind with her dessert chef gone for the entire week.

"Of course, I'll pay you for the week, Hannah," Sally told her.

"Yes, I'll do it, if I can ask Andrea to help me. And no, you don't need to pay me. You can give Andrea a small salary if you want to, but I doubt she'll take it. And I owe you one, Sally."

Sally looked puzzled. "Why? You owe me for . . . what?"

"You helped me out when Connie Mac was killed in my kitchen at The Cookie Jar and Mike roped it off with crime tape."

"But . . ."

"No," Hannah interrupted her. "I refuse to take a salary, but I want to enjoy your noon buffet with Andrea. That's payment enough for both of us."

A huge smile spread over Sally's face. Obviously, she was very relieved. "Both you and Andrea? What fun! For the first time since my dessert chef left, I'm feeling really happy!"

It took Hannah more than a split second, but then she had the perfect response. "Then you'll actually give me your Caramel Pecan Roll recipe?"

Sally laughed. "You drive a hard bargain, Hannah, but of course I will. I was going to give it to you anyway."

"Thanks, Sally. Are you going to make them for your breakfast buffet?"

"No, you are, but I'll help you make them on the first day."

"What's going to happen on the first day?" Hannah asked.

"Wally wants the contestants to explore the lake and choose the spots they want to fish. Wally is going to welcome them and have them introduce themselves so everyone knows each other. And when he's through, Sonny is going to explain the rules and tell them when to weigh in."

"So the first day is just to acclimate them?"

"Yes, and to tell them when meals will be served, and explain the tournament judging. It's a social day for the contestants to get them used to the venue and our Lake Eden Inn."

"Is there a special dinner that night?"

"Yes, we're having Walleye with drawn butter and a special dessert."

"And I'm in charge of the special dessert?"

"You got it!" Sally gave her a big smile. "Think of something really phenomenal, Hannah. I have the feeling that most of these fishermen will be dessert hounds."

Hannah thought for a moment and then she gave a nod. "Okay. I've got several things in mind."

"Good. Let me know when you decide and we'll print it on the menu. And I guess that means that you accepted my job offer?"

"Yes. It'll be a change of scenery for me, and I can use that right now. This'll be even easier if you have an extra room you can give me so I can stay at the inn, Sally."

Sally looked puzzled. "Of course I do, but . . . I thought you were happy staying at Norman's house."

"I am. Norman's been great about giving me his master suite and staying in the guest room. It's just that . . ." Hannah's voice trailed off and she winced slightly. "I think the people in Lake Eden are getting the wrong impression about our relationship."

"That's a very politic way of saying that you think everyone suspects you're sleeping with Norman."

"Yes," Hannah admitted. "And it's beginning to really bother me. I don't like being the subject of Lake Eden gossip, and I can't go back to the condo without Moishe."

"He's still afraid to go there?"

"Yes, Norman and I tried to take the cats with us a couple of times, but he's deathly afraid to go up the steps." Hannah stopped and looked sad. "I don't know if he'll ever want to go back home, Sally."

"But you do?"

"Yes, I miss my own home. It's just that I can't bear to leave Moishe behind." Hannah did her best to explain past the lump in her throat at the thought that Moishe might not be able to come home with her.

"So Moishe's happy at Norman's house?"

"Yes. He adores Cuddles. But I can't stay there forever, Sally. I'm . . . well, frankly . . . I'm afraid I'll wear out my welcome. And I love my condo."

"I understand. You want to go home and you can't. Does Norman know that?"

"Yes, and he says he understands how I feel. He told me he wants me to stay with him forever, but . . . I can't do that, Sally."

"Did Norman offer to keep Moishe with him?"

Hannah gave a nod. "Of course he did, but he understands that I can't just leave Moishe there."

"Did Norman offer any kind of a solution to your dilemma?"

"Not yet. Norman thinks Moishe might get over his fear eventually, but we tried to carry him up the stairs a couple of times but it didn't work. The moment Moishe gets close to my stairs, he begin to tremble and make little crying noises. He sounds so pathetic that I don't even want to think about what might happen if we actually took him up the stairs and forced him to go inside!"

"Have you told Sue and Doc Haggaman about it?"

"Yes. They think Moishe will get over his fear if we just keep trying, but I'm not so sure."

Sally took a sip of her coffee. "How about you, Hannah? Are you upset when you climb up the stairs to your condo?"

Hannah swallowed past the lump in her throat. "Yes. I keep remembering the sight of . . . of *him* on the floor."

"You really loved him, didn't you?"

It was more of a statement than a question, and Hannah gave a little sigh. "I did. And then, when I found out what kind of a man he really was, I felt like a fool for believing him! But I still get a lump in my throat when I think about seeing him there, so . . . so . . ."

"I know. We all make mistakes, Hannah. But sometimes an even bigger mistake is not trusting ourselves to love again."

LEMON CURD
(A Stovetop Recipe)

3 whole eggs
4 egg yolks (*save the whites in a mixing bowl and let them come up to room temperature—you'll need them for the meringue*)
½ cup water
⅓ cup lemon juice
1 cup white sugar (*granulated*)
¼ cup cornstarch
1 to 2 teaspoons grated lemon zest
1 Tablespoon butter

Hannah's Note: Using a double boiler makes this recipe foolproof, but if you're very careful and stir constantly so it doesn't scorch, you can make the lemon filling in a heavy saucepan directly on the stove over medium heat.

Put water in the bottom of a double boiler and heat it until it simmers. (*Make sure you don't use too much water—it shouldn't touch the bottom of the double boiler top.*) Off the heat, beat the egg yolks with the whole eggs in the top of the double boiler. Add the ½ cup

water and the lemon juice. Combine sugar and cornstarch in a small bowl and stir until completely blended. Add this to the egg mixture in the top of the double boiler and blend thoroughly.

Place the top of the double boiler over the simmering water and cook, stirring frequently until the Lemon Curd thickens (5 minutes or so).

Lift the top of the double boiler and place it on a cold stovetop burner.

Add the lemon zest and the butter. Stir thoroughly.

If you are using your Lemon Curd for a Lemon Meringue Pie, you can pour it into a pre-baked pie shell while it is hot. Otherwise, let the Lemon Curd cool to room temperature.

When your Lemon Curd is cool, you can use it in Lemon Danish or Miniature Lemon Cheesecakes.

LEMON DANISH

DO NOT preheat your oven yet.
You must do some preparation first.

Hannah's 1ˢᵗ Note: Frozen puff pastry dough is good for all sorts of things. When you buy it for this recipe, buy 2 packages. You'll only use one package in this recipe, but keep that second package in your freezer for later. Thaw it when you want to dress up leftovers by putting them inside little puff pastry packets and baking them, or make some turnovers from fresh fruit. Puff pastry can also be used for appetizers.

The Pastry:

One 17.5-ounce package frozen puff pastry dough (*I used Pepperidge Farm, which contains 2 sheets of puff pastry*)

1 large egg

1 Tablespoon water (*right out of the tap is fine*)

White (*granulated*) sugar to sprinkle on top

The Cream Cheese Filling:

8-ounce package brick cream cheese, softened to room temperature (*I used Philadelphia*)
⅓ cup white (*granulated*) sugar
½ teaspoon vanilla extract

The Powdered Sugar Drizzle Frosting:

1 and ¼ cups powdered (*confectioners*) sugar (*pack it down in the cup when you measure it*)
1 teaspoon vanilla extract
⅛ teaspoon salt
¼ cup whipping cream (*that's heavy cream, not Half & Half*)

Directions:

Thaw 1 package of Puff Pastry (*2 sheets*) according to package directions. Do this on a lightly floured surface (*I used a bread board*). To prepare the surface, sprinkle on a little flour and spread it around with your impeccably clean palms.

Directions for the Cream Cheese Filling:

In a microwave-safe mixing bowl, combine the softened cream cheese with the sugar and the vanilla extract. Heat the mixture in the microwave for 30 seconds, then take it out, place on a folded towel, and give it a final stir until it is smooth and creamy. When it's cool, cover the bowl with plastic wrap and leave it on the counter.

Hannah's 2nd Note: You will not be making the Drizzle Frosting yet. You will do this after your Lemon Danish are baked and cooling.

Preheat your oven to 375 degrees F., rack in the middle position.

While your oven is preheating, prepare 2 baking sheets by lining them with parchment paper.

Check your puff pastry to see if it is thawed. If it is, it's time to prepare it to receive its yummy contents.

Unfold one sheet of puff pastry on your floured board. Sprinkle a little flour on a rolling pin and roll your puff pastry out to a twelve-inch square.

Hannah's 3rd Note: I use a ruler to make sure I have a 12-inch square when I'm through.

Use a sharp knife to make one horizontal line through the middle of the square and one vertical line through the middle of the square. This will divide it into 4 equal (or nearly equal) pieces.

Break the egg into a cup. Add 1 Tablespoon of water and whisk it up. This will be your egg wash.

Transfer one of your cut squares of puff pastry to your prepared cookie sheet.

Use a pastry brush to brush the inside edges of the square with the egg wash. This will make the edges stick together when you fold the dough over the cream cheese and Lemon Curd.

Measure out approximately ¼ cup of the cream cheese filling and place it in the center of the square.

Spread the cream cheese over the square evenly to within ½ inch of the edges.

Spread 2 Tablespoons of the Lemon Curd from the previous recipe over the cream cheese.

Pick up one corner of the square and pull it over the filling to cover just a little over half of the filling. Then pick up the opposite corner and pull that over to overlap the first corner.

Since the egg wash you used on the square of puff pastry dough acts as a glue, that second corner should stick to the first corner. If it doesn't, simply use a little more of the egg wash to stick the two overlapping corners together.

Hannah's 4th Note: This sounds difficult, but it's not. You'll catch on fast once you complete the first one. It takes much longer to explain than it does to actually do it.

When you've completed the first 4 squares, repeat this procedure for the second sheet of puff pastry.

Once you have all 8 Lemon Danish on the cookie sheets, brush the top of the pastry with more egg wash and sprinkle on a little granulated sugar. You won't drizzle your Danish with the Powdered Sugar Drizzle Frosting until AFTER you bake them.

Preheat your oven to 375 degrees F., rack in the middle position.

When your oven comes up to temperature, bake your Lemon Danish for 25 to 30 minutes, or until they're golden brown on top.

Remove the cookie sheets from the oven and place them on a cold stovetop burner or a wire rack and let the pastries cool for 10 minutes. While your Lemon Danish are cooling, make the Powdered Sugar Drizzle Frosting.

The Powdered Sugar Drizzle Frosting:

Place the powdered sugar in a small bowl and mix it with the vanilla extract and salt. Add in the whipping cream slowly, while stirring, until the frosting is the proper consistency to drizzle on top of your Lemon Danish.

Use your favorite method to drizzle frosting over the tops of your Lemon Danish. A pastry bag *(or a plastic bag with one of the corners snipped off)* works well for this.

Hannah's 5th Note: If you don't want to use a pastry bag to do this, simply mix in a little more cream so that the frosting will drizzle off the tip of a spoon held over the pastries.

When all the Lemon Danish have been decorated with the frosting, pull the parchment paper and the Lemon Danish off the cookie sheets and place them onto a wire rack.

These pastries are delicious eaten while slightly warm. They're also good cold.

If any of your Lemon Danish are left over *(I don't think this will happen!)*, wrap them loosely in wax paper and keep them in a cool place.

Hannah's 6th Note: The Lemon Curd recipe I gave you will make more than you need for your Lemon Danish. Store the leftover Lemon Curd in a tightly covered jar in the refrigerator and use it to make Miniature Lemon Cheesecakes. The recipe is on the next page.

MINIATURE LEMON CHEESECAKES

Preheat oven to 350 degrees F., rack in the middle position.

Ingredients:

24 vanilla wafer cookies (*I used Nabisco Nilla Wafer Cookies*)
2 eight-ounce packages softened cream cheese (*room temperature*)
¾ cup white (*granulated*) sugar
2 large eggs
1 Tablespoon lemon juice
1 teaspoon vanilla

24 cupcake liners (*48 if you're like me and you like to use double papers*)
Leftover Lemon Curd from the Lemon Danish recipe OR 1 can lemon pie filling, chilled (*21 ounces net weight*)

Hannah's 1st Note: Make sure you use brick cream cheese, the kind that comes in a rectangular package. Don't use whipped cream cheese or low-fat, or Neufchatel.

Hannah's 2nd Note: If you're using your leftover Lemon Curd from the Lemon Danish recipe, you may not have enough Lemon Curd to fill all 24 miniature muffin cups. If you run out of Lemon Curd, get out a jar of strawberry jam, seedless raspberry jam, or any other kind of berry jam, and use that on the tops of the other miniature cheesecakes.

Prepare Your Pans:

Start with filling two (2) muffin pans *(the kind of pan that makes 12 muffins each)* with paper cupcake liners. There is no need to spray the inside of the muffin cups with Pam or any other nonstick food spray.

Put one vanilla wafer cookie in the bottom of each cupcake paper, flat side down.

Hannah's 3rd Note: You can mix the filling by hand, but it's easier with an electric mixer.

To Make the Filling:

Using LOW speed, mix the softened cream cheese with the white sugar until it's thoroughly blended.

With the mixer still running on LOW speed, add the eggs one at a time, beating after each addition. Continue to mix until everything is well-blended and of a uniform color.

Mix in the lemon juice and the vanilla extract. Beat until the resulting mixture is light and fluffy.

Shut off the mixer, scrape down the insides of the bowl, and take the bowl out of the mixer.

Spoon the cheesecake batter into the muffin tins, dividing it as equally as you can. When you're through, each cupcake paper should be between half and two-thirds full. *(They're going to look skimpy, but they'll be fine once they're baked and you put on the Lemon Curd or jam topping.)*

To Bake the Cheesecake Filling:

Put both cupcake pans in the preheated oven and bake the cheesecake filling at 350 degrees F. for 15 to 20 minutes, or until the top of the filling has set and has a satiny-looking finish. *(The center may sink a bit, but that's okay—the topping will cover that.)*

Take the muffin pans out of the oven and set them on cold stovetop burners or wire racks. Cool your Miniature Lemon Cheesecakes until they reach room temperature.

To Add the Lemon Topping:

When the cheesecakes have cooled, take the leftover Lemon Curd out of the refrigerator and give it a stir with a spoon from your silverware drawer. Then add topping to bring the muffin cups to about ¾ full.

When, and if, you run out of Lemon Curd, fill the remaining muffin cups with berry jam.

Refrigerate your Miniature Lemon (or Berry) Cheesecakes in the muffin tins for 30 minutes to 1 hour before serving.

To Serve:

Take your cheesecakes out of the refrigerator and carefully remove them, still in their cupcake papers. Place them on a pretty platter for an elegant dessert. Make sure to have hot, strong coffee and icy cold glasses of milk available.

BUTTERSCOTCH SAUCE

A Stovetop Recipe

Ingredients for Butterscotch Sauce:

½ cup salted butter (*1 stick, 4 ounces, ¼ pound*)

1 cup brown sugar (*pack it down in the cup when you measure it*)

⅓ cup whipping cream (*heavy cream—I used Knudsen*)

Hannah's 1st Note: Sally serves this Butterscotch Sauce with her pancakes, waffles, and French toast at her breakfast buffets. Everyone raves about it!

Hannah's 2nd Note: Gather up all your ingredients before you start to make this recipe.

If you find that your brown sugar has clumped up in hard little nuggets, don't panic. There's an easy way to make your own brown sugar as long as you have white (granulated) sugar and molasses. Simply place the cup of white sugar in a small bowl and drizzle one teaspoon of molasses over the top of the bowl.

Then mix in the molasses until it is thoroughly combined with the sugar and the result is a nice, even color of brown. I always keep molasses on hand at The Cookie Jar for this reason. All you have to remember is to mix it with white sugar to get brown sugar.

Directions:

Place the salted butter in a medium-size saucepan on the stovetop. Turn the burner on medium heat and melt the butter.

Once the butter is melted, use a whisk to add the brown sugar to the melted butter. Whisk until the brown sugar and butter are thoroughly combined.

Add the heavy cream to the mixture in your saucepan and continue to whisk until the cream is combined.

With the burner still on MEDIUM heat, whisk until the mixture comes to a boil.

Set a timer for 3 (three) minutes and continue to whisk for EXACTLY 3 (three) minutes.

Pull the saucepan off the heat and over to a cold burner. Then shut off the hot burner. You won't need it again.

Let the Butterscotch Sauce cool until it comes to room temperature. Then pour it into a glass jar with a lid or a sealed container. Refrigerate your Butterscotch Sauce until you need it. If it's tightly sealed and refrigerated, it will keep for weeks.

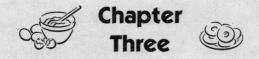

Chapter Three

Hannah stood in back of the breakfast buffet table, watching to see which dishes needed to be replenished. Andrea was several feet from her, by the stacks of pancakes and large pan of crispy bacon. The pan with the breakfast sausages was between them, and Sally stood at the other end, helping to dish up squares of the breakfast bakes the three of them had prepared earlier.

The array of breakfast dishes was impressive. While Hannah and Andrea had baked the cookies they'd need for mid-morning and mid-afternoon snacks, Sally and her kitchen crew had assembled a variety of breakfast bakes, scrambled egg and cheese casseroles, and biscuits. Then, leaving her crew to finish their tasks, Sally had joined Hannah and Andrea to teach them how to make her Caramel Pecan Rolls.

The Caramel Pecan Rolls were not as difficult as Hannah had thought they would be. And the fishermen seemed to love the buttery breakfast treat. So far, Hannah had refilled the large platter three times and it was almost time to do it again. She could understand why more than one contestant had come back for multiple rolls. She'd had one for breakfast once the baking was finished, and they were incredibly good. Despite the fact she'd already eaten one, she'd had to squelch the urge to snatch another every time she'd refilled the platter.

"How's it going, Hannah?" Sally asked, walking over to her.

"Everything's going like hotcakes, including the hotcakes."

Sally laughed. "Very clever, Hannah. How about my Butterscotch Sauce? Are they using it on the pancakes?"

"Yes, and they love it. I think you should serve it every time you make pancakes."

"Good to know."

"Your Caramel Pecan Rolls are a huge hit, too."

"They always are. I wish I could have found my grandmother's recipe. It was written on the back of an old telephone bill."

"I hope it was paid."

"I'm sure it was. My grandfather paid all the bills. He didn't think that women should handle money."

"Did your grandmother agree with that?"

"Certainly not, but she never told him that! She had a chicken coop and she sold the eggs."

"Did your grandfather know about her egg money?"

"Yes, but he didn't think it was important. Actually, she made quite a bit of money from the eggs, but he never bothered to find out how much."

"What did she use the money for?"

"For us. My grandparents lived way out in the country and they only went into town once a month. While

Grandpa was paying the bills, Grandma used to get groceries and go to the mercantile stores to buy clothes and presents for the grandkids."

"And that was all right with your grandfather?"

"Oh, yes. It wouldn't have been all right if she'd worked outside the home, but he felt that farm wives were entitled to their egg money."

Hannah noticed that a man dressed in fishing clothes was walking up to the podium that had been set up next to the stage Sally used for entertainment. "Is that Sonny?" she asked.

"No, that's Wally. I'll introduce you later. Wally's going to greet the contestants and then he'll turn things over to Sonny and Joey."

Wally clicked a button on the microphone and tapped it to make sure it was working. "Hello, fishermen!" he said. "It's good to see a group of sportsmen all ready to enjoy the great outdoors." There was a smattering of applause, and he smiled before he went on. "Today is the first unofficial day of the Walleye Fishing Tournament. Today is the day you'll get time to explore Eden Lake and get acclimated. I know that most of you have fished for walleyes before, but our fishing expert, Sonny Bowman, is going to go through the rules of the contest with you and give you a few tips about walleye fishing. How many of you have fished in Eden Lake before?"

Hannah was glad to see at least a dozen men raise their hands. There were quite a few locals signed up for the competition.

"Our tournament doesn't officially begin until tomorrow morning, so use today to explore the lake and find your favorite spot to fish," Wally went on speaking. "Come up here, Sonny, and explain the competition rules and tell them about the prizes."

Hannah couldn't help but stare as Sonny Bowman walked up to the podium. He was criminally handsome with sun-bleached hair and a physique that had obviously benefitted from frequent workouts at the gym.

"He's something, huh?" Andrea whispered, coming up to Hannah.

"He's certainly handsome."

"And he knows it," Andrea added. "He looks good on camera, though, and that's probably why Wally chose him for the show."

"But he's an expert fisherman, too . . . isn't he?"

"I don't know. I asked Bill about that. I figured he'd know since he always watches all the fishing shows."

"What did Bill say?"

"Bill said he'd never heard of Sonny before Wally put him on the show."

"Really?" Hannah asked. "I thought he was famous?"

"He is now, but we drove to Wally's flagship store and Bill met Sonny. Bill asked him a couple of questions about fishing and was not impressed!"

"Why? What did Sonny say?"

"He said he had to cut his time short because Wally wanted to meet with him. And he told Bill to find Joey Zee and ask him."

Hannah reached the obvious conclusion. "So you don't think Sonny knew the answers to Bill's questions."

"That's right. Sonny could hardly wait to get away."

"Did Bill find Joey and ask him?"

"He did. And Joey answered every one of his questions and even gave him some fishing tips. He likes Joey, but he thinks that Sonny is a fake. That's one of the reasons Bill didn't sign up for the tournament."

Hannah began to frown. "I thought Bill didn't sign

up because he was going to the big sheriffs' conference."

"You're right, but if he'd really wanted to enter the competition, Bill would have done it. As it turns out, it's a good thing since they changed the dates on the sheriffs' conference."

"So he's going to the conference instead?"

"Rick Murphy's going with him. Bill asked Mike and Lonnie to stay here in case there was any kind of an emergency."

Hannah heard the arpeggio that Andrea used for her ringtone and watched as Andrea pulled her cell phone out of her apron pocket. "Here's Bill now. He probably wants to know what time I'm coming home so I can help him pack. That man can't fold a shirt to save his soul! If he had to do it himself, he'd roll them up in a ball and throw them in the bottom of his suitcase."

Hannah filled the Caramel Pecan Roll platter again as Andrea answered her husband's call. She was just putting the platter back on the table when she saw the shocked expression on her sister's face. "Is Bill okay?" she asked quickly.

Andrea gave a quick nod and turned back to her phone. "I'll leave here just as soon as I can, honey. And don't be nervous. Your speech is wonderful, and everyone's going to love it."

"Problems?" Hannah asked when Andrea dropped her phone back into her apron pocket.

"Not really. It's just that Bill always gets nervous when he has to give a speech. And this one is a lot more important than either one of us thought it would be."

"How so?"

"They just called him from the convention center and told him that their keynote speaker had to cancel. And then they asked *Bill* to be the keynote speaker!

They told him it's going to be televised and everything!"

"That sounds like a real honor, Andrea! Bill's going to do it, isn't he?"

"Yes, but you know how nervous he gets speaking in public. It's a good speech, Hannah." Andrea gave a little laugh. "I should know. I had to listen to him go through it four times last night!"

Hannah laughed. "Will we be able to see him on television?"

"Yes, KCOW-TV is going to run it as a community service program. You can see him, but you'll have to record it. I checked with Lynn and they're going to air it at eight in the morning and we'll be out here working with Sally."

"Call Mother and tell her about it. She'll record it and we can all watch it at the penthouse."

"Good idea! Mother and Doc just got a new big screen and we can all watch it there."

Andrea reached into her apron pocket and pulled out her cell phone once again. "That's probably Bill, telling me that he's arrived at the hotel." One glance at the display and she frowned slightly. "It's Michelle." She clicked on her phone to answer. "Hi, Michelle. What's up?"

Hannah refilled one of the buffet dishes while Andrea spoke into her phone. She was smiling as she hung up.

"What did Michelle want?" Hannah asked.

"She invited us to join Lonnie and her at Dick's bar at five for drinks tonight. She's going to invite Mike, too."

"I'll have to ask Norman first, but that's fine with me."

Andrea looked around the room. "Where *is* Norman? I thought he'd be here."

"He planned to be, but he got a call from Doc

Bennett. He was supposed to fill in for Norman every day this week, but Doc Bennett forgot he had a doctor's appointment this morning."

"Doc Bennett's okay, isn't he?" Andrea sounded worried.

"He's fine. This is just a checkup, but he didn't want to cancel at the last minute. He told Norman he'd probably be through by noon and Norman's coming out here then." Hannah reached out to move a platter slightly so that it would be easier for the breakfast crowd to reach. "How about you, Andrea? You can make it out here tonight, can't you?"

"No problem. Grandma McCann is taking the kids out to a movie tonight, and I wasn't exactly looking forward to sitting at home all alone."

"I'll call Norman when we finish with the buffet and ask him about tonight, but I'm sure it'll be fine with him. He has to run back to his house to feed the cats, but that won't take long." Hannah stopped speaking and began to frown. "It's not Karaoke night tonight, is it?"

Andrea laughed. "No, Michelle told me that right away."

"Good! I don't think I could take another rendition of Alice and Digger singing together. It's even worse than Mother and Carrie singing *Bye Bye Love*."

Andrea looked extremely doubtful. "They can't be *that* bad!"

"Take my word for it, they are! If anyone's an expert about singing off-key, it's me," Hannah said, laughing.

"Do you want me to pick up you and Norman?" Andrea said.

Hannah hesitated. "Uh . . . no. I'll be here already. I'm staying out here for the week of the fishing contest."

"How about Norman? I could pick him up."

Hannah hesitated. "Um . . . thanks, but that's not necessary."

Andrea gave her a long level look. "You mean you and Norman are staying out here together?"

"Not together," Hannah said quickly. "Sally told me she'll probably have a room available for Norman if he wants it."

"But how about the cats? If both of you stay out here, you'll have to go back to Norman's house to feed them and everything, won't you?"

"I don't think so. Mother said that she misses the cats and Doc's grown really fond of Moishe. I'm going to ask Mother if she'll keep the cats for the week. Doc's been working long hours, and she told me that she was a little lonely. I'm just hoping that she can keep Moishe and Cuddles for the week."

"That's a good idea, Hannah, and she'll probably agree. She told me that Stephanie Bascomb comes over every afternoon for tea and they both love to watch the cats try to catch ladybugs in the garden."

"I know. Everyone gets a kick out of that, especially because the cats never catch them. And Doc says that Moishe always looks completely amazed when the ladybugs fly off."

Andrea looked highly amused. "Moishe caught one the other day. Mother told me."

"Oh, dear! I hope he didn't eat it!"

"He didn't. Mother said he just stared at it for a minute and then he reached out and nudged it until it flew away."

"Hello, ladies!" A male voice broke into their conversation. "I've got a question for you."

It was Sonny Bowman, and Hannah watched as Andrea began to blush slightly.

"What can we do for you?" Hannah asked him.

"I need some information. Which one of you made those Caramel Pecan Rolls?"

Since Andrea looked totally flustered by the handsome fishing show star, Hannah answered. "Both of us did, along with a little help from Sally. Do you like them?"

"They're great! I've already had three and I'll probably have another one for dessert. Are you going to make them again tomorrow morning?"

"We can if you want them," Andrea recovered enough to say.

"I do. Make three extra for me, will you?"

"We'd be happy to," Hannah said quickly. She wasn't sure if Sally had planned to serve them again tomorrow, but she was almost certain that Sally would agree with a request from the fishing competition celebrity.

"Of course we will!" Andrea chimed in.

"Package them up for me. I'm going to take some out on the boat with me after the buffet."

"Do you want a few more for Joey?" Andrea asked him.

"No. He can get his own if he wants them. Besides, he's going out early to find the best spots. He'll pick me up after the breakfast buffet."

"So Joey's not coming to the breakfast buffet?" Hannah asked, drawing the obvious conclusion.

"No, he can wait until noon to eat. Joey needs to lose a little weight anyway. I don't want anybody fat in the boat with me."

Without another word, Sonny turned and walked toward a table where two attractive ladies were sitting alone. He pulled out a chair between the two and sat down, giving the women his famous smile.

"He's a conceited you-know-what, isn't he," Andrea said, and it wasn't a question. "It's just too bad he's so good looking. He didn't even thank us when we said we'd make a package of rolls for him. And when we asked if he wanted a package for Joey, he looked positively amazed that we'd even suggested it."

"I noticed that," Hannah said, not going into detail but already deciding that she'd make an extra package of Caramel Pecan Rolls and leave them outside Joey's room. "You said you watched his fishing show?"

"Yes. Bill likes it because he always goes to a different lake in Minnesota. He says it's good advertisement for our state."

"That's probably true. Has he gone to Eden Lake before?"

"I don't think so, and I've watched every episode with Bill. We always record it and watch it together."

"I didn't realize that you liked fishing that much."

"I don't. I watch because it's something I can do with Bill. It's time that we get to spend together. If I didn't watch, he'd probably turn on the TV in his office and watch it there."

Hannah was impressed. Her sister was doing her best to be a good wife.

"You ought to watch it sometime," Andrea told her. "It's just a crime the way Sonny treats Joey. I think they just chose Sonny because he looks really good on television."

"You're probably right. I'm sure it all has to do with demographics. Fishing shows are primarily a guy thing, but women will watch it for Sonny." She glanced over at the table where Sonny was sitting with the two women.

"You're right." Andrea was obviously impressed with Hannah's insight. "I encourage Bill to come home in time to watch the fishing show. Now that you mention it, a lot of wives probably do the same thing. And that means Sonny's show does better in the ratings."

"Exactly right," Hannah said, turning to greet Sally, who was coming over to their buffet station. "Hi, Sally. How is it going?"

"Great, but I'm keeping an eye on Sonny's table," Sally said. "Just look at those two women. They are practically salivating over him!"

"We noticed," Andrea answered her.

"Well . . . their husbands just walked in, and both of them looked a little upset that their wives hadn't saved enough chairs for them. I wonder if I should go there and add another couple of chairs."

"Wait a second," Hannah said, noticing that Wally was heading for Sonny's table along with a waiter carrying more chairs. "I think Wally just took care of things for you."

The three women watched as Wally shook hands with the men and the waiter put the chairs in place. Right after the two men sat down next to their wives, Wally motioned to Sonny.

"You're right," Sally said, and they watched as Sonny said goodbye to the women and followed Wally from the room. "Is Wally going to chew Sonny out?" Andrea asked.

Sally shook her head. "I doubt it, but watch. I saw Wally motion to Joey right before he left with Sonny."

"Very smart," Andrea said, watching Joey get up from his chair and walk over to the table that Sonny had vacated.

"Look at the men now," Sally commented. "They're all smiles."

"That's probably because they have the chance to ask Joey fishing questions," Sally suggested, beginning to smile. "Dick got a chance to talk to Joey last night and he said that Joey knows more about fishing than anyone else he's ever met." She turned to Hannah. "I hope you girls are going to make those rolls for Sonny in the morning. Personally, I can't stand the guy, but I need him to convince Wally to come back here every year for a Walleye Fishing Tournament. We've already made more money this month than usual."

"Don't worry, Sally. We'll make as many rolls as you want us to," Andrea assured her.

"Yes, we will," Hannah agreed. "Don't worry, Sally, Andrea and I will make sure Sonny's *well* taken care of!"

"We will?" Andrea asked, looking slightly shocked.

"Absolutely!" Hannah gave a mischievous smile. "Besides, there's always arsenic."

CARAMEL PECAN ROLLS

(The easiest Caramel Pecan Rolls you'll ever make)

DO NOT preheat your oven yet—these rolls have to sit in the baking pan for approximately 15 to 20 minutes before baking.

3 cans Pillsbury Grand Cinnamon Rolls *(you'll find these in the refrigerated section of your grocery store – if you can't find the Grands, get 3 cans of the Pillsbury regular cinnamon rolls)*

½ cup salted butter *(1 stick, 4 ounces, ¼ pound)*

1 cup brown sugar, firmly packed *(make sure you pack it down in the cup when you measure it)*

½ cup heavy cream *(whipping cream or manufacturer's cream)*

Approximately 4 ounces of pecan halves or approximately 50 pecan halves.

Prepare your pan:

Spray a 9-inch by 13-inch pan with Pam or another nonstick cooking spray. Make sure to spray the bottom of the pan and at least 2 inches up the insides of the pan.

54

Directions:

Set the cans of Pillsbury Cinnamon Rolls on the counter. Don't open them yet.

Place the stick of salted butter in a 3 cup microwave-safe bowl. Melt it in the microwave on HIGH for 30 seconds.

Let the bowl sit in the microwave for one minute. Then check to see it's melted. If it is, take the bowl out of the microwave and set it on the counter. If the butter hasn't melted yet, microwave it on HIGH for another 20 seconds and let it sit in the microwave for another minute.

Measure out one cup of brown sugar. Use the palm of your impeccably clean hand to pack it down in the measuring cup.

Add the brown sugar to the bowl with the melted butter and use a wire whisk to whisk it in. Keep whisking until the resulting mixture is smooth and without lumps.

Hannah's 1st Note: If your brown sugar has lumps in it, pick them out by hand or use a sieve to take out the lumps. Then re-measure to make

sure you have a full cup. Remember, you can always make brown sugar by adding molasses to white, granulated sugar and mixing it in until the resulting mixture is the proper brown color.

Measure out the half-cup of heavy cream and add it to the bowl with the butter and brown sugar. Whisk until the resulting mixture is smooth and creamy.

Spoon the butter, brown sugar, and cream mixture into the bottom of your prepared baking pan. Use a heat resistant spatula to spread it out evenly over the bottom of the pan.

Once the caramel mixture is in place, sprinkle the pecans over the bottom of the pan as evenly as you can.

Hannah's 2nd Note: If you love pecans, you can always sprinkle on extra.

Open the packages of Pillsbury Grand Cinnamon Rolls.

Place three unbaked rolls across the top of your baking pan.

Place another 3 unbaked rolls in a row under the first roll.

Place another 3 unbaked rolls under the second row of rolls.

Place another 3 unbaked rolls under the third row of rolls, which should bring you to the bottom of your baking pan.

Hannah's 3rd Note: You now have a choice. You will have 3 Pillsbury Grand Cinnamon Rolls left over. You can either spray the bottom of a bread pan with Pam (or another nonstick baking spray) and place the remaining 3 rolls in the bottom of the bread pan. Once they are baked, frost them with the icing that came with the canister of rolls. Alternately, you can cut the 3 rolls in half and squeeze 3 halves, rounded side up, between the 2nd and 3rd row and another 3 halves rounded side down between the 3rd and 4th row. I've done it both ways and I prefer to bake them separately and frost them after baking.

Hannah's 4th Note: If you couldn't find the Pillsbury Grand Cinnamon Rolls and you bought the regular Pillsbury Cinnamon Rolls instead, open the 3 cans of rolls and arrange them with four rolls on the top row, 2 rolls in the second row, another 4 rolls in the middle row, 2 rolls

in the next row and 4 rolls in the bottom row. This will total the 16 rolls that are contained in 2 regular cinnamon roll cans.

Once the unbaked rolls are arranged in your pan, preheat your oven to 350 degrees F., rack in the middle position.

Cover your baking pan loosely with a sheet of foil or plastic wrap while you're waiting for your oven to come up to temperature.

When your oven is at the proper temperature, take the covering off your baking pan and put the pan in the center of your oven.

Hannah's 5th Note: If you used a bread pan for your 3 extra Pillsbury Grand Cinnamon Rolls, put them in the oven on one side of your baking pan.

Bake your Caramel Pecan Rolls for 30 to 35 minutes, or until they're nicely browned on top. (If you used the smaller cinnamon rolls, bake those for 25 to 30 minutes.)

Take your baking pan out of the oven and set it on a cool stovetop burner or a wire rack to cool.

Let your rolls cool, uncovered, for 15 minutes.

Once the time is up, line a serving platter or a cookie sheet with sides with foil.

Place the serving platter or the cookie sheet with sides over your pan of rolls and use potholders or oven mitts to flip the hot rolls over onto the platter or cookie sheet.

If some of the caramel sticks to the bottom of your baking pan, use a heat-resistant spatula to scoop it up and transfer it to the top of your rolls.

To Serve:

Let your Caramel Pecan Rolls cool for at least another fifteen minutes and then serve them to your guests or your family. These rolls are good warm or cold. Make sure to provide soft butter for those who want it, plenty of hot coffee, orange juice, or big glasses of milk. If there are any rolls left over (Which is highly unlikely!), you can reheat them for 15 seconds or so in the microwave.

Chapter Four

Hannah had just finished mixing up a batch of Molasses Crackles to bake in the morning when Norman came through Sally's kitchen door.

"Hi, Hannah," Norman greeted her. "Sally said you were working in here and I should just come in."

"Hi, Norman." Hannah began to smile. "I'm just mixing up some things to bake tomorrow. Would you like a cup of coffee? I've got some left in Sally's kitchen coffeepot."

"Thanks. That sounds good. Do you have anything I can eat, Hannah? Doc Bennett just got back from his doctor's appointment and I drove straight out here. Do you have any leftover cookies I can munch on? I missed the lunch buffet and all I had for breakfast was a couple pieces of toast."

"How about a big piece of quiche? I have one that was left from the lunch buffet."

"That sounds perfect. Thanks, Hannah. What time did you leave this morning? I didn't even hear you, and when I woke up, you were gone."

"I left early. The weather's not really predictable this time of year and I didn't want to be late."

"What time did you get up?"

"I got up at three. I wanted to make sure I could get out here to start the baking by four." Hannah poured a cup of coffee for Norman and then she made a quick trip to the walk-in cooler. "What time did you leave the house?"

"I left at six. It was lonely without you, Hannah, and I thought I'd be here in time for the lunch buffet."

"How was Doc Bennett's appointment?" Hannah asked, carrying a huge piece of quiche to the microwave to heat it for Norman.

"He said it went just fine. He saw one of Doc's interns and he got a clean bill of health. He told me that the intern couldn't believe he was the age that was listed on his chart."

"That's great." Hannah turned on the microwave and came back to get another sip of her coffee at the little table Sally had in the kitchen.

"Is that your Corned Beef Hash Quiche?" Norman asked.

"Yes. Is that all right with you?"

"That's great with me! I love your Corned Beef Hash Quiche. That and your Quiche Lorraine are my favorites."

The microwave dinged, Hannah removed the plate and brought it and a fork to Norman. Then she sat back down at the table.

Norman took a bite, smiled at her, and took another sip of his coffee. "You shouldn't have to get up at three in the morning, Hannah. Why don't you see if Sally has a room you can use for the week of the fishing contest? It would be a lot easier on you if you stayed out here. Then all you'd have to do is take a quick shower, get dressed, and go downstairs to the kitchen."

"Sally suggested that," Hannah said truthfully. "But that would mean we'd have to run back to your house after the contest closed for the day to feed the cats."

"I don't mind. I don't have to get here until seven-thirty."

"I know, but . . ." Hannah paused and took a deep breath. "I might have another solution."

"What's that?"

"Sally thinks they may have another vacant room and you could stay out here, too."

"But what about the cats?"

"I'm not absolutely positive about this, but Mother's been saying she's lonely lately with Doc working so many hours. And she loves to watch the cats play in the garden. She might agree to keep the cats with her if I asked her."

"But she's finishing another Regency Romance book, isn't she?"

"Yes, but there's a limit to how many hours a day she can work. The cats come in the office with her when she's there, and they sleep while she's working. And then Mother takes them out in the garden, under the dome, and watches them play. She told me that it's very relaxing. Then, when Stephanie drops by after the mayor's office closes, they sit out there, drink champagne, and watch Moishe and Cuddles play."

Norman began to smile. "Is there another piece of that Corned Beef Hash Quiche left, Hannah?"

"Yes. Are you still hungry?"

"No, but Doc Knight might be. And we can ask him what he thinks about keeping the cats for a week."

"That's a good idea, but I don't think we should disturb him in the middle of his work day."

"You're right. Let me go check his office and see if he's busy."

Hannah felt her confusion grow. "You're going to drive out to the hospital to see if Doc's busy?"

"No. Doc's right here. Wally asked him to stay here during the day to take care of any fishing-related accidents that might happen. Sally gave him the empty office across the hall from you, and he's in there now."

"I didn't know that! When did he get here?"

"Just a little while before I did. He was setting up his office when I walked by to come here." Norman got up from his stool. "I'll go see if he wants to join us, Hannah. Then we can ask him about keeping the cats."

Hannah hurried to put on another pot of coffee and got the rest of the Corned Beef Hash Quiche out of Sally's walk-in cooler. By the time Norman came back, she was ready with a hot cup of coffee.

"Hi, Doc," she said as Doc came in. "I didn't know that you were working out here this week."

"Neither did I, until Wally called me," Doc said, spying the full cup of coffee and wasting no time in sitting down to take a sip. "I meant to come see you earlier, Hannah, but I was getting organized. Tomorrow's the first day of the contest, and Wally said we're bound to get a couple of HRIs."

"One of them won't be me!" Norman promised him. "I always wear gloves when I'm fishing."

"I wish everyone did," Doc told him. "HRIs are a pain in more ways than one!"

"Excuse me, guys," Hannah said, holding up a hand. "I don't know what you're talking about. What are HRIs?"

"Hook-related injuries," Doc told her. "You have no idea how careless fishermen can be with fishing hooks."

"And those barbs can dig in there," Norman added.

"Doc told me he gets at least a dozen HRIs every week during fishing season."

Hannah shuddered, remembering how sharp the barbs looked on a fish hook. "I'm glad that's never happened to me," she said, retrieving Doc's plate with the quiche from the microwave and setting it down next to him. "Just in case you didn't have lunch, I heated a piece of quiche for you."

Doc began to smile. "Smells like your Corned Beef Hash Quiche," he said, reaching out for the plate. "Thanks, Hannah. I was going to have lunch at the hospital but then Wally called and I came straight out here. Your mother should be here soon. She said she'd finished work for the day and she was coming out early."

"How is she coming along with the book?" Hannah asked, hoping that her mother was on schedule.

"Great! She worked late last night and she was still working when I got home. Did Michelle call you about tonight, Hannah?"

"She called Andrea, and Andrea told me."

"Good." Doc turned to Norman. "You're coming, aren't you, Norman?"

"Coming to what?" Norman asked.

"Sorry, Doc," Hannah said quickly. "I haven't had the chance to ask him yet." She turned to Norman. "Michelle wants all of us to meet up in Dick's bar tonight. Dick's has a couple of new appetizers for us to try."

"I'm in," Norman said quickly. "Hannah's going to stay out here and we'll run back to my place to feed the cats first, but I always enjoy Dick's appetizers."

"I talked to Dick earlier," Doc said quickly, a huge smile spreading across his face. "Dick said they were making Scotch Eggs tonight just for me!"

It was Hannah's turn to look confused. "I thought Scotch Eggs were deep-fried."

"They are . . . usually," Doc told her. "Dick found a recipe for Scotch Eggs that are baked in the oven, and he wants to try it tonight. Sally said he made it for her a couple of nights ago and it was phenomenal."

Hannah smiled. "If Sally said it was phenomenal, it must be."

"I saw Sally on the way in here and she mentioned the Scotch Eggs," Norman said. "She said she's going to help him behind the bar tonight and she's making her recipe for Special Boursin Cheese-Filled Mushrooms."

"No dinner for me," Hannah declared, resisting the urge to lick her lips. "I love all of Sally's appetizers!"

"What time can you leave to go feed the cats?" Norman asked Hannah.

"I'm through now," Hannah told him, glancing over at Sally's bakers rack. "I don't have to do anything else until we do the Caramel Pecan Rolls tomorrow morning."

"Good! Why don't you get settled in your room and then we can go back to my house, feed the cats and play with them a little, and come back in time to stake out a big table in the bar for all of us?" Norman suggested.

"Sounds good to me," Hannah agreed. "What time is Mother going to get here, Doc?"

"Any minute now. Stephanie isn't coming by today because she's got a late city council meeting."

"When Delores gets here, we can ask her about the cats," Norman said just as the door opened and Delores walked in.

"Hi! Sally said you were all in here." She turned to

Hannah. "You were talking about the cats when I came in . . . they're all right, aren't they?"

"They're fine, Mother, but I'm out here this week. Sally's pastry chef had a family emergency and I'm taking his place," Hannah hurried to explain. "Sally offered to let me stay out here, but Norman and I need to find someone to keep the cats for the week."

A smile spread over Delores's face. "Doc and I will keep them," she said quickly, and then she glanced at Doc. "That's all right with you, isn't it, dear?"

"That's fine with me," Doc agreed.

"Oh, good!" Delores said, and then she frowned slightly. "*Both* of you are staying out here?"

"Yes, but we'll have separate rooms," Hannah reassured her. "I checked with Sally and she's got an extra room for Norman. There's enough gossip about us around town already, and Sally's going to make it clear that Norman and I have separate rooms."

"That's good, dear," Delores said quickly. "I think all this speculation about the two of you is ridiculous. You and Norman are adults, and people should have the courtesy to mind their own business and let you make your own decisions about your living arrangements!"

Hannah bit back a smile, remembering the shock she'd felt when she'd spotted her mother's car at Doc's house in the middle of the night. She'd never told anyone about that, not even Andrea or Michelle, and she probably never would.

"You're right, Mother," Hannah said. "And you won't have to do any damage control for us. I checked with Sally and she's going to make it clear to anyone who asks that Norman and I have separate rooms."

"Good. That might stop some tongues from wagging, unless . . ." Delores stopped speaking and looked a little worried. "They're not connecting rooms, are they?"

"No, Mother. Sally told me that Norman's room is down the hall from mine."

"Oh, good. That'll help." Delores turned to Norman. "Will you bring the cats over to us tonight? Doc and I are going to try Dick's appetizers and then we'll go straight home and get things ready."

"Yes, but we'll bring everything you need, Delores," Norman promised.

"That's nice, dear, but I think I probably have everything. I have their favorite food and water bowls, and I picked up some beds at the pet store. And of course I have treats. I bought the fish-shaped, salmon-flavored ones that Moishe loves, and the little triangular ones that Cuddles likes. And I have cat food, the same kind you feed them at home."

Norman smiled. "That was good of you, Delores."

"Thank you, but that's not all. The cats really like to stay in the office with me when I work, and I bought one set of kitty beds for there and another set for our bedroom."

"Do you really think they'll actually sleep in *pet* beds, Lori?" Doc asked her.

Delores laughed. "Of course not, but the pet store had a two-for sale and I thought it was worth a try."

"Are those all those packages I unloaded from your trunk, Lori?" Doc asked her.

"Yes, but only part of them. I remembered how Moishe always crowds you off your pillow, so I bought two more goose-down pillows at CostMart, one for Moishe and one for Cuddles."

"But Cuddles never tries to get my pillow," Doc reminded her.

"I know, but it's not fair to get one for Moishe and

leave Cuddles out in the cold. It could hurt her feelings."

Hannah exchanged amused glances with Norman. "What else did you buy, Mother?"

"Only a few more things. They had cat tuna and cat salmon at the pet store, but I noticed that you usually give them regular salmon and regular tuna. I picked those up at the grocery store, along with a couple packages of frozen shrimp."

"It sounds like you had a cat shopping spree," Norman said.

"Oh, that's not all!" Delores began to smile. "I ordered a couple of things online too."

"Like what?" Hannah asked, having trouble keeping a straight face.

"Not much, dear," Delores said, and then she looked slightly embarrassed.

Doc laughed. "I have a feeling this is going to be good! Out with it, Lori!"

Delores sighed. "All right. Well . . . I know it's probably silly, but I ordered this floppy fish toy for them to play with. And then I saw a little box where a mouse popped out of a series of holes and ducks down again, and I got that, too. They'll probably ignore those, but they came yesterday and they look very cute. And I can hardly wait to try everything out!"

"Anything else?" Norman asked, grinning at Delores.

"Just one thing, and I probably wasted money on that. I got one of those new litter boxes that cleans itself. I'm not entirely sure how it works, but it came with instructions and Doc's really good at figuring out things like that."

"Thank you, dear," Doc said sweetly, but Hannah could hear the laughter in his voice.

"Well, you are!" Delores declared, flashing him an ingratiating smile. "I never would have figured out the new microwave without you. It's very complicated."

"How about other cat toys, Mother?" Hannah asked. "I always get stuck buying something new when I go to the pet store."

"You're right," Delores admitted. "I did forget a couple of things."

"Like what?" Doc asked her.

"Like . . . kitty sweaters to wear if it's cold. And new collars, nice ones with a light-up feature so we can see where they are in the garden in the dark. And a few of the little mice that Moishe likes and a couple of yarn balls for Cuddles. She likes to chase balls when Doc throws them. And I got a squeaking squirrel for the garden."

"A squeaking squirrel?" Doc asked. "Are you talking about a toy that squeaks if they bite it?"

Delores shook her head. "Heavens no! I wouldn't get them something like that because it might teach them to bite and then the ladybugs in the garden wouldn't be safe. The squeaking squirrel has a remote control and I thought I'd hide it behind a bush in the garden. Then we could use the remote to make it squeak and let the cats hunt for it."

Norman turned to Hannah. "Your mother is going to spoil our fur kids, Hannah."

"I know," Hannah said, giving a fake sigh. "But there really isn't anything we can do about it, Norman. That's what all grandparents do!"

Chapter Five

Hannah glanced around at the other tables in the bar. She'd managed to take a short nap this afternoon while Norman had gone out on the lake to check out the likely spots to fish, and she felt rested and more than a little hungry to try Dick's new appetizers.

"Over here, Mike!" Lonnie stood up to wave at Mike as he came through the old-fashioned saloon-style entrance. "I ordered a lemonade for you."

"Thanks," Mike responded, taking the vacant chair next to Michelle. "Sorry I'm late, but I had to finish up some paperwork at the station." He turned to smile at everyone at the table. "Glad to see you here, Andrea. Bill called and he and Rick are getting settled in."

Andrea nodded. "I already set my TV to record it."

"So did we," Delores said.

"And I checked it to make sure she got it right," Doc added. "How about you, Norman?"

"I set mine when Hannah and I went back to the house to feed the cats. Since Hannah and I are staying out here for the week, Delores and Doc are going to babysit."

"And I didn't even touch it," Hannah said with a smile. "As a matter of fact, I didn't even step inside the den. Unless I can cause havoc remotely by just walking past the doorway, it's going to work."

Everyone laughed. They all knew that Hannah was severely challenged when it came to anything electronic.

"I set the one in Hannah's condo, too," Michelle told them. "I had Lonnie check it, and he said I'd done it right."

"That's true." Lonnie gave a little nod. "And since all of us set our equipment to record, we're bound to get at least one good recording of Bill's speech."

"Don't jinx us, Lonnie," Mike warned.

"Right." Lonnie nodded in agreement.

"We can all watch it together," Delores said.

"Great idea, Delores," Mike chimed in.

"Thank you, Mike." Delores smiled. "We'll work out the details later."

Just then Sally came up to their table. "Hello, guys! Hannah told me that all of you were coming tonight." She turned to Doc. "She said that you wanted to try Dick's Baked Scotch Eggs."

"Scotch Eggs are my favorite," Doc said with a smile. "Can we start with those?"

"Yes, but I need a glass of wine first," Michelle told him. "Today's my only night off this week, and I plan to enjoy myself."

"Our drink order first is a good idea," Doc said quickly. "What kind of wine do you want, Michelle?"

"A chardonnay," Michelle answered. "I'll let Dick choose it, Sally. I've never been disappointed in a wine that he's recommended."

"That's good to know." Sally turned to Hannah. "How about you, Hannah?"

"Does Dick have any champagne open?" Hannah asked.

"I'm sure he does. And if he doesn't, I'll open a bottle. Anyone else for champagne?"

Delores nodded. "Count me in. How about you, Andrea?"

"I'll have the same chardonnay Michelle does," Andrea decided. "Just one glass though. I have to drive home later."

"You do, tonight," Hannah told her. "But I'm staying over here at the inn, and I have two beds in my room. Just pack up what you need for the rest of the week and bring it with you in the morning. If it's okay with Grandma McCann, you can stay over with me."

"Great!" Andrea looked very excited. "I haven't been away from home in forever, and since Bill's not there, I'll take you up on that."

"It'll save you from having to make that early morning drive," Sally told her. "What would you like to drink, Doc?"

"Jameson's with a water back," Doc told her. "How about you, Mike?"

"Cold Spring Export. Since Lonnie and I don't start our shift until tomorrow morning, we can relax a little tonight. Red wine for you, Lonnie?"

Lonnie nodded. "I'll have cabernet, whatever Dick recommends. He knows what he's doing when it comes to choosing wine."

Sally looked pleased. "I'll tell him you said that. And Baked Scotch Eggs all around once you finish your first drink?"

Everyone nodded and Sally hurried off to place their order. Since they'd all arrived early, they were the first table filled in the bar. They made conversation for a few minutes, and gradually the other fishing contestants began to arrive.

"There's Sonny Bowman," Andrea said, as the handsome fishing star walked in.

Mike nodded. "Yes, I recognize him from the fishing show." They all watched as Sonny walked over to a table and pulled out a chair. "I think this isn't his first trip here today," he commented, as Sonny sat down rather awkwardly.

"Either that or he's got a bottle in his room," Lonnie said with a nod. "It's a good thing he's got a suite out here. I wouldn't want to run into him if he was driving on the road."

"Right you are," Mike agreed, watching as Sonny reached out for some of the chips Dick had placed in a basket on every table. "I'm glad he's eating something. Maybe it'll help. He's a big guy and I wouldn't enjoy carrying him up to his room."

"I've got a gurney in my office and Sally has an elevator," Doc said. "It's the kind that folds flat so we could just roll him on."

Mike smiled. "Good to know."

"Here comes Sally with a tray," Hannah told them, spotting Sally weaving her way past several tables to get to them. "Let's make room for her to set it down."

Michelle picked up the basket of chips, and Lonnie grabbed the stack of bowls. "Got it," Michelle said.

"Thanks," Sally said, lowering the tray and setting it on the table. "I brought you a little extra surprise. Dick's serving these with the appetizers tonight."

Hannah stared at the miniature martini glasses on the tray. "Martinis?"

"Yes, special martinis. Dick calls them Walleye Martinis."

"Why does he . . ." Hannah stopped speaking in the middle of the question she had been about to ask. "Never mind. I see and it's too cute for words!"

"What . . . ?" Andrea started to ask, but she began to laugh. "Never mind. I get it!"

They all watched as Sally added two large green pimento-stuffed olives to the rim of each glass. She placed the olives across from each other and facing out so they looked like two green eyes with red pupils staring out at opposite sides of the room.

"Walleyes," Doc said with a chuckle. "That's very clever. What's in the drink, Sally?"

"It's a miniature dirty vodka martini. The olive juice looks a little like cloudy lake water."

"My compliments to the bartender," Norman told her. "That's very clever."

It was Sally's turn to laugh. "That's Dick. He's always trying something new. It took him a while to figure out how to cut the right slices in the side so the waitress could hang them on the rims of the glasses. And once he got that figured out, he gave me a job to do."

"To serve them?" Delores asked her.

"Yes, but I always do that. My difficult job was to find the miniature martini glasses. That took me an hour and a half online before I finally found a company that made miniature disposable glasses."

Doc gave a little nod. "And Dick wanted them to be miniature because vodka martinis are all liquor and he didn't want any of the competitors to get too drunk?"

"Exactly right," Sally said, smiling at Doc. "Enjoy your Walleye Martinis and I'll go get your first appetizer."

"Our *first* appetizer?" Delores looked puzzled. "But we only ordered one, didn't we?"

"Yes, but there's a new appetizer that I'm trying out in the bar tonight. If everyone likes it, I may add it to the dinner menu in the restaurant."

"What is it?" Hannah asked.

"Special Boursin Cheese-Filled Mushrooms."

"I love filled mushrooms," Michelle told her.

"Good. Have you ever had them with a French cheese called Boursin?" Michelle shook her head and Sally went on to explain, "It's a kind of cream cheese, and I use the type that's flavored with garlic and herbs."

"That sounds heavenly!" Andrea commented. "Maybe it's a good thing Bill's in Chicago if we're going to have something with garlic. We made a pact when we were first married."

"A pact?" Doc was clearly puzzled.

"Yes, neither one of us could have garlic unless the other one did."

"What happened if you broke the rule?" Lonnie asked her.

"The one who ate garlic had to sleep alone in the guest room."

"How often did that happen?" Michelle wanted to know.

"Never. The bed in the guest room was a couch you had to pull out and it was hideously uncomfortable."

Sally laughed, picked up her tray, and hurried off to get their Special Boursin Cheese-Filled Mushrooms.

"Uh-oh!" Hannah said, after a glance at Sonny's table. "Guess who just arrived at Sonny's table."

"Don't tell me they're back!" Andrea said, looking over at the table and giving a little sigh. "Those two wives are just asking for trouble."

"Why? They're just sitting there," Delores said, observing the guests who'd just arrived at the fishing star's table.

"They're sitting there without their husbands again," Hannah explained. "They did the same thing this morning and their husbands looked extremely unhappy when they got downstairs to the breakfast buffet."

"Well, at least they're not . . ." Andrea stopped speaking and gave another groan. "Dick just put on the music. I hope Sonny doesn't ask one of them to dance."

Mike laughed. "Hope and a buck might buy you a cup of coffee, Andrea. Sonny just motioned to the blonde, and she's getting up from her chair."

"It might be okay," Doc told them. "I've been watching Sonny, and he just polished off all three Walleye Martinis at the table, plus a full-sized Martini to boot!"

"He drank all of them?" Hannah asked.

"Yes, it didn't take him long! He's probably too inebriated to get out of his . . . I'm wrong! He's up!"

They watched as Sonny led the blonde to the small dance floor and grabbed her around the waist. "I think he's using her for balance," Lonnie conjectured.

"Let's hope that's *all* he's doing!" Norman said, glancing toward the doorway. "Two guys are coming in right now with Joey and they don't look very happy."

"It's the husbands," Andrea confirmed. "Joey and Wally took care of it when there was trouble at the breakfast buffet this morning. I hope Joey Zee can calm them down again."

"Joey's got it," Hannah told her, watching as Joey steered the two men over to the table where one of the wives was still sitting.

Doc gave a little nod. "I saw Joey handle several problems this afternoon. I get the feeling that he's used to doing damage control when it comes to situations with Sonny."

Everyone watched as Joey pulled out chairs for the two husbands and went to the dance floor to escort the blonde wife back to the table.

"Sonny looks completely puzzled," Michelle commented.

Delores gave a slight laugh. "You're right, dear. I don't think he has any idea what happened to his dance partner."

"Maybe that's a good thing," Andrea said, giving a little smile.

"And it would be an even better thing if he forgot where his table was and went back up to his room," Hannah added.

"It doesn't look like that's going to happen," Lonnie said, watching as Sonny headed in their direction. "Do you think he forgot where his table was?"

"Maybe," Mike said, "unless . . . nope, he's headed this way," Mike corrected himself. "I wonder if he thinks that Andrea is the woman he was dancing with."

"Me?" Andrea looked completely shocked. "But I don't look anything like her!"

"You've got blonde hair, and he's so drunk he probably doesn't remember *what* she looked like!"

"Whatever are you going to do, dear?" Delores asked, looking slightly amused.

"I . . . I don't know." Andrea appeared terribly conflicted. "I don't want to alienate him. I know Sally and Dick are hoping that the fishing tournament will become a yearly event. But . . ." She turned to Hannah. "Do I have to actually *dance* with him?"

"Yes, but not for long," Michelle jumped in. "As soon as you take a turn around the dance floor with him, I'm going to cut in."

"Thank you, Michelle!" Andrea looked very relieved. "But then you'll be stuck with him."

"No, she won't," Hannah said quickly. "We'll let Michelle dance with him for a minute, and then I'll cut in."

"And once you take your turn with him, I'll cut in," Delores spoke up. "And once I do what I'm going to do, you men can pick him up and take him to his room."

"What are you going to do, Lori?" Doc asked her.

"I'm going to trip him. It won't be hard because he's already practically falling on his face. You go get your fancy gurney. This won't take long at all."

Doc chuckled. "You are something else, Lori!"

"You should have known that when you married me," Delores told him. "There's no way I'm going to let my girls dance with a drunk for long. Believe me, Doc. Sonny will never know what happened in the morning. Now get going! This won't take long at all and you're going to need that gurney."

They all watched as Sonny weaved his way over to their table. "Come on, babe! Dance with me. I'm a big star, you know."

"I've heard," Andrea said, doing her best to be pleasant. "Are you sure you want to dance? We ordered appetizers and they should be here soon."

"I'm sure. I love to dance," Sonny said, grabbing Andrea by the arm and practically pulling her off her chair. "Let's go! The night's young and I wanna hold you!"

"His night's almost over," Michelle said, as Andrea let Sonny push her across the room to the dance floor.

"Play something slow," Sonny shouted at Dick. "This one's even cuter than she was before."

Andrea made a face, and Hannah had all she could do not to laugh. "Once around and that's it," she reminded Michelle. "Andrea doesn't look very patient and you know what a temper she's got."

Michelle nodded. "You bet I do! Don't worry, Hannah."

Hannah watched as Andrea tried her best to keep a little space between herself and Sonny. "And to think Andrea told me she thought Sonny was handsome this morning!"

"He looks pretty gross now," Michelle said, pushing back her chair. "I'd better go rescue Andrea before she coldcocks him. She's been working out at the gym, and I want to get to her before she decides she's had enough."

They all saw Andrea shoot Michelle a grateful glance as she stepped onto the dance floor. Michelle smiled at her sister and gave Andrea the okay sign. "I'm cutting in," Michelle said, grabbing Sonny's arm and pulling him away from Andrea.

"What . . . wha's goin' on?" Sonny asked, giving Michelle a blank look.

"You've got me now," they heard Michelle say. "Let me teach you how to dance, big boy!"

"Whoa!" Sonny began to laugh. "I got a tough girl now! A regular little . . ."

"Don't say it!" Michelle interrupted him. "I wouldn't want to have to wash your mouth out with soap."

"Hoo-hah!" Sonny said with a laugh. "I like 'em mean, babe!"

"Dance," Michelle ordered, pulling him around the floor. "Somebody said you were a star. Is that right?"

"Tha's right. Fishin' star."

Michelle managed to step away slightly as Sonny attempted to pull her closer. "No handling the merchandise," she said. "You pick it up, you have to buy it and you don't have *that* much money."

"Where did she get that line?" Lonnie asked, and Hannah could tell he was trying not to look shocked.

"It's from a play she was in at college," Hannah told him.

"What play was that?" Lonnie asked, but he still looked a bit rattled by this new side of Michelle.

"It was a one-act play and Mother and I drove down to Macalester to see it. She directed it, and she also played the lead. I don't remember the exact title, but I think it had something to do with beach blankets. Mother and I were a bit shocked, and Michelle thought that was hilarious."

"I'm back!" Andrea said, gasping for air as she flopped into her chair. "That was awful! I think I need a drink!"

"Finish mine," Hannah said, shoving her miniature martini glass over to Andrea.

"Thanks!" Hannah watched as Andrea downed the rest of the martini in one gulp. "He's really awful!" she said. "I hope Michelle will be all right."

"She will be if Hannah gets out there," Delores responded. "Michelle's trying to get a little breathing space, but Sonny keeps leaning over her and trying to kiss her."

"I'm going to . . ."

"No, you won't," Mike said quickly. "Stick to the plan, Lonnie. The ladies have got it all figured out."

"That's right," Hannah told him. "You're going to sit there while I go take care of it, and Michelle will come right back to the table."

Norman looked slightly concerned and he turned toward Hannah. "Are you okay, Hannah?"

Hannah patted his shoulder as she stood up. "Don't worry, I got this, Norman. He'll never know what hit him!"

Lonnie didn't look convinced but he stayed seated as Hannah headed for the dance floor.

There were several other couples out on the dance floor, and Hannah skirted them to get to Michelle and Sonny. "My turn," she said, grabbing Sonny by the shoulders and turning him around to face her.

"Not . . . not same," he mumbled, almost falling as she picked up his arm and released Michelle from his grasp. "Back to the table," she hissed to her sister. "Lonnie's getting anxious."

"Very glad to see you," Michelle said quickly, taking her opportunity and running with it. "Good luck, Hannah."

"Han . . . nah," Sonny said, squinting at her. "I know you. Rolls."

"That's right," Hannah said, grabbing his shoulders and turning him toward her. "Dance."

"Roll . . . girl," Sonny said again, wavering a bit on his feet. "Make more."

"You'll have them tomorrow morning," Hannah promised, shoving him around the floor. "Move your feet, Sonny. Don't pass out on me. I'm not going to catch you."

"Catch me, catch me if you can," he mumbled, but he did move his feet. And that's when she saw Delores standing up at the table.

"I didn't have that much time on the ice," she said, echoing one of her favorite hockey expressions. "Just don't fall down yet, Sonny, and spoil Mother's fun."

Delores was smiling as she came across the room with Doc, Mike, and Lonnie. "My turn," she said to Sonny, lifting his arms, putting them around her shoulders, and tromping on his foot.

"Owwww!" Sonny groaned. "Wha's you do tha' for?"

"For this," Doc said, motioning to Lonnie, who grabbed Sonny's left arm, and Mike, who grabbed Sonny's right arm.

"Owwww!" Sonny complained again, limping a bit as the two men half walked, half carried him across the room. "Say bye-bye, Sonny," Delores said, escorting them as far as the door.

"Looks like Doc's got a D.R.I.," Hannah said, sitting down next to Norman.

"Dance-related injury?" he guessed.

"Either that or Delores-related injury. They both apply." Hannah turned to Delores. "Nice footwork, Mother."

Delores smiled. "Thank you, dear. Here comes Sally with our drinks."

Sally arrived at their table slightly breathless. "You did a really good job handling Sonny," she told them, setting the tray on the table and distributing the glasses. "Dick said Mike called down to say they were on their way back. He's keeping your appetizers warm and he'll bring them over when everyone gets here. And by the way, tonight's drinks are on us. We appreciate all the help you gave us with Sonny."

"Joey called Wally to tell him what happened, and Wally thanks you, too."

"Where is Wally?" Hannah asked, realizing that the organizer of the fishing tournament wasn't in attendance.

"He had to drive up to Brainerd tonight. They're opening a new store tomorrow and he promised them he'd be there for the opening. He'll be back tomorrow afternoon, though." Sally looked up as Doc, Mike, and Lonnie returned to the bar. "Here come the rest of your group. I'll go help Dick bring the appetizers. He can hardly wait to see what Doc thinks of his Baked Scotch Eggs."

It only took a few moments to serve the appetizers, and Doc began to smile as he bit into his Baked Scotch Egg. "Perfect," he said. "I like these even better than the deep-fried kind."

"And they're healthier, too . . . aren't they, dear?" Delores asked him.

"I suppose they are," Doc said quickly. "I never thought about that before. Scotch Eggs are so good, I didn't really care."

"And that's why Doc's a great doctor!" Sally said.

"Agreed," Hannah added. "It's one of the reasons we all love him. Doc always says that sometimes eating great food is worth sacrificing a few calories or grams of cholesterol."

BAKED SCOTCH EGGS

**DO NOT preheat oven until you have read
Hannah's 1st Note.**

Hannah's 1st Note: There is a bit of preparation you must do before you can make these Baked Scotch Eggs. The day before you plan to make them, hard-boil 4 large eggs. (Or 8 large eggs if you plan to double this recipe.)

Once the eggs are hard-boiled, place them in the refrigerator overnight to chill. Baked Scotch Eggs are much easier to make if the hard-boiled eggs are chilled.

Ingredients:

>   4 large eggs, hard-boiled
>   12 oz. bulk pork sausage *(I used Farmer
>   John's Premium Original pork
>   sausage, it comes in a chub)*
>   1 teaspoon dried, minced onion *(you can
>   find this in the spice aisle)*
>   1 teaspoon salt
>   ¼ cup all-purpose flour *(pack it down in
>   the cup when you measure it)*
>   ¾ cup Progresso Italian Style Bread Crumbs

1 fresh egg, beaten *(just crack it into a glass and beat it up with a fork)*

Instructions:

When you're ready to bake, preheat oven to 400 degrees F., rack in the middle position.

While your oven is preheating, prepare your baking sheet by lining a cookie sheet or jelly roll pan with parchment paper.

Take your hard-boiled eggs out of the refrigerator.

Peel the eggs, making sure no shell remains.

In a large bowl, mix the 12 ounces of pork sausage with the teaspoon of dried, minced onion.

Sprinkle on a teaspoon of salt and mix everything up together.

Divide the sausage mixture into 4 (four) equal portions.

Make each portion into a flat patty.

Place ¼ cup of all-purpose flour in a flat bowl. Spread out the flour in the bowl. *(When I made these, I used a pie plate to hold the flour.)*

Roll each peeled, hard-boiled egg in flour to coat it.

Place one floured egg on one of the sausage patties.

Shape the sausage around the egg, covering the egg completely.

Repeat for the other eggs until all of them are coated with sausage.

If you haven't done so already, crack the fresh egg into a bowl and whip it up with a fork.

If there is flour left over in the flat bowl, dump it out and replace it with Progresso Italian Style Bread Crumbs.

Dip each sausage-coated egg into the beaten egg mixture, coating the outside with beaten egg.

Quickly roll the resulting creation in the breadcrumbs, making sure it is coated completely.

Place the finished hard-boiled egg on the parchment-lined baking sheet.

Repeat with the other eggs, leaving an inch or two between the eggs.

Bake your eggs at 400 degrees F. for 35 to 40 minutes or until the sausage has been cooked.

Remove the baking sheet from the oven and let your Baked Scotch Eggs cool on the baking sheet for at least 10 minutes before serving them to your guests.

Hannah's 2nd Note: If you have trouble dipping the sausage-coated eggs in the egg wash, you can brush the egg wash on the outside of the sausage. Be sure to coat the eggs with the wash completely.

Hannah's 3rd Note: Rather than rolling the eggs in the bread crumbs, you can place the egg in the flat bowl with the bread crumbs and sprinkle them over the whole surface.

Yield: 4 delicious treats or appetizers that everyone will enjoy.

SPECIAL BOURSIN CHEESE-FILLED MUSHROOMS

Preheat oven to 350 degrees F., rack in the middle position.

Ingredients:

20 large fresh mushrooms (*get a few extra, just in case*)

5-ounce container of Boursin cheese (*I like to use the kind that comes mixed with herbs*)

¼ cup bread crumbs (*I used Progresso Italian Style*)

⅛ teaspoon salt

Directions:

Start by preparing your baking sheet. Line a baking sheet (*I prefer a jelly roll pan because it has sides*) with parchment paper.

Begin by washing and drying your mushrooms. (*Do this gently and pat them dry using paper towels.*)

If your mushrooms have stems, twist and then pull them out. Throw away the stems. You won't need them for this recipe.

Place your mushrooms on your baking sheet.

Get out a microwave-safe bowl that will hold at least a cup and a half.

Take your Boursin cheese out of the refrigerator, remove the top of the container, scoop out the cheese, and place it in the microwave-safe bowl.

Heat the cheese in the microwave for 30 seconds on HIGH.

Stir in the salt.

Let the cheese rest in the microwave for another 30 seconds.

Remove the bowl from the microwave and stir the cheese around with a fork from your silverware drawer. If it stirs easily, set it on the kitchen counter.

Measure out the quarter-cup of bread crumbs. If the kind you bought doesn't contain seasonings, add a few Italian seasonings to the crumbs.

Hannah's 1ˢᵗ Note: My Italian style bread crumbs had onion powder, garlic salt, parsley, and a few other Italian spices.

Add the bread crumbs to the bowl with the salt and the softened cheese, mixing them in as you go.

Hannah's 2ⁿᵈ Note: This is easier if you don't just dump in the bread crumbs all at once. Add them little by little, mixing with the fork before you add more.

Pick up one of the mushrooms and wipe the outside of the cap with softened salted butter. This is easy to do if you use a square of folded cheesecloth to dip into the butter and wipe it on the outside of the mushroom cap. Do this with all of your mushrooms before you begin to fill them with the cheese mixture.

Choose a small spoon from your silverware drawer to scoop out a spoonful of the cheese mixture and fill the cavity of the mushroom caps.

Hannah's 3ʳᵈ Note: Fill your mushrooms all the way to the top of the cavity, but don't mound

them too much on top. You don't want your delicious filling to melt over the sides of the mushrooms.

HANNAH'S MAKE AHEAD TIP: If you like, you can do all this in the morning before you want to serve your Special Boursin Cheese-Filled Mushrooms. If you fill all of the mushrooms ahead of time, cover the baking sheet securely with plastic wrap, and place it in the refrigerator, you can get them out when your company arrives, let them warm up 15 minutes on the kitchen counter, and then bake them.

Bake your mushrooms at 350 degrees F. for 15 minutes. Then take them out of the oven and let them cool on a cold stovetop burner or a wire rack. DO NOT serve these immediately. They must cool for at least 10 to 15 minutes before you serve them.

To serve, place each mushroom on a salted cracker, salt side down, and arrange them on a pretty platter. It's best if you prepare to make a double batch and have more ready to go in the refrigerator. Believe me, your guests will gobble them up and beg you for more!

Yield: At least 20 large Special Boursin Cheese-Filled Mushrooms that everyone will enjoy as an appetizer. They are especially good with dry white or red wine.

Chapter
Six

Hannah groaned when the alarm clock rang at four the next morning. It was time to get up, and she felt as though she'd just gone to bed. After Andrea had gone home to pack her overnight bag and Norman had taken the cats and their things to Delores and Doc's penthouse, the three of them had stayed up late in the lobby talking.

Reluctantly, Hannah got out of bed, put on her robe, and was just trying to decide if she was awake enough to take a shower without drowning when she heard a soft knock on the door. Puzzled, she went to answer it and found one of Sally's kitchen workers standing outside with a tray.

"I hope I didn't wake you," the woman said, handing the tray to Hannah. "Sally said to bring up coffee. She's in the kitchen starting the rolls and she said to tell you that she started breakfast for you two."

Hannah hoped she didn't look quite as shocked as she felt. "Sally's up already?"

"Yes. Sally always gets up at three-thirty. There's a

lot of prep work to be done in the kitchen and she likes to help."

"But does Sally ever sleep?"

"Oh, yes. She takes a two-hour nap every afternoon right after the lunch buffet."

"Sounds like Sally gets about as much sleep as you do," Andrea said, climbing out of bed so that she could pour herself a cup of coffee. "Shall I pour one for you, Hannah?"

"Not yet. I'm awake now so I'll take a quick shower and get dressed first."

"I love room service," Andrea said, sitting down on the side of her bed and sipping coffee. "It's coffee you don't have to make and food you don't have to cook. What could be better than that?"

"Not a whole lot," Hannah replied, heading off to the shower.

Taking a shower didn't take long. Hannah stepped out of the spacious shower enclosure ten minutes later, wrapped in a large bath sheet. She reminded herself to go to CostMart to pick up the kind of bath sheets that Sally used as she toweled off. Then she wrapped herself in the old-fashioned chenille robe she'd picked up at Lake Eden's thrift store, Helping Hands, and walked back out into the bedroom. "Your turn," she said to Andrea. "The shower's set on hot and it's hot enough to cook shrimp in a couple of minutes, so reduce the temperature if you don't like it very hot and almost scalding."

"Will do," Andrea said. "Thanks for telling me. There's a croissant left on the tray if you want it. And Sally sent us two dishes of cut-up fruit. I ate mine and left yours."

"Thanks," Hannah said, heading to the closet to

choose the long-sleeved billboard tee shirt she wanted for the day. She pulled a forest green one with the words "The Cookie Jar" emblazed across the chest in red and spread it out on her bed. Then she dressed quickly, slipped on a forest green sweater, and went to pour her first cup of what many people of Scandinavian descent called "Swedish Plasma" in Lake Eden, Minnesota.

The coffee she poured was hot and strong and Hannah drank it greedily. As she sipped, she decided that she agreed with Andrea. Room service was one of the joys of staying in a hotel on vacation. And even though this wasn't exactly a vacation, there were times, like now, when she almost felt like it was.

One glance at the pastry basket told her that Andrea had eaten her croissant and one of the muffins that had probably been there. She picked up the second muffin, slathered it with butter, and smiled as she tasted it. The butter was salted and the muffin was delicious. It took her a moment to recognize the flavor of the fruit inside, and she began to smile as she realized that it was rhubarb. Rhubarb was a favorite fruit in Minnesota. Almost everyone Hannah knew who owned a house had rhubarb growing somewhere in their yard. Because it was so plentiful and people didn't have to go to the grocery store to buy it, it was used in a multitude of bakery goods. There were rhubarb muffins, rhubarb pie, rhubarb cookies, rhubarb cakes, and rhubarb cookie bars. There was also a plentiful supply of rhubarb sauce in almost every household. It was served even more often than cranberry sauce. It graced the table with every meat, fish, or poultry, and some people, including Hannah's great-grandmother Elsa, had even spread it on bologna sandwiches to add a little interest. Actually, now that she thought about it, Hannah could only think of one baked item using rhubarb that she'd never heard of.

"I'm ready," Andrea said, coming out of the bathroom fully dressed. "Is there any more coffee?"

"There's plenty. Sally sent up two pots," Hannah told her. "Do you know anyone who's ever made a rhubarb soufflé?"

Andrea thought about that for a moment and shook her head. "No. Did the rhubarb muffin bring on that train of thought?"

"Yes. I was trying to think of some baked item that hadn't used rhubarb."

Andrea thought it over for several seconds and then she shook her head. "I don't think I've ever heard of a rhubarb soufflé."

"Neither have I. Maybe I should try making one."

"You could, but . . . maybe it'll be like Michelle's duck soup."

Hannah was slightly taken aback. "Michelle makes duck soup?"

"That's past tense. Michelle *made* duck soup," Andrea corrected her. "Only once, and everyone agreed that she should never make it again."

"What was wrong with it?"

"It was dreadful! She tried it while you were away at college and invited Bill and I over for dinner. That was before Tracey was born."

"Did she make it like turkey soup?"

"Yes. She told us she used a turkey soup recipe and just substituted the duck. It was awful, Hannah."

"But why?"

"I'm not sure. Bill and I like duck and so did Dad and Mother. I'm not exactly sure why we didn't like the soup, but none of us could eat more than a spoonful before we had to go pick up pizza."

Hannah considered that for a moment. "I'm not sure why it wouldn't work, but now that I think about it, I've never seen a recipe for duck soup. There's baked duck, warm duck salad, and duck pate, but no duck soup."

"Take it from me, there's a reason. Once you've tried Michelle's Duck Soup . . . you'll *duck* soup for the rest of your life."

Hannah groaned and rolled her eyes,

"Are you going to eat that croissant?" Andrea asked.

"There's another?" Hannah asked, pulling the napkin back a little farther.

"Yes, and I think it's a chocolate croissant."

"Ah yes. I see it. Do you want it, Andrea?"

"Yes, if you don't. I miss Bill a little and I think the chocolate might make me feel a little happier."

Hannah bit back a smile. It was one of the lamest excuses she'd ever heard, but Andrea deserved to have it. Sally had mentioned that Andrea had refused to take a salary and she was working long hours right along with Hannah. "You can have it," Hannah said, passing the basket to Andrea. "And when you're finished, we'd better get down to the kitchen. The woman who brought up the breakfast tray said that Sally had already started the Caramel Pecan Rolls."

"Right," Andrea said, taking a bite of the chocolate croissant, giving a little sigh of enjoyment, and retrieving her socks and shoes. "This won't take me long and then I'll be ready to go."

True to her word, Andrea was ready to leave the room in less than five minutes. Hannah picked up her saddlebag-size purse to follow her sister when she realized that Andrea was carrying the bag she usually carried with her when she went to work at the real estate office.

"Why are you taking your work bag, Andrea?" Hannah asked her.

"I'm taking it because I have to run back to the office right after we finish with the buffet and I didn't want to have to go back up to the room again. It's okay if I leave it in the kitchen while we're doing the buffet, isn't it?"

"I'm sure it is," Hannah said quickly. "You're coming back later then, aren't you?"

"Of course I am. I just need to go in to print some flyers and show one house. I'll be back in time to watch the weigh-in for the fishing contest and take a couple of pictures to send to Bill. He's going to call me on my cell phone later and he wants to know who's ahead on the first day."

The two sisters walked down the hall, and Hannah pointed to the door on the end. "That's Sonny's suite," she said.

"That's one of Sally's bridal suites, isn't it?"

"Yes. It's the same one that I stayed in," Hannah said, feeling a slight pang of regret. "It's beautiful, Andrea. The bedroom is huge and the living room has everything you could ever want in a living room. And the bath has its own Jacuzzi."

"Sounds nice," Andrea commented. "Somehow, I don't think Sonny was in any shape to appreciate all that space last night."

Hannah gave a little laugh. "I'm pretty sure you're right. Mother told me that Doc gave him something to keep him asleep until this morning so he couldn't cause any more trouble in the bar."

"I wonder if he's up yet," Andrea said.

"I doubt it. Doc told Mother that he would probably sleep until noon."

"But Wally's not here. Who's going to handle the fishing contest?"

"Joey. Doc warned him that he might have to take over in the morning, and Joey said that was fine with him. Everybody really likes Joey."

"I know, and I bet they won't miss Mr. Fishing Star at all," Andrea said.

"Probably not." Once the elevator stopped and they got off, they walked through the lobby and headed directly to the kitchen. When they got there, they found Sally sitting at the kitchen table, drinking a cup of coffee.

"Hi, Sally," Hannah greeted her. "What do you want us to do first?"

"Have a cup of coffee with me," Sally said with a smile. "Did you two girls sleep well?"

"I did," Andrea responded immediately.

"So did I," Hannah said. "Are you sure there isn't any prep work you need us to do, Sally?"

"Nothing yet. I'll get started on the cakes for the lunch buffet. The crew in the other kitchen is making the other dishes for the breakfast buffet, so all we have to do is bake some cookies for the bags the fishermen are taking out on the lake with them."

"That sounds good to me," Hannah said, heading for the kitchen coffeepot. "Thanks for the tray this morning, Sally. I'm not sure I would have made it without the coffee you sent up to us."

"Me neither," Andrea said quickly. "Thank you, Sally. That was a real help."

"I told Beatrice to bring the same thing up to you every morning," Sally told them. "We had ten walk-in late contestants last night and that brings the total up to the contest limit. Joey told me that this is the best-attended event they've ever had, and Wally was extremely happy about that."

"Here you go, Andrea," Hannah said, handing her sister a full cup of coffee. "When I pour mine, it's going to drain the pot. Do you want me to put on another one, Sally?"

"Heavens yes! I'm not entirely caffeinated yet."

"Me neither," Andrea said.

It didn't take them long to drink their coffee and then the three women went to work. There were moments of silence when all three of them were concentrating on the tasks they were completing, but there was also some conversation about the fishing competition, the contestants, and the work that remained to be done.

"Break time!" Sally announced when the rolls had been baked, the cakes for the lunch buffet were cooling on the bakers rack, and the cookies had been shaped and were baking in one of the ovens.

"I smell coffee," Doc said, coming into the kitchen. "Is there a cup for a hardworking doctor?"

"Of course there is," Sally said quickly, "but would you like a cup too, Doc?"

Doc laughed. "You're a piece of work, Sally. And so early in the morning, too!"

"I've been up since three," Sally told him. "How about you?"

"Not me. Lori wanted to talk last night and we were up late. She was still sleeping when I left the penthouse, and I didn't want to wake her by rummaging around in the kitchen."

"I'll get you a cup, Doc," Hannah offered, hurrying to the coffeepot to pour him a cup. "You take it black, don't you?"

"Yes, but not this morning. I need a little carb jolt."

"Is that doctor's advice?" Andrea asked him.

"Yes, but don't tell anyone, especially Lori. She says I'm gaining weight."

"Are you?" Hannah asked him.

"I don't know. I haven't weighed myself. And just between the four of us, I plan to keep it that way."

"How's Sonny this morning?" Hannah asked him.

"Up and getting dressed. I checked on him about ten minutes ago and he said he felt great."

"Did you ask him if he remembered anything about last night?" Andrea wanted to know.

Doc shook his head. "I didn't think that would be a good idea. It might be best if he doesn't remember."

"Did he mention it at all?" Sally asked.

"No. He just said he felt fine and he was going to wake up Joey and they were going to go out on the lake before the breakfast buffet."

"Then he won't be at the buffet?" Hannah drew the obvious conclusion.

"It didn't sound like it." Doc took a sip of his coffee and then he gave a deep sigh. "I probably shouldn't say this because it's conjecture on my part. I don't have any real proof, but I have the feeling that what happened last night was not a first for Sonny. I bet he's done this sort of thing before other fishing tournaments."

"That wouldn't surprise me a bit," Sally said. "As a matter of fact, Dick said the same thing to me last night. Dick thinks Sonny may be a functional alcoholic."

"What's a functional alcoholic?" Andrea asked her. "I thought most alcoholics weren't functional at all."

"Functional alcoholism is interesting," Doc told them. "I've done some research on it. Most people don't

even realize they're dealing with someone with a
drinking problem. When I was in medical school, I
rented an apartment with three other guys, and our
neighbor next door was a functional alcoholic. He held
down a job during the week and didn't drink a drop of
alcohol. Then, when he got off work on Friday, he started
binge drinking and he didn't stop until six o'clock in
the evening on Sunday. The four of us watched him
rapidly fill up the garbage bin with alcohol bottles.
But, when he went to work on Monday morning, he
was stone-cold sober."

Hannah gave a little shiver. "That's an awful way to
live," she commented.

"Yes, but it worked for him. I talked to him one
Friday when he got home from work and I asked him
about it. He told me he'd been doing it for years and he
never drank during the week because he had such a re-
sponsible job."

"What did he do?" Andrea asked.

"He worked at a munitions factory in Minneapolis."

"That's frightening!" Sally sounded nervous about
what she'd just learned. "Are you absolutely sure he
never drank at work?"

"No." Doc shook his head. "All I have is my own
opinion, but I believed him when he said he never
touched alcohol during the week. I did manage to
check his work record, and he'd been working at the
same place for twenty-seven years and there wasn't a
single employee complaint in his file. I also found out
he'd been promoted several times, and he was a shift
supervisor in charge of hundreds of workers. That convinced me that he was telling the truth."

"That's still pretty frightening," Andrea said. "What
if one of those workers had made a mistake when they

were making bullets or whatever they made. They could have blown up and killed people."

"That's true," Doc said. "I often wondered what happened to him after we left our apartment for one in a better area. Then, one day, I saw a photo of workers who had retired from that munitions factory and he was in the front row."

"That makes me feel a little better," Sally told him.

"It made me feel better, too," Doc admitted. "Since they retired him with honors, I guess he must have managed to get through his whole work career without any alcohol-related mishaps." Doc finished his coffee and got up. "I'd better let you ladies get back to work. I have to call the hospital to check in and see how my interns are doing."

"That was interesting," Hannah said when Doc had left. "I learned something new. I knew there were functional alcoholics, but I always thought they'd slip up eventually."

"I think a lot of them do," Sally said. "I'll ask Dick if he knows any more about it. Since we bought this place and he became the head bartender, he's been learning a lot from his bar customers."

"Like what?" Andrea asked, obviously unwilling to give up their conversation quite yet.

"Like how to cut someone off without making them angry. That takes a certain talent. There's only one person I can think of who's better at that than Dick is."

"Who's that?" Hannah asked.

"Your mother. Stepping on Sonny's foot and pushing him into Mike and Lonnie's arms was a stroke of pure genius."

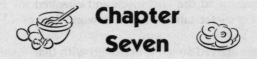

Chapter
Seven

Three hours later, the morning baking was finished, and Hannah and Andrea were standing behind the breakfast buffet table. They were serving those who needed help and refilling various platters and dishes as needed. They'd had a few minutes to run up to their room to freshen up and now they were back on duty again.

"There's the blonde wife and her friend," Andrea said as the two women walked into the dining room.

"I see them," Hannah told her. "The blonde looked around for a few moments and now they're heading for an empty table."

"I bet she was looking for Sonny," Andrea said. "It's a good thing he's not here at the buffet this morning because here come their husbands."

Both sisters watched as the husbands spotted their wives and joined them at the table.

"At least there won't be a problem this morning," Andrea commented, sounding relieved. "Do we have a backup pan of breakfast enchiladas, Hannah? This pan only has two left."

Hannah lifted the tablecloth and checked the shelf under the buffet table. "Do you want the red or the green?"

"These are red so we'd better go with that," Andrea told her. "I can add these two to the full pan."

"Sally's breakfast enchiladas are really popular with this crowd," Hannah remarked.

"I know. I was a little surprised when Sally told us that we were making enchiladas for breakfast."

"So was I until I read the recipe. Everything inside is practically a staple for breakfast."

"You're right. You can't go wrong with scrambled eggs, cheese, potatoes, and ham. If we have any left, I'm going to try one to see what it tastes like."

"I'm going to try two, a red and a green," Hannah decided. "Do you want me to hold out one of each for us?"

"Yes, if you can."

"I can," Hannah said, salting away the two red enchiladas that were still in the pan and passing a full steam table tray to Andrea.

"I wonder why Sally's so fond of Mexican food," Andrea said. "I could understand if we lived in a big city where there were lots of ethnic restaurants."

"I think I know why . . ." Hannah said. "Sally and Dick spent a week in Mexico on their honeymoon, and they went back a couple of times after that. I think that's when Sally fell in love with Mexican food. I know she can make it the traditional way, but she told me that she likes to play with the recipes and do new things with them."

"Like these Breakfast Enchiladas?" Andrea asked.

"Yes. Check the tray of green enchiladas, will you, Andrea? There's another full pan under here."

"Three left," Andrea said, moving to the second pan.

"Okay. Give me that pan and I'll pass you the full one. And when those are eaten, we'll just have to tell everyone that the enchiladas are gone."

"I don't think it'll take very long," Andrea said, taking the full pan and setting it out. "The guys at the closest table saw that I was putting out new pans and now they're standing up and heading this way. Did you make a copy of Sally's recipe, Hannah?"

"Of course I did."

"Oh good! I really think that I could make those some morning for Bill."

"I think you could, too." Hannah refilled the pan of bacon and set it out. "The fishermen are hungry this morning."

"I know, and so am I. I know we had breakfast, but that was hours ago. And standing back here, looking at all that good food, is just about killing me."

"I heard that," Sally said, coming over to join them. "Do you want to take a little time off to eat? My third waitress just came on and she can refill trays with me. And I've already made the rounds of the tables and greeted everyone."

"Could we?" Andrea looked almost pathetically eager. "I think I'm starving, Sally."

"Then go fill a plate, find an empty table, and enjoy yourselves. You girls worked hard this morning and you deserve a meal break. We only have a couple more hours to go and you two are through for the day."

"Are you sure?" Hannah asked.

"I'm sure. Get out of here and eat. And let me know what you think of the Breakfast Enchiladas."

It was time to reveal her small theft, and Hannah

drew the two nearly empty pans out from under the buffet table. "We planned on it, Sally. And I saved two apiece for us."

"Good! I'll take that as a compliment. Let me know how you like them."

"We will," Hannah promised, handing Andrea a plate. "Thank you, Sally. I'm really looking forward to this breakfast."

Hannah and Andrea filled their plates and turned around to find a table when Norman stood up. "Hannah! Over here!" he called out to her. "We have two empty chairs for you."

"Norman to the rescue," Andrea said, following Hannah to the table. "You know . . . you really ought to . . ."

"Not now," Hannah said, setting down her plate and greeting his tablemate. "Hello, Doc."

"Hi, Hannah. I hope you tried the Breakfast Enchiladas. They're really terrifi—never mind. I see you held out some for yourself."

Hannah laughed. "Of course. Andrea and I have been filling those pans all morning and the scent of those Breakfast Enchiladas was just about killing us. I really had to work to keep myself from reaching out, snatching one, and ducking down behind the buffet table to scarf it down."

Norman laughed. "If I'd been back there, I think I would have done it. They're great, Hannah. Did you make them?"

"All three of us did. Sally perfected the recipe and Andrea and I put them together and baked them."

"Well, you did a great job," Doc praised them. "Tell Sally to put them on the breakfast buffet again and I'll roust Lori out of bed and bring her out here. I know she'd love them."

"You're probably right," Hannah agreed, forking her first bite of the Breakfast Enchilada. "Mmmmm!"

"Would you ladies like coffee?" one of the waitresses asked, coming up to the table.

"Mmmmmm," Hannah replied, still chewing.

"Yes, please," Andrea, who had already swallowed her first bite, told her. "Hannah drinks it black and I like mine with a little cream."

"How's Sonny?" Hannah asked Doc when she could talk again.

"Better than I expected," Doc told her. "He was pretty chipper this morning when I went to see if he needed anything and he went out on the fishing boat with Joey."

"He certainly wasn't chipper last night!" Norman said, frowning a bit. "Do you think all that drinking he did will catch up with him later?"

"I don't know, but we'll see. It's like I told the girls this morning. I think he's used to binge drinking and he'll probably get through this episode without any problems."

"That's more than a little scary," Hannah commented.

"It is," Doc agreed. "Let's just hope that he can do everything he's supposed to do for the fishing competition today. I'll be around for the weigh-in at one this afternoon and we'll see."

Norman rose from his chair. "Speaking of weigh-ins, I'd better get out there if I'm going to catch any fish. Do you have any tips, Doc?"

Doc laughed. "Not unless you run into a school of suicidal Walleyes."

Andrea looked surprised. "Are there suicidal fish?"

Doc laughed. "I think every fish I've ever caught was suicidal, because I sure don't have any talent as an angler. It's too bad Bill couldn't be here, Andrea. He was quite a fisherman in his day."

"He was?" Andrea looked surprised. "I didn't know that!"

"Just ask him and he'll tell you about the big one he caught that somehow managed to get away. He's told me that story before, and every time he tells it, the fish gets bigger and bigger."

Norman, Hannah, and Andrea laughed. Doc was pulling their legs and it was funny. "How about you, Doc?" Andrea asked. "Did you ever catch any really big fish?"

"Hundreds. Just buy me a shot of scotch whiskey and I'll tell you all about it. And now, you two had better get back to work and Norman had better get out on the lake to see if he can win this tournament."

"Do you think you stand a chance?" Andrea asked Norman as they stood up to leave the table.

"About as much as a snowball in Hades," Norman replied, grinning at her. "I've never been a great fisherman, but I really enjoy being out on the lake. And that's why I'm here." He turned to Hannah. "Do you want to go out on the lake with me when you get off work this afternoon?"

"I do," Hannah said quickly, making up her mind immediately.

"But how about your afternoon nap?" Andrea asked, looking slightly worried.

"I'll forgo it today," Hannah told her. "I've never seen a suicidal fish before, and I want to be there to save its life and throw it back into Eden Lake."

Hannah yawned as she changed into jeans and a sweatshirt. It was a warm day, but it was always a bit chilly on the water. She pulled her hair back in a makeshift ponytail, picked up a cloth hat with a brim, and hurried down the stairs to meet Norman.

They'd agreed to meet in the lobby, and Hannah found Norman waiting for her. "Sorry that I'm a little late," she apologized. "I went back to the kitchen to pack up a couple of sandwiches and some cookies."

"Thanks, Hannah," Norman said, looking slightly amused. "I don't think I'm going to get hungry."

"Maybe not, but I brought something just in case. Sally had some of her Pear Cobbler left so I wrapped up a couple of pieces for us."

Norman glanced at the large bag that Hannah was carrying. "We've only got a couple of hours left on the lake before the end-of-day weigh-in. I really doubt we'll be able to eat everything you brought."

"Oh, this isn't all food." Hannah gestured toward the bag. "I've got a lightweight jacket, an extra pair of sunglasses, and some sunscreen in there."

"It's a cloudy afternoon, Hannah," Norman reminded her.

"I know, but you can get sunburned on cloudy days, too."

"You're right about that," Norman agreed. "When I was a kid and I went fishing with my dad, I got the worst sunburn of my life."

Hannah gave a little nod. "The same thing happened to me. It was a hot day and I was wearing my bathing suit at the time. I got a sunburn so bad, I couldn't wear any clothes except my bathing suit for three days!"

Norman slipped an arm around her shoulders and they walked down to the lakeshore. "I'm glad you're going with me, Hannah," he told her as she climbed into the rented fishing boat.

"It's a beautiful boat," Hannah told him, heading for

one of the bucket seats in the front. "Do you want me to untie us from the dock?"

"Yes, if you don't mind."

Hannah loosened the rope that tethered the boat and Norman started the motor. "It's not an outboard motor?" she asked, glancing at the back of the boat.

"There's an outboard back there, but it's a small one and it's just for trolling. This one's an inboard and it starts like a car. All I have to do is turn the key and press the Start button."

"Things have changed since the last time I went fishing," Hannah said, once they'd pulled away from the dock. "I remember my dad pulling the cord about a million times to start the motor."

"Same here. Everything is easier now, Hannah. I've been thinking about buying this boat, or one just like it. I talked to Dick about it and he said he rents summer dock space for fishermen who want to leave their boats here."

"He has that much room?" Hannah asked, surprised.

"Not on the dock we just left, but he has another dock right past the convention center. I brought the boat up and tethered it here while I was waiting for you to get ready to go. The other dock is U-shaped and it's a lot larger. It's the perfect setup for fishing, Hannah. Dick even has a bait shop and a boat rental business down there."

"Are you going to be using live bait?" Hannah asked, crossing her fingers for luck. She really hoped Norman wouldn't ask her to put angleworms or grubs on the hook. Everybody said that worms couldn't feel it, but she didn't believe it and she always felt sorry for them.

"Live bait isn't permitted in this contest," Norman said, causing Hannah to give a little sigh of relief.

"Wally's promoting his new line of tackle, and he gave every contestant a full tackle box with his gear in it when we signed up for the tournament."

"What's in it?" Hannah asked.

"Take a look. It's right in back of your seat and it's a really nice tackle box. I'm sure Wally is hoping that everyone will come to Wally's Sporting World when the competition is over and add some of his new lines of tackle."

"Does he have very many lines?"

"Yes, and he has other tackle boxes for them. If you want to, you can buy a tackle box for every kind of fish, depending on whether you're lake fishing or fly fishing."

"And you got the Walleye tackle box?"

"Yes. Take a look, Hannah. There's all sorts of goodies in there."

Hannah turned around and spotted a small red tackle box. She retrieved it, placed it on her lap, and opened it.

"There's practically everything in here and it's all labeled," she said, impressed at the way the tackle box was organized. "I bet this would cost a fortune if you bought it at one of Wally's sporting goods stores."

"You're probably right."

"The tackle box has got a whole section in here labeled *spoons*. They look like something my dad would have used when we used to go fishing. What do you do with this one, Norman?" Hannah inquired.

"That's called a Silver Streak mini. I would probably rig that on a line weighted down to run at about 25 or 30 feet deep and troll along at about 3 miles per hour or so. Some people really like to use crankbait on Walleyes but you have to go slower with crankbait at those depths. I like to fish a bit deeper than most Lake

Edenites, because I have a feeling that is where the really big fish hang out!"

"Have you ever caught a really big Walleye, Norman?"

"Hmm, that's quite a leading question to ask any fisherman, Hannah. I suppose I could tell you about the one that got away."

"Really?" Hannah asked with a small smile. "The one that got away, huh? Just how big was it?"

"It was so big that for a minute I thought that Jonah would pop out of his mouth!"

Hannah laughed. "Seriously, is there anything I can do for you, Norman?"

Norman turned to smile at her. "Just keep me company, Hannah. You've been working all morning. There's a bench seat in the back of the boat, and if you get sleepy you can take a little nap while you enjoy the breeze on the lake."

"But you might need me to help you net a fish. Dad taught all three of us girls to handle a net."

"I'll let you know if I need help. I thought we'd head out to that area by the water lily pond. It seems the most likely place to catch Walleyes."

"Really?" Hannah asked, a bit surprised. "Why is it the most likely place?"

"Because Walleyes have very photosensitive eyes. They like the shadows when it's bright daylight, so in the daytime they prefer water with some plant cover or overhanging limbs. The plant cover protects them from predators, yet it spreads out enough to still let some light get through the water so that they can identify their prey."

"That makes sense, I guess. What do Walleyes usually eat?"

"Smaller fish like minnows, shads, insects, and other small live things."

"Then why did Wally say no live bait?"

"I'm sure it's partially because he wanted us to try his new line of Walleye tackle, but there's probably another reason, too. Using live bait can contaminate the water, and Eden Lake is known for its clear water. I'm sure Wally didn't want to do anything that might hurt the environment."

"That makes sense and I'm sure Wally was concerned with public opinion, too. I doubt he'd want the conservationists on his back."

"You're right." Norman smiled at her. "Most fishermen care about the environment, especially in Minnesota. We try to keep our lakes clean and our wildlife, including our fish, healthy."

Hannah smiled back at Norman. Even though he'd spent some of his adult life in other states, he was a true Minnesotan at heart.

As they made their way out on the lake, Hannah looked up at the sky. What she saw made her frown. The moment she'd left the air-conditioned Inn, she'd noticed that it was very muggy. The air was heavy and very still. Normally out on Eden Lake, you could hear the gulls and some of the shore birds. This afternoon, it was silent. Except for the occasional buzzing of an insect, there were no sounds at all.

"It's quiet out here today," she said, turning to look up at the sky. It was grey, and as she swiveled to look toward the West, she realized that it was growing darker. "Do you think it's going to rain?" she asked.

"Maybe. I've got two raincoats in the bench seat. All you have to do is lift it and pull it out if you need one."

"Thanks," Hannah said quickly. "I used to always

bring a poncho with me when I went fishing with my dad. He really liked to fish in the rain. He said the fishing was better then."

"I've heard that before, but I'm not sure I believe it. We can go in if it starts raining, Hannah."

Hannah shrugged. "Rain doesn't bother me all that much. I don't melt."

"Keep your eye on the sky, Hannah. If it starts to turn a kind of greyish yellow, point it out to me right away and we'll head for the dock at full speed."

"Because it could be a tornado?" Hannah asked.

"Yes. I've never been out on a lake during a tornado before, and I don't think I want to experience it."

"Fine with me!" Hannah gave a little laugh. "Have you ever been through a tornado, Norman?"

"Not outside, but Mom used to rush me down in the basement every time the tornado warning siren went off. Actually, I'm not sure which one would be worse— the tornado or the cellar. The cellar smelled musty, and except for one lightbulb hanging from the ceiling, it was dark down there."

"My mother did the same thing," Hannah said, remembering how she'd hated going down the stairs into the gloom. "It always seemed to take forever for the siren to sound an all-clear."

They rode in silence for several minutes until Hannah spotted another boat in the distance. It was moving, too, but there was something strange about it. The boat looked as if it were making big circles in the water, following some sort of pattern. It was a strange way to troll, and she decided to ask Norman about it.

"Look at that boat ahead of us, Norman. I think it's going in circles. Is that some new kind of trolling for Walleyes?"

"Where?"

Hannah pointed off in the distance. "It's fairly close to the water lily garden."

"I see it," Norman said when he'd located the other boat. "There's a pair of binoculars in back of my seat, Hannah. They're in a green case with a strap. Can you get them for me so I can take a closer look?"

Hannah leaned back in her seat and located the bag with the binoculars. She took them out of the case and handed them to Norman. "Here you go, Norman."

Norman slipped the strap around his neck and slowed the progress of his boat. Then he adjusted the binoculars and nodded. "Okay. I can see it better now. It looks like . . . hold on a second. I'm going to adjust the magnification."

"Is there something wrong?" Hannah asked as Norman made a distressed sound.

"I think so. I'll have to get a little closer to see for sure, but it looks like someone's bent over the wheel and that's why the boat is going in circles."

Hannah took the binoculars when Norman handed them to her and watched as he drove toward the other boat. "Hand me the binoculars again, Hannah. I don't want to disturb one of the other contestants if there's nothing wrong."

They had gotten close enough so that Hannah could see the other boat clearly now. Norman was right. There was someone draped over the wheel and that's why the boat was circling. "Should we go closer?" she asked.

"I'm not sure. Just let me . . . no! Do you have your cell phone with you, Hannah?"

"Yes. It's right here in my purse. Is something wrong, Norman?"

"Yes, I think there may be. Do you have Mike's number? He told us all that we could reach him at any time during the contest."

"Even out on the lake?"

"Yes. Wally arranged for a cell phone tower right next to the Inn. Call Mike and tell him where we are and then I'll talk to him."

Mike's number was on Hannah's speed dial, and she got him on the phone almost immediately.

"What's up, Hannah?"

"I'm out here with Norman and he wants to talk to you." Hannah handed her phone to Norman. She listened as Norman quickly explained the situation with the other fishing boat.

"I didn't want to get too close," Norman said, "but I thought you should know there may be something wrong." He listened for a moment and then he gave a nod. "Okay. Hannah and I will wait until you get here. We're fairly close to the water lily garden, if you know where that is." He listened again and then he said, "Thanks, Mike. It's probably nothing, but we'll see you in a few."

"Mike knows where we are?" Hannah asked, dropping her cell phone back into her purse.

"Lonnie does. Mike said the Murphy boys fished this lake every summer with Cyril."

"What do you think is wrong?" Hannah asked, hoping she wouldn't regret asking the question.

"I don't know, but it's odd. Hand me the binoculars again, Hannah. I'm going to keep an eye on that boat until Mike arrives."

"Do you think the fisherman who's bent over the wheel is sick?"

"Maybe." Norman adjusted the binoculars again. "It doesn't look like he's moved at all."

"Do you think he could be . . . really sick?" Hannah asked, not wanting to ask the dire possibility that was running through her mind.

"Don't think about it now, Hannah. We'll find out exactly what's wrong when Mike and Lonnie get here."

BREAKFAST ENCHILADAS

DO NOT preheat the oven yet—you can make these ahead of time, put them in the pans, and refrigerate until you wish to finish this dish.

Ingredients:

- 1 ounce *(2 Tablespoons, ¼ stick)* salted butter
- 12 large eggs *(Yes, that's a whole dozen!)*
- 1 pound shredded pepper Jack cheese *(use regular Jack cheese if you don't want it spicy)*
- 2 pounds pork breakfast sausage *(I got the kind in the chub, 1 pound each)*
- 1 pound bacon *(regular and NOT thick sliced)*
- 2 cups frozen Potatoes O'Brien *(if you can't find those, you can use ½ cup chopped onions with round hash browns or tater tots cut in half)*
- 2 cups shredded Mexican cheese *(I used Kraft Finely Shredded Mexican Four Cheese)*
- 2 four-ounce cans chopped green chilies, drained *(I used Ortega green chilies)*
- Hot sauce, optional *(I used Slap Ya Mama brand hot sauce)*

24 soft-taco sized flour tortillas
1 can or jar (*28 ounces*) red enchilada
sauce (*I used Las Palmas*)
1 can or jar (*28 ounce*) green enchilada
sauce (*I used Las Palmas*)
1 jar (*15.5 ounce*) medium-heat salsa (*I
used Tostitos*)

Directions:

Prepare your pans. You will need two 9-inch
by 13-inch cake pans sprayed with Pam or another nonstick cooking spray.

Hannah's 1st Note: If you're having company
for breakfast, you can prepare the pans of ingredients the night before, cover them with foil,
and put them in the refrigerator overnight. Then
all you have to do in the morning is take out the
pans, let the contents warm up to room temperature, and pour on the enchilada sauce.

Hannah's 2nd Note: If you can't find shredded pepper Jack cheese, just buy it in a block
and grate it when you get ready to use it. Pepper
Jack cheese is difficult to shred because it's a
soft cheese, so keep it in the 'fridge until you are
ready to grate it.

Hannah's 3rd Note: if you can't find shredded Mexican cheese, you can use shredded Italian cheese or shredded cheddar.

Place the ounce of salted butter in the bottom of a large frying pan.

Crack the eggs into a medium-sized bowl and beat them up with a wire whisk.

Put the shredded *(or grated)* pepper Jack cheese in a second bowl.

Heat the frying pan over MEDIUM heat, moving the ounce of salted butter around with a spatula so that the entire bottom of the pan is covered with melted butter.

Pour in the eggs you've whisked and move them around with the spatula. Make sure they don't stick to the bottom of the pan.

Continue to stir and add the pepper Jack cheese to the frying pan. Make sure the cheese and the eggs don't stick to the bottom of the frying pan.

Stir everything around until the eggs are beginning to scramble. Then switch to a heat-

resistant fork to make sure the contents are scrambling in small pieces.

Once your eggs are scrambled, pull the frying pan off the heat and shut off the burner.

Rinse out the bowl you used to whisk the eggs and transfer the scrambled eggs to the bowl.

Cut the chub of pork breakfast sausage into pieces.

Place the pork sausage and the bacon in the frying pan you used for the eggs and cheese.

Fry the sausage pieces and bacon at MEDIUM-HIGH heat until the meats are brown and crisp, and can be crumbled when they are cool.

Take the frying pan off the heat, turn off the hot burner, and use a slotted spoon or slotted spatula to drain the meats into a medium-size bowl lined with layers of paper towels.

Carefully *(the meats could still be hot)* pat the top of the meat with paper towels to blot the grease.

Scrape the bottom of the frying pan to re-move any bits of meat that may have stuck to

the bottom and place it on the burner you used to fry the meats. Turn that burner on MEDIUM-HIGH heat again.

Add the Potatoes O'Brien *(or your substitute potatoes)* to the frying pan and fry them until they're brown and crisp.

Pull the frying pan off the heat and transfer the potatoes to another MEDIUM-SIZE bowl.

Open the can of chopped green chilies and use the strainer again to drain them. *(Mine didn't need draining—this may depend on which brand of chopped green chilies you use.)*

Stir the chopped green chilies into the bowl with the Potatoes O'Brien.

When the pieces of meat are cool enough to crumble, remove the paper towels from the bowl and use your impeccably clean fingers to crumble up the sausage and bacon.

After your meats are crumbled, stir in half of the shredded Mexican cheese.

You now have three bowls on your counter. There's the scrambled egg bowl, the meat and cheese bowl, and the potato bowl.

Eye the contents of the three bowls and get out a bowl that is large enough to hold all three. Then add the contents of the scrambled egg bowl, the meat and cheese bowl, and the potato and green chili bowl.

Use your impeccably clean fingers to mix everything up together in the large bowl.

Once you've mixed everything together thoroughly, use a spoon from your silverware drawer to taste a sample of the mixture. If you think it needs to be spicier, add a few drops of Slap Ya Mama hot sauce and mix that in.

Check for seasoning and add salt and pepper if needed. If you add anything at this point, make sure that you mix it in thoroughly.

Hannah's 4th Note: Rather than make things too spicy, make sure you have an extra bottle of Slap Ya Mama hot sauce to put on the table. That way, people can choose the level of spicy that they prefer.

It's time to assemble your Breakfast Enchiladas. Take the flour tortillas out of the package and make sure that you have at least 24 tortillas.

Spread out a sheet of plastic wrap on your counter. It should be about 12 inches long when you tear it off the roll.

Center a flour tortilla on the sheet of plastic wrap.

Place ⅓ cup of your filling in the center of the flour tortilla. Check to make sure you have some of the scrambled egg mixture, the meat and shredded cheese mixture, and the potato and green chili mixture.

Spread 1 Tablespoon salsa over the top of the filling.

Pull the bottom edge of your tortilla over the filling and up to meet the top edge. This will roll the filling into the proper place.

Fold one side of the tortilla over the filling to the middle.

Fold the opposite side of the tortilla over the filling to the middle of the tortilla. *(The sides may overlap a bit and that's the way it should be.)*

Starting from the bottom, roll the enchilada up tightly, creating a cylinder that will not leak when you transfer it to the baking pan. Repeat

until you have used all the filling. (This should be approximately 24 enchiladas.)

Open both cans or bottles of enchilada sauce. Pour a little red enchilada sauce in one baking pan and use a spatula to spread it around the bottom of the pan.

Pour a little green enchilada sauce in the other baking pan and use a spatula to spread that around to cover the bottom of the pan.

Place your unbaked enchiladas in the baking pans. *(You will be placing approximately 12 enchiladas in each baking pan.)*

As you place your enchiladas in the baking pans, make sure you leave at least ½ inch of space between each roll. If you pack them in too tightly, you will not be able to separate them easily when you serve them to your guests.

Hannah's 5th Note: If you don't want to bake both pans, you may cover one with foil, put it in a freezer bag, and freeze it until you want to use it.

When you have finished rolling and placing your enchiladas in the baking pans, pour the

rest of the red enchilada sauce over the pan with red sauce in the bottom. Then pour the rest of the green enchilada sauce over the pan with the green sauce in the bottom.

Sprinkle the rest of your Mexican shredded cheese evenly over the top of both pans.

When you have used up all the enchilada sauce, you're ready to bake your creation.

Preheat your oven to 375 F., one rack in just above the center position and the other rack just below the center position. Make sure your cake pans fit on the racks before you begin to pre-heat the oven.

When your oven has come up to tempera-ture, bake your pans of enchiladas at 375 de-grees F. for 20 to 25 minutes or until the enchilada sauce is hot and bubbly.

Take your pans of enchiladas out of the oven and let them cool on cold stovetop burners or on wire racks.

Wait at least 5 minutes before serving your enchiladas. Then, if you wish, put a bowl of sour cream and another bowl of extra shredded

Mexican cheese on the table. Make sure you have a bottle of Slap Ya Mama hot sauce *(especially if you invite Mike!)*.

Yield: This recipe serves from 8 to 12 people, depending on their appetites.

Hannah's 6th Note: If you have any enchiladas left over, simply cover the pan with aluminum foil and stick it in the refrigerator. If you have overnight guests, it shouldn't surprise you if you find you don't have many left in the morning.

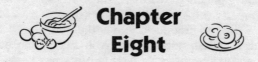

Chapter Eight

"So where's this boat you called me about?" Mike asked when Lonnie got close enough to talk to Hannah and Norman.

"Up there." Norman pointed at the boat in the distance. "We didn't want to interfere if there was nothing wrong, but I looked through the binoculars and there was someone draped over the wheel, facedown. Maybe he's sleeping, but I thought it was odd enough for me to call you."

"Is there anyone else in the boat?"

"It didn't look like it to me."

"Okay. I'll take a look." Mike got out his binoculars and studied the boat for a minute. "You're right, Norman. There could be something wrong. The only way to tell is to get a lot closer." He turned to Lonnie. "If the guy's passed out or something, I may have to get into his boat. Can you match his speed?"

"I can try, but it'll be tricky," Lonnie told him.

"I think I can help," Norman offered. "I can get alongside him and slow him down."

Hannah glanced at Norman, surprised by his offer. "Do you really think you can?" she asked.

"Yes. I used to practice a move like that when I was racing. It's called sidedrafting. You match the other driver's speed and move up next to him, match speeds, then slow so your teammate can slingshot by them. It's not that easy, but I know how to do it."

"In a boat?" Lonnie asked.

"Why not?" Mike asked him.

Norman gave a little shrug. "It can't hurt to try."

Mike glanced at Lonnie and he nodded. "It's worth a try," Lonnie told him. "Can you get into Norman's boat now, Mike?"

"Sure," Mike said. "Just pull up beside him and I'll switch boats."

"What do you want me to do?" Lonnie asked him.

"Just get close enough and I'll jump over."

Hannah watched as Lonnie pulled up beside them and Mike stood up. Hannah grabbed on to the side of Mike's boat and Mike jumped in.

"Nice," she said, admiring his balance.

"Thanks. I've been doing some balance practice at the station gym. We have one treadmill that bumps and tilts when you're walking on it. At first I had to hold on to the side rails, but after a week or so, I could stay on without any handholds."

"I bet you never thought learning how to do that would come in handy," Norman said, driving his boat forward.

"You're right, I didn't," Mike admitted. "I just wanted to see if I could learn to do it without falling down."

"That's the same way I felt when I was a kid and I finally learned to ice-skate," Hannah said.

Mike held his binoculars up to his eyes as they drew

closer to the runaway boat. "He's still in exactly the same position. You were right, Norman. Something's wrong and I think that's Sonny!"

Hannah opened her mouth to say something about Sonny's drinking the previous evening, but she quickly shut it again. Mike knew about it. He'd been there. Besides, this could be something completely different and she had to give Sonny the benefit of the doubt. "I thought Joey was going out in the boat with him," she said.

"So did I," Norman agreed.

"Maybe he ditched Joey somewhere," Mike suggested. "I talked to a couple of the other contestants, and they mentioned that Sonny didn't seem to like Joey very much."

"That's the impression Andrea got, too," Hannah told him. "She said he wasn't very nice to Joey on the show."

"Andrea watches a fishing show?" Mike sounded surprised.

"Yes. Bill wants to watch, and Andrea told me it was something they could do together."

Mike thought that over for a second or two, and then he smiled. "That's nice. Hannah, were you up when Sonny left to go out on the lake this morning?"

"Yes, but I didn't see them leave, if that's what you're asking."

"That's exactly what I was asking, because it looks like Sonny's alone now."

Hannah felt a chill. She hoped Joey was all right. He seemed like a very nice, polite person. Wally certainly seemed to like him, and she idly wondered why Sonny didn't get along with him.

"Here we are," Norman said. "Are you ready, Mike?"

"I'm ready," Mike said, patting his pocket.

"Be careful," Hannah warned, and then she wished she hadn't. It had looked to her as if Mike was checking to make sure his service revolver was still on his hip.

"Just tell me when you're in the best position," Mike said to Norman. "And Hannah?"

"Here we go!" Mike said, jumping to Sonny's boat. "I'm okay! You can let go now, Hannah. Drop back a little, Norman, I'm going to shut her down."

Norman cut his speed and got behind Sonny's boat. Both of them watched as Mike moved between the seats and reached Sonny, who was still slumped over the wheel in exactly the same position.

Neither Hannah nor Norman said a word as they watched Mike leaning over Sonny. Both men seemed frozen in their positions for a moment, and then Mike cut the motor on Sonny's fishing boat.

Norman reacted immediately, cutting his motor so that they were floating behind Sonny's boat. They waited for what seemed like an eternity before Mike straightened up and reached for his phone.

"Your phone, Hannah," Norman said as Hannah's cell phone began to ring.

Hannah answered quickly. "Yes, Mike. Is everything okay?"

"No. Listen carefully, Hannah. I need you and Norman to go back to the Inn and get Doc."

"Okay. Do you want us to bring him back out here?"

"No, Doc knows Eden Lake. Just find him and tell him I'm out here at the lily garden. And if Doc's got a patient, you can tell him that there's no need to hurry."

Hannah winced. "Does that mean that Sonny is . . . " She stopped speaking and swallowed hard, reluctant to voice that final word.

"Yes. You can tell Doc I'm calling the crime scene

boys and I'd like him to get out to establish the time of death before they arrive."

Hanna took a deep breath. "Is there anything else you want Norman and I to do?"

"Yes, after you send Doc out here, try to find Joey. And if you find him, keep an eye on him."

Hannah gave a little nod even though she knew that Mike couldn't see her. "Then Sonny was . . . murdered?"

"Sure looks like it to me, but don't mention that to anyone else."

"How about Dick and Sally? Can I tell them that Sonny was murdered?"

There was silence for a moment and then Hannah heard Mike sigh. "You can tell them that Sonny's dead, but warn them not to tell anyone else until I get back to the Inn. You got that?"

"I got it," Hannah promised. "Is there anything else you need us to do?"

"Not really, but if you run into Joey, keep an eye on him. Stick to him like glue and don't let him wash his hands or take a shower."

"Does that mean that Sonny didn't die of natural causes?"

"Not unless those Caramel Pecan Rolls Mr. Bowman was eating were poisoned."

"Of course they weren't! I made them myself."

Mike laughed, but there was no humor in it. "You ask too many questions, Hannah. Just don't mention this to anyone except Dick and Sally. I'll tell you more about it when the crime scene boys are finished out here and I get back to the Inn."

Mike disconnected the call and Hannah turned to Norman. "Mike wants us to go back to the Inn and find Doc."

"Is that all he told you?"

"That's all he said, but he called Sonny Mr. Bowman."

"And what does that mean?"

"Mike always uses the formal term of address when he refers to homicide victims."

"Got it," Norman said, starting his motor and heading back toward the Inn.

They rode for several minutes and then Norman turned to Hannah. "I almost asked Mike if he needed me to come back to keep him company."

"He would have told you no," Hannah replied, leaning close so that Norman could hear her over the sound of the motor.

"That's what I thought, so I didn't ask. I guess it doesn't bother Mike to keep murder victims company until other officers arrive."

Hannah thought about that for a moment, but she didn't comment. She wasn't sure whether it bothered Mike or not. But deep down she suspected it was one of the parts of his job that Mike really didn't like.

Chapter Nine

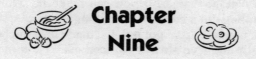

Once they got to the Inn, Hannah and Norman went straight to Doc's office to tell him what had happened. Doc grabbed his bag, ushered them out of his temporary office, assured them that he knew exactly where the water lily garden was located, and hurried out to get his boat.

"Where to next?" Norman asked as they walked down the hallway.

"Let's go see if we can find Dick. He may have seen Joey."

They found Dick in the bar, restocking the shelves with bottles. Norman and Hannah pushed through the saloon-type doors and walked up to the long mahogany bar.

"Bar's closed," Dick told them apologetically.

"No problem," Norman assured him. "We didn't want a drink. Do you have a minute to talk to us, Dick?"

"I always have time for you two," Dick said. "How about something nonalcoholic to wet your whistles?"

"An Arnold Palmer, if you can make it," Norman said, pulling out a barstool and sitting down.

Dick nodded. "I've got it. I just made up a pitcher of lemonade and I've always got iced tea." He turned to Hannah. "How about you?"

"I'll have the same," Hannah said, pulling out the barstool next to Norman and seating herself.

"What brings you so early? I thought you were out for the afternoon," Dick asked them, once he'd poured their drinks.

Hannah and Norman exchanged glances. Mike had told them to tell Doc what had happened, but they hadn't thought to ask about Dick.

Hannah considered that for a moment, and then she gave Norman a slight nod. They needed to get some information from Dick and that meant they had to share the reason they needed it.

Norman gave a nod back, and Hannah suspected he'd guessed what she was thinking. "Okay, Dick," she said. "There's a problem and I can tell you about it, but it can't go any further than you."

"How about Sally?" Dick asked. "Shall I call her to come here so the four of us can talk in private?"

"Good idea!" Norman said immediately. "Please do that, Dick."

Hannah felt a bit uncomfortable. Would Mike be upset that they'd told Dick and Sally what had happened? She took a few moments to consider the possibility, and she decided that Dick and Sally had the right to know that one of their guests had been murdered. Mike had asked them to locate Joey, and they couldn't search the whole hotel without giving Dick and Sally a reason.

It didn't take long for Sally to arrive once Dick had called her. She came through the doors to the bar, looking extremely curious. "What are you two doing back here so early?" she asked, spotting Hannah and Norman at the bar.

"There's a problem, Sally," Norman told her.

"With one of the contestants?" Sally asked, beginning to look worried.

Hannah shook her head. "It's Sonny. He's . . ." She stopped and motioned to the barstool closest to her. "Sit down, Sally."

Sally slid onto the barstool. "What about Sonny?" she asked. "Did he get into some sort of trouble again?"

"You could say that." Hannah gave a quick nod. "It's big trouble this time, Sally."

"With another one of the contestants' wives?" Sally guessed, giving an exasperated sigh. "We all saw what happened in the bar last night, and I'm really grateful that all of you were here. You saved us from a situation that could have gotten really bad."

"That's right," Dick agreed. "You saved us from even bigger trouble. I hate to think of what would have happened if those two husbands had walked in and noticed what was going on before you defused the situation."

"Wally warned me that Sonny got out of line when he drank too much," Sally told them. "He really thought that having his daughter here would keep Sonny from acting up again."

"I must be missing something," Hannah said. "What does Wally's daughter have to do with it?"

"Wally's daughter, Lily, is Sonny's fiancée," Sally told them. "Wally thought that if anyone could calm Sonny down, it would be Lily. Wally knew he had to have someone to keep an eye on Sonny so he called Lily last night."

Hannah's mind went into warp speed. Had Lily

been so upset with Sonny that she'd murdered him? It was definitely a possibility, and that made Lily a suspect right along with Joey. "Could we talk to Lily?" she asked.

Dick shook his head. "She's not here anymore. I checked and the night desk clerk said that she left early this morning."

"I didn't know Sonny was engaged!" Hannah said, still surprised at that fact.

"He is, and that's not in his publicity release," Dick told them. "Sonny's publicist thought that it might hurt his image." Dick refilled their glasses and brought Sally a glass of lemonade. Once he'd done that, he turned to Hannah. "You haven't told us about Sonny's latest trouble yet."

Hannah took a deep breath. She hated to be the one to deliver bad news, but it seemed to fall on her shoulders more often than it should have. She swallowed once, took another breath for courage, and then she said, "Sonny's dead."

"Dead?" Sally repeated, setting her lemonade glass down with a thump.

Dick's eyes narrowed slightly. "Dead . . . how?" he asked.

Hannah looked at Norman and gave him a slight nod. She'd delivered part of the shocking news, and now it was his turn.

"He was murdered," Norman said. "At least that's what Mike thinks. Doc is on his way out to Sonny's boat right now to confirm that fact."

Sally took a moment to compose herself. "Does Wally know?" she asked.

"No one here at the Inn knows except you, Dick, and Doc. Mike asked us to come back here to tell Doc and to have us try to locate Joey."

"Joey?" Dick looked surprised. "You saw him this morning, didn't you, Sally?"

"I did. It was early and he was getting ready to go out on the boat with Sonny when I ran into him in the lobby. He told me he was sorry that he was going to miss our great breakfast buffet, so I asked him if he wanted us to pack up some breakfast for them to take out on the lake. He said no, that he was in too much of a hurry and Sonny had already gone out to the boat."

"What time was that?" Hannah asked her.

"I'm not completely sure, but it was well before dawn. The sky wasn't even beginning to lighten yet and I'd just run out to the lobby with coffee for the desk clerk. Craig's a college kid and he's up all night, so I always bring him coffee."

Hannah nodded. "It must have been before five, because I came down from the room a little before that. Andrea was still sleeping and I didn't wake her. I just started making the day's Caramel Pecan Rolls."

"Did you see Joey get into the boat?" Norman asked Sally.

Sally shook her head. "No, it was too dark to see the dock from the window."

"So you don't know, for sure, if Joey actually went on the boat with Sonny," Hannah concluded.

"That's true, but I don't have any reason to think he didn't." Sally stopped speaking and frowned. "Was Joey on the boat when Mike found Sonny?"

Hannah hesitated a moment, and then she shook her head. "No, and I'm sure that's the reason Mike asked us to try to locate Joey."

"I hope he's all right." Dick looked worried. "Joey's a good guy. He was always polite and nice to Sonny, and Sonny treated him like . . . well, you know."

"It's true," Sally confirmed. "All you have to do is

watch one of the fishing shows and you can see he treated Joey like a hired servant." Sally stopped speaking and looked thoughtful. "Rosa's cleaning Joey's room today. Do you want me to call her and ask her if Joey's in his room?"

"Yes, please," Hannah said quickly.

"Hello!" a voice called out from the doorway. "Is this a private meeting, or can anyone come in and get something wet to drink?"

"Joey!" Sally gasped. "We were just about to ask Rosa if she'd seen you."

"Not a word about Sonny," Hannah warned Dick and Sally. "You know nothing, okay?" When both of them nodded, she turned around on her barstool and waved at Joey.

"Come in, Joey," Dick said, gesturing toward the barstool next to Norman. "Lemonade? Iced tea? Or an Arnold Palmer?"

"Lemonade, please," Joey said, sliding onto the barstool. "What's going on? It looked like serious business in here."

"Serious enough," Hannah said, taking the lead. "We thought you went out on the boat with Sonny this morning."

"I did. I was with him for over an hour before he got mad at me and dropped me off back here."

"Was it still dark when you got back here?" Norman asked him.

"Yeah. It didn't even start to get light until after I'd taken a shower."

"When you came back, you took a shower in your room?" Hannah asked him, doing her best not to look as disappointed as she felt. If Joey had taken a shower, there was no longer a possibility of gunpowder or any other residue. "So you took a shower and dressed in clean clothes?" she asked.

"Yeah. I threw my clothes in a laundry bag and put it out in the hall. That's what it said to do."

"Exactly right," Sally confirmed.

"Why was Sonny mad at you? Was Sonny drinking this morning?" Dick asked.

"Of course he was! He keeps bottles stashed in his live well. I didn't know it when I got on the boat. All he had out was a thermos and I thought it was coffee!"

"Was he acting drunk?" Sally asked.

"Yes, but at first I thought he could have still been drunk from last night. You guys saw him. He tied one on and then some. I don't know whether he kept on drinking all night or started drinking when he woke up this morning. All I know is that he was a bit shaky when we went out on the lake this morning."

"Did Sonny mention that Lily was here last night?" Hannah asked him.

"No." Joey looked very surprised. "Is she still here?"

"No," Dick answered. "The desk clerk said she checked out early this morning."

"That makes sense. Lily was probably disgusted by the fact he fell off the wagon again."

"That's happened before?" Hannah asked.

"At least twice that I know of. This is the third alcohol treatment program he's been in, and we all thought he was doing okay."

"So you didn't realize that he was still drunk when you got in the boat with him?" Hannah asked.

Joey shook his head. "Sonny was good at hiding it. I knew he'd been completely blotto last night in the bar, but I thought he'd be sober this morning. If I'd known he was buzzed, I wouldn't have let him handle the boat. Maybe I was still sleepy or just not observant enough, but I didn't catch on to what was happening until Sonny spilled his thermos all over me and I smelled it."

"So, what *was* in the thermos?" Dick asked.

"Smelled like Bourbon or some sort of whiskey. That's why I had to peel off my clothes and take a shower the minute I walked into the room. I could hardly wait to get out of those clothes!"

"You must be hungry, Joey," Sally said, changing the subject. "We missed you at the breakfast buffet."

"I missed you, too!" Joey replied, smiling widely. "And I especially missed all that delicious food. My stomach's growling like crazy. Is there any way I can get something to eat, Sally?"

"Why don't you take Joey to the kitchen, Dick?" Sally suggested. "I'm sure you can find someone to rustle up something for Joey to eat."

"Sure," Dick said, coming out from behind the bar and motioning to Joey. "If everyone there is busy, I'll make Joey one of my famous Reuben Omelets."

"A Reuben Omelet?" Joey looked interested. "Is that like a Reuben sandwich?"

"Yes, except there's no bread. It's corned beef, sauerkraut, and Swiss cheese."

"That sounds good to me," Joey said, sliding off his barstool to follow Dick. My dad used to make Reuben sandwiches every time Mom had one of her meetings."

Hannah waited until Joey and Dick had left and then she turned to Sally. "Will you call Rosa and ask her to get Joey's laundry bag? Mike's going to need the clothes Joey wore on the boat. And you'd better tell her not to clean Joey's room. Mike may want to send his crime scene people up there to check it out for any trace evidence."

Sally pulled out her cell phone and did what Hannah had asked, but she looked worried after she'd put away her phone. "You don't think Joey killed Sonny, do you?"

"Not really, but everyone's a suspect at this point."

"Does that mean that you're going to help with the investigation?" Sally asked.

"I'd like to," Hannah answered quickly, and then she thought she'd better qualify that. "At least I think Mike might ask me to help. Norman and I will just have to wait and see what he wants us to do."

"What do you think he'll say?" Sally asked.

"I'm not sure, but he may tell us that he wants us to leave everything to him."

Sally looked amused. "You could be right, but that's never stopped you before!"

"That's true," Hannah admitted. "But I don't really have a vested interest in this case. It's not like I knew Sonny well. Actually, the only dealings I had with him all took place at the breakfast buffet."

"Yes, except for dancing with him," Norman pointed out.

"That's true, but it wasn't like I wanted to dance with him. It was my turn and I had to rescue Michelle."

"How about watching the fishing show?" Sally asked her.

"I've never seen it. I just heard Andrea talk about it." She took a deep breath and tried to explain. "It's been different in the past, Sally. Either I've found the victim or someone close to me has. This time, all I did was spot Sonny's fishing boat circling out of control. Mike was the one who discovered that Sonny was murdered. If he tells me that he doesn't need my help, then I'll have to step back."

Sally still didn't look convinced. "You said you

didn't have a vested interest, but you do. You were here when the murder was committed. You were kind enough to help me out with the cooking and Sonny ate the food that you prepared. He even told you that he liked the Caramel Pecan Rolls. You might not have liked him that much, but he paid you a compliment by saying that." She turned to Norman. "That's a vested interest, isn't it?"

"Absolutely," Norman agreed quickly. "Not only that, Hannah was with me when we spotted Sonny's boat, and both of us suspected that something was wrong."

"There you go," Sally said, smiling at Norman. "And don't forget that Mike sent you two back here to tell Doc about the murder."

Hannah gave a reluctant nod. "That's all true," she said.

Sally was obviously pleased at Hannah's response. "Since you agree with us, you can't just step back and do nothing. Just by sending you back here to the hotel to notify Doc, Mike was asking for your help."

"There's something else, too," Norman added. "Mike asked both of us to locate Joey and keep an eye on him. We're part of this investigation, Hannah. And don't forget that Bill is gone and so is Rick. The new guy's on vacation, and Mike and Lonnie are the only detectives left. Mike and Lonnie are going to need us to do some of the legwork for them."

"Well . . . maybe," Hannah conceded.

"Not to mention that you and Norman are friends of ours," Sally pointed out.

"Of course we are," Hannah said quickly.

"And this whole mess with Sonny could reflect badly on the Lake Eden Inn. You want to help us, don't you?"

"Yes, of course I want to help."

Sally began to smile. "Thank you, Hannah. Dick and I have a lot at stake here."

"I know you do," Hannah said.

"And you do want to investigate, don't you, Hannah?" Norman asked her.

"Of course I do!"

"So then that's a yes, you're going to investigate?" Sally pushed for a definite commitment.

Hannah sighed. Sally and Norman were relentless. "It's a yes," she said. "I promise that I'll do my best to find out who killed Sonny."

REUBEN OMELET

DO NOT preheat the oven yet—you will only use the oven to keep finished omelets warm while others are being cooked.

This is a stovetop recipe.

Hannah's 1st Note: This recipe is designed to serve 4 people unless you invite Mike. He ate 3 out of 4 omelets when Michelle and I invited him for breakfast.

Ingredients:

> 1 cup sauerkraut
> 4 Tablespoons Thousand Island dressing
> 5 gherkins *(small sweet pickles)*
> 4 Tablespoons salted butter
> 8 large eggs
> ½ cup water
> 8 slices Swiss cheese, thinly sliced
> ¾ pound corned beef brisket, thinly sliced

Hannah's 2nd Note: I get all these ingredients from the deli section of Florence's Red Owl Grocery. She slices the corned beef and the Swiss cheese for me.

Hannah's 3rd Note: Gherkins are small sweet pickles. If you can't find them in your grocery store or deli, you can substitute 2 Tablespoons of sweet pickle relish.

Prepare your pan:

If you have an omelet pan, you'll use that. If you don't, you can use any frying pan that is large enough to hold 2 large eggs with room to maneuver a spatula to flip one side of the omelet over the other. You will use this frying pan for all 4 omelets. Do not spray the inside of your pan with any nonstick cooking spray or grease it in any way. You will be heating it up and then adding salted butter.

You will also need a serving platter that can hold 4 omelets and can be placed in an oven to warm.

Hannah's 4th Note: Michelle, Andrea, and I have large crockery serving platters that Mother gave us for Christmas one year. She bought one for herself, too. I'm sure that she was hoping we'd fill them with something to serve at her house.

Directions:

Measure out one cup of sauerkraut, leaving as much juice behind in the jar as possible.

Drain the cup of sauerkraut in a strainer over a bowl, reserving the juice to pour back into the jar with the sauerkraut left in the jar.

Pat the sauerkraut dry with several layers of paper towels.

Hannah's 5th Note: I sometimes line my strainer with a large coffee filter. It's surprising how dry the sauerkraut gets when it's on top of the coffee filter.

Place the 4 Tablespoons *(that's ¼ cup)* Thousand Island dressing in a small bowl on the counter.

Use a sharp knife to chop the gherkins into very small pieces.

Add the minced gherkins to the bowl with the Thousand Island dressing and stir them in.

Choose a larger bowl, one that will hold all 8 eggs and a half-cup of water.

Break the eggs into the bowl and whisk them together.

Add the half-cup of water and continue to whisk until the mixture is light and fluffy.

Turn one of your stovetop burners on MEDIUM heat.

When your pan is hot, add the Tablespoon of butter and swish it around until the bottom and sides of the pan are coated with butter.

Turn the burner up to MEDIUM-HIGH heat.

Give the egg mixture a quick whisk and then pour one-quarter (¼) of it into the heated frying pan.

Using a wide heat-resistant spatula, lift the edges of the eggs around the outside of the pan and tilt the pan to let the uncooked portion flow underneath.

While the top of the eggs are still moist and look creamy, add two slices of cheese to one half of your omelet and add one quarter of the corned beef brisket on top.

Hannah's 6th Note: Don't forget that you're making an omelet and you will fold one half of the eggs in the pan over on the other half to finish your creation.

Once the meat is in place, top it with ¼ of the sauerkraut.

Use the wide spatula to flip the bare side of the omelet over to cover the side with the Swiss cheese, corned beef brisket, and sauerkraut.

Slide the wide spatula under your omelet to loosen it and immediately remove it from the frying pan.

Transfer your omelet to a serving platter and place it in your barely warm oven. Cover the platter loosely with foil so it's ready to receive the rest of your Reuben Omelets. Repeat three more times!

To Serve:

Once all 4 of your omelets are on the serving platter, top them with the Thousand Island dressing that you mixed with the finely chopped gherkins.

Yield: 4 two-egg omelets that will serve 4 people (*unless you invite Mike—Re-read Hannah's 1st Note*).

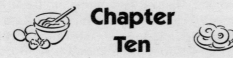

Chapter
Ten

"I have to get this," Hannah said, standing up and walking to another table to take the call. It was Mike, and she wanted him to know that they'd told Sally and Dick that Sonny was dead.

"Doc's here." Mike wasted no time on preliminary politeness. "He's confirmed that Sonny's death is definitely a homicide."

"We managed to locate Joey," Hannah told him, relating the conversation they'd had with Joey in the bar.

"Okay. Just make sure he stays with Dick," Mike cautioned. "Do you happen to know if Joey is a good shot?"

"Was Sonny shot?" Hannah asked.

"Yes, in the back. Whoever shot him from a distance was a heck of a marksman."

Hannah shuddered slightly. "I'm having trouble believing that Joey could do something like that."

"I know. Joey seems like a really nice guy. But you've got to remember that nice guys can go off the deep end and take their revenge. And Joey must know how to handle firearms."

"You're right," Hannah said, going on to tell Mike about the laundry bag of Joey's clothes that Rosa was saving. "When Dick and Joey come back to the bar, do you want us to ask Joey if he knows how to handle firearms?"

"No, you can leave that to me. I'll take care of it when I get there. Just keep him at the Inn, Hannah. Lonnie and I will question him later."

Hannah was thoughtful as she ended the call. It was difficult to believe that Joey could execute anyone, but, as Mike had pointed out countless times, the most unlikely people could turn out to be killers.

"Is everything all right, Hannah?" Norman asked as she climbed back on her barstool.

"Yes, everything's fine," Hannah replied. "How are you two doing?"

"We're fine," Sally told her. "We were just talking about the prizes Wally's giving for the fishing competition." Sally stopped and took a deep breath. "Was that Mike on the phone?"

"Yes."

"Is Doc with him?"

Hannah gave a nod. "Mike said he should be back soon." She took another swallow of her Arnold Palmer, and then she turned to Norman. "Mike wants us to stay here until Dick and Joey get back."

"Is Joey still a suspect?" Sally asked.

"I think so," Hannah said.

"And Mike's sure it was murder?"

Hannah nodded. "That's what he said. Doc will have to confirm it with an autopsy, of course, and establish the time of death, but Mike sounded very positive when he told me. And Mike told me that Doc was ninety-nine percent certain that no one committing suicide would shoot themselves in the back."

Sally looked a bit sick at the thoughts that were probably running through her mind, and Hannah almost wished she hadn't said anything. "When do you think Mike will be back?" Sally asked.

Norman glanced at his watch. "That probably depends on the crime scene people that Mike called in, but it can't take as long as a large murder venue."

"True," Hannah agreed. "A fishing boat isn't that big."

Sally gave a little smile. "No, but Wally's fishing boats are a lot bigger than the ones Dick rents. They're equipped with everything you could ever want in a fishing boat."

"They sure are!" a voice spoke from the doorway, and all three of them turned to see who was there.

"Mike!" Hannah was pleased. "You certainly got here quickly! Did your crime scene people come back with you?"

"Yes. I wanted them to go through Joey's room, and Rosa was in the hallway outside. She said Sally told her not to let anyone inside the room and she handed me the laundry bag with the clothing that Joey put out this morning when he got back to the Inn."

"Oh, good." Hannah was relieved. "I asked Sally to talk to Rosa, and keep everyone else out of that room."

He turned to Hannah and Norman. "I'm glad you found Joey."

"Actually, he found us," Hannah said. "I was about to ask Dick and Sally about him when Joey walked into the bar."

"Where is he now?"

"He's still with Dick in the kitchen," Sally answered. "Joey said he was hungry, and Dick offered to make him one of his special omelets."

Mike turned to Hannah again. "Does Dick know not to mention Mr. Bowman's death to Joey?"

"Dick knows," Hannah assured him.

"And so do I," Sally told him. "Hannah and Norman told us to keep mum about everything until you and Lonnie came back. And since everyone knows the bar's not open yet, there haven't been any other people in here."

"Good work," Mike said, smiling at all three of them. "You're making our job a lot easier."

"Would you and Lonnie like something to drink, Mike?" Sally asked him.

"Yes, but nothing alcoholic. Doc will be here in a minute and he'll probably want something, too."

"How about lemonade?" Sally suggested, going behind the bar to serve them.

"Sounds great," Mike said with a nod.

"Sure does!" a voice from the doorway called out, and Doc came into the bar. "This isn't a private meeting, is it?"

"Yes, and you're in it," Mike replied. "Right here, Doc." He patted the stool beside him. "I need to caution you not to mention anything about Mr. Bowman to anyone."

Doc gave a nod. "Noted. Then you're not going to let anyone know that he's deceased?"

"Not tonight. And maybe not tomorrow morning, either."

Sally looked surprised. "Why is that, Mike?"

"Because I'm going to hang out in the bar tonight

with Lonnie and pick up any information about Mr. Bowman that we can."

"You need to know what the other competitors thought of Sonny?" Norman asked.

"Yes. We'll be looking for any long-term or new grudges, any motives any of the other fishermen or their wives may have had for wanting him dead, and anything else that might apply in some way to the case."

"I can help with that, and so can Delores," Doc offered.

"Good," Mike agreed immediately, and then he turned to Hannah and Norman. "You two are staying out here, aren't you?"

"Yes, and we'll be in the bar if you need us," Norman promised.

"I do."

"How about Andrea?" Hannah asked him. "She's staying out here, sharing my room with me."

"Andrea could be really helpful," Mike said. "Bill always says that she could charm the birds right out of their trees."

"I'll be there, too," Sally told him. "I'm helping Dick in the bar this week. It's going to be crazy busy."

"One more thing," Hannah said quickly when Mike pushed back his barstool. "What are you going to tell everyone when Sonny doesn't show up at the bar tonight?"

"That's where you and Dick come in," Mike told Sally. "I want you two to tell everyone that Sonny is up in his room sleeping."

"We can do that," Sally promised. "How about Wally? What if he calls to check in? Shall I tell him?"

Mike shook his head. "Just say that Sonny left a message with the desk asking that no one disturb him."

Hannah frowned slightly. "How about Lily? Are you going to call to tell her that Sonny is dead?"

"Not yet . . . at least not until we find out if she's a suspect or not."

"Everybody's a suspect." Lonnie walked into the bar, grinning. "Everybody's a suspect until *we* clear them, right, Mike?"

"That's right!" Mike told him. "Stay here, Lonnie. I need to go check on the crime scene boys to see if they're done yet. When they are, I will tell Rosa that she can clean Joey's room." He turned to Sally. "Can you and Dick keep Joey here for another twenty minutes or so?"

"No problem," Sally said quickly. "Just ask Rosa to give me a call when Joey's room is done so I can let him go back upstairs."

Mike asked, "What time is dinner, Sally?"

Sally glanced up at the clock behind the bar. "Not 'til seven, Mike."

Mike gave a long-drawn-out sigh. "I'm really hungry now," he said. "What's in those special omelets that Dick made for Joey?"

"Corned beef brisket, Swiss cheese, and sauerkraut," Sally answered. "Dick calls them Reuben Omelets and he serves them with Thousand Island dressing with chopped gherkins on top."

"Sounds good!" Mike said, beginning to smile. "I like Reuben sandwiches, so I should like Dick's omelets, right?"

"Right," Sally said. "Shall I call Dick and ask him to make one for you?"

"Yeah, that'd be great!" Mike turned to Lonnie. "You want one, too?"

"Sure," Lonnie agreed.

"Consider it done," Sally told them as they got up from their barstools. "Head on back to the kitchen right now and I'll tell Dick you're coming. There may even be a couple of Caramel Pecan Rolls left from the breakfast buffet, if Joey didn't eat them already."

Once Mike and Lonnie had left, Doc turned to Sally. "Better tell Dick to make more than two omelets," he warned her. "If Mike wasn't here for the breakfast buffet, he'll probably eat at least three."

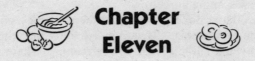

Chapter Eleven

There was a knock on the door, and Hannah opened it. "Andrea!" she said, as her sister rushed into their room.

"I just ran into Mike in the hallway, and you should have called me right away!" Andrea said, and she looked as shocked as she obviously felt. "I can't believe he's dead!"

"Believe me, he is," Hannah assured her, "and you can't tell anyone about it."

"I understand, but . . ." Andrea gave a little shiver. "Why can't I tell Bill when he calls me tonight? He's the sheriff, and he ought to know that there's been a murder."

"That's not wise, Andrea. Do you really want him to come home early and miss the opportunity to give his televised keynote speech?"

Andrea thought about that for a moment. "You're right," she said. "I just hope Bill isn't mad that we kept him in the dark about the murder."

"I don't think he will be," Hannah said quickly.

"After all, Bill chose Mike to fill in as acting sheriff while Bill was gone. Bill expects Mike to make his own decisions and not to check in with him every other minute."

"I guess that's true," Andrea said, but she still sounded slightly doubtful. "I just hope he's not mad at me for not telling him."

"He won't be," Hannah assured her, although she wasn't sure at all. "Since Mike is the acting sheriff while Bill is gone, we have to do what he tells us to do."

Andrea started to smile. "I don't believe you just said that, Hannah!"

"Neither do I." Hannah gave a little laugh. "But I really do think we'd better trust Mike's judgment when it comes to alerting Bill."

"All right," Andrea reluctantly agreed. "I won't tell Bill until Mike says it's okay."

Andrea lifted the suitcase she'd brought in with her and put it on her bed. "This is heavier than I thought it would be, but I promised Tracey I'd bring it."

"You brought more clothes?" Hannah asked.

"No, it's something Tracey thought of, so we went shopping right before I drove out here."

"What did you buy?" Hannah asked, moving a little closer.

"Goldfish. We got a whole carton of them."

"You bought live goldfish??"

Andrea began to laugh. "No, silly. Tracey and I bought Goldfish crackers. They're for Dick to put out in the bar in the baskets he uses for bar snacks. Tracey thought it would be perfect for the fishing tournament."

Hannah smiled. "That *is* perfect! When you talk to

Tracey, tell her I think she had a great idea! Dick and Sally are going to love it!"

"We're going down to the bar tonight, aren't we?" Andrea asked, taking the large box out of her suitcase.

"Yes. Since you're okay with not telling anyone that Sonny is dead, will you help us listen for gossip in the bar tonight?"

"Of course I will! I'm good at things like that. People tell me gossip and they trust me not to tell anyone else."

"We know, that's why Mike and I and Lonnie don't tell you any secrets."

Andrea looked shocked. "Oh . . . Really?"

"I'm kidding, Andrea! Actually it's one of the reasons we need you with us in the bar. People do tell you secrets."

Andrea smiled. "Thank you! You're good at it, too, Hannah. And so is Mother. Everybody tells Mother all their secrets."

And she tells them to us, Hannah thought, but she didn't share that thought with Andrea. "The local competitors know who you are, but the ones from out of town don't. Do you think you can circulate tonight and talk to the out-of-towners? We need to find out what they thought of Sonny."

"Of course I can!" Andrea replied immediately.

Hannah smiled. "I know. We need to know if anyone who came here had a past history with Sonny."

"I get it," Andrea said. "You want to find out if any of them had a motive for wanting Sonny dead."

"Exactly right. The only thing you can't do is tell anyone the real reason that Sonny isn't down in the bar drinking the way he did last night."

There was a knock on their door, and Hannah went

to answer it. She was surprised to see Rosa there with a tray. "Hi, Rosa," she greeted Sally's head housekeeper. "What's all this?" She gestured toward the tray.

"Sally sent me up with coffee and something they just baked in the kitchen. Can I come in?"

"Of course," Hannah said, opening the door all the way. "Whatever it is smells really good."

"It's Blueberry Coffee Cake and it is good. I had a piece before I came up here."

"Do I smell blueberries?" Andrea asked, coming out of the bathroom wearing one of Sally's Lake Eden Inn robes.

"Blueberry Coffee Cake," Rosa said, setting the tray on the dresser. "Help yourself, both of you."

"Do you know if Sally needs help in the kitchen?" Hannah asked. "I'm all ready for tonight, but I could run down there if she does."

Rosa shook her head. "She's training a new helper for the pastry chef, but she told me that he was doing great. She was all smiles when I went to pick up your tray."

"Okay, then. If you go back down there, tell her that we'll see her in the bar tonight, and . . ."

"What did you just think of?" Andrea asked, when Hannah began to frown.

"I was just wondering if the blonde will be there."

Rosa smiled. "Oh, she'll be there."

Hannah just stared at Rosa for a moment. "Will you please tell us what you know that we don't know?" she asked.

"I don't know if . . ." Rosa stopped speaking and gave a huge sigh. "I'm just not sure if I should be the one . . ." She stopped speaking again and frowned heavily.

"What is it, Rosa?" Hannah asked her.

"I don't know if I should say anything to you or not," Rosa blurted out. Then she stopped, drew a deep breath, and asked, "Are you two girls investigating?"

Both Andrea and Hannah were dead silent for a moment, and then they exchanged glances. "Would that make a difference?" Hannah asked Rosa.

"Maybe. Look, girls . . ." Rosa sighed again and looked terribly uncomfortable. "I know I shouldn't tell tales out of school, but . . . I put two and two together and I figure Mr. Sonny is dead. Am I right?"

"Oh, Lord!" Andrea said, not entirely under her breath.

"Of course you put two and two together," Hannah said directly to Rosa. "And you're right, Rosa, but please don't tell anyone, especially Mike or Lonnie, that I said that. And yes, we are investigating."

"Then it's murder?" Rosa asked.

Hannah nodded. "That's the conclusion that Mike, Lonnie, and Doc came to."

"That doesn't surprise me at all," Rosa admitted. "He was bound to come to a bad end the way he was drinking and womanizing. And Lily is the sweetest thing! I sure hope she's not the one who killed him, although I wouldn't blame her a bit if she did!"

"Sit down, Rosa," Hannah said, patting the side of her bed. "Tell us what you know, and maybe it'll help Lily. You sound as if you think she's a nice person."

"I do, and I'm pretty sure she is. No woman should have to put up with the grief that man gave her! I would have been out of that relationship in two seconds flat if my man ever treated me that way!"

"Because he flirted with other women?" Andrea asked.

"Not just flirted!" Rosa exclaimed, looking irritated.

"I don't know how he could treat her like that when Lily got him the best job he'd ever had. Wally knew that Sonny didn't know anything about fishing, but his daughter was so insistent, he told her he'd give Sonny a try. And Sonny was good on television," Rosa concluded. "Wally's daughter was right when she told him that the wives would watch the fishing shows because Sonny was so . . ." Rosa stopped and looked uncertain. "What is the word I want?"

"Handsome?" Andrea guessed.

"And sexy," Hannah added. "Is that what you mean, Rosa?"

"Yes. There's another word for it, but I don't want to say it. It's not . . . very nice."

Andrea laughed. "That's okay, Rosa. We know exactly what you mean."

Hannah nodded, but her mind was going a million miles a minute, trying to fit pieces of information and theories about the murder together. "Dick told me something this morning in the bar," she told Rosa. "He said that Lily was here last night."

Rosa nodded. "She was. I went up to let Lily into Sonny's suite. And now . . . I wish I hadn't. It might have been better if Lily hadn't seen Sonny last night."

"Why?" Andrea asked.

"Because Sonny had . . . how you say . . . company."

"You're talking about female company?" Andrea asked, and it was a cross between a statement and a question.

"Yes. *She* was there in the bed with him."

"The blonde?" Hannah guessed.

"Yes. I saw her there when I came in to turn down the lights. He was sleeping, but she wasn't. She was not nice to me."

"What did she do?" Andrea asked.

"She told me to get lost and she said she'd have me fired if I ever told anyone I'd seen her. So I haven't . . . until now."

"That's okay," Hannah reassured her. "It's just an empty threat, Rosa. There's nothing she could do to you."

"That's right," Andrea agreed. "You work for Sally, and Sally knows how valuable you are."

Rosa gave a big smile. "Thank you for telling me that. I love working here. Sally gave me my own room for the whole fishing tournament so I don't have to drive back home. And I don't have to pay for the room, or the food, or anything."

"That's wonderful, Rosa," Andrea said. "And it proves how much Sally values you as her head of housekeeping."

"That's true," Hannah agreed. "And Sally obviously trusts you to take care of any problems with the guests."

"Was Lily very upset when she got here?" Andrea asked.

"Oh, yes! I was in the lobby when she came in and asked for the key to Sonny's suite. The desk clerk wasn't sure what he should do, so I told him to give her a key."

"And he did?" Hannah asked.

"Yes, but I knew there'd be trouble so I went upstairs with her."

"How did you know?" Hannah asked.

"I was in the hallway when *that woman* knocked on the door. And I saw how fast Sonny opened it and pulled her inside."

Hannah and Andrea exchanged glances. What Rosa had told them gave Lily a plausible reason for murder.

"Did you go in with Lily?" Hannah asked the housekeeper.

"No, I just walked her to the door and waited to make sure that she could get in. And I was worried because I didn't know if *that woman* was still there."

"What time was this?" Andrea asked, and Hannah felt like applauding. Andrea was establishing a time line, something she'd forgotten to do.

"It was after midnight. I know because I stop working at midnight and go down to the kitchen to get the tray that Sally always leaves out for me. Then I go to my room, eat the snack that she leaves for me, and go to bed."

"Is that what you did last night?" Andrea asked.

"No! I was too worried to leave. I was afraid there could be trouble!"

"What did you do?" Andrea asked.

"I stayed in the hallway behind the door to the housekeepers' closet to keep my eye on things, just in case." Rosa began to frown. "You don't think I was wrong to stay there and watch, do you?"

"Absolutely not!" Hannah said quickly. "That sounds entirely reasonable."

"I think so, too," Andrea agreed.

Rosa gave a sigh of relief. "I was curious," she admitted. "I wanted to know what would happen. I thought maybe I could help Lily in some way."

"You like Lily?" Hannah drew the obvious conclusion.

"Yes. Very much."

"I'm glad you stayed in the hallway, Rosa," Andrea said.

Rosa looked grateful for Andrea's words. "I wasn't spying on them. It's just that I was afraid that something bad was going to happen."

"And did something bad happen?" Hannah asked.

Rosa nodded. "Oh, yes. It was very bad for *that woman*."

Hannah exchanged a warning glance with Andrea. It was time to let Rosa tell them what had happened in her own way. "Please tell us, Rosa," Hannah encouraged her.

"There is a clock in the housekeepers' closet and I looked at the time when I opened the door. It was twenty past midnight."

Hannah watched as Andrea pulled out the small notebook that her sister had begun to carry in the outside pocket of her purse. Andrea's notebook had an attached pen, and Andrea held it at the ready.

"I didn't want to stay in the closet all night watching the hallway, and I was just thinking about leaving when the door to Sonny's suite opened and someone . . . someone without any clothes came out!"

"What?!" Hannah gasped.

"That's right." Rosa gave a little smile. "I didn't ask, but I think Lily found *that woman* in Sonny's bed and chased her right out of the suite without a stitch of clothes on!"

"Do you know what time that was?" Hannah asked.

"Yes, I was getting ready to leave because it was almost twelve-thirty and I needed to get some sleep."

Hannah and Andrea exchanged glances again. Neither one knew exactly what to say.

"She deserved it!" Rosa said, giving a little laugh. "She deserved to be locked out in the hallway with no clothes."

"Yes, she did," Hannah agreed.

"Good for Lily for kicking her out!" Andrea added, "I'd do exactly the same thing if I ever walked in and found another woman in my husband's bed!"

The thought of her standing in the hallway without her clothes at half-past midnight made all three of them begin to laugh.

"I grabbed one of the robes we put in the rooms. It was funny, but I didn't want *that woman* to be out in the hallway naked. Something like that could give the Inn a bad name," Rosa told them.

"I guess it could," Hannah managed to say, although she was still fighting to keep from chuckling. "Did you take the robe to her?"

Rosa nodded. "Yes, and I told her to hold out her arms so I could put it on her. She was shaking and I think she was really scared. I'm not even sure she knew exactly where she was."

"Was she drunk, too?" Andrea asked.

"No, not drunk. It was like she just woke up and she didn't really know where she was. Once I got the robe on her, I asked her if she had her room key."

"And of course she didn't," Hannah said.

"That's right. So I grabbed her arm and marched her to the room she was supposed to be sharing with her husband," Rosa continued. "I had the passkey with me and I was all ready to let her go back inside when I thought of something that scared me a little."

"What was that?" Hannah asked her.

"I asked her if her husband would be mad at her for leaving in the middle of the night."

"What did she say?" Andrea asked.

"She said he wouldn't even wake up because she'd given him a sleeping pill. So I let her into the room, shut the door, and waited a couple of minutes to make sure that everything was all right."

"Was it?" Hannah asked.

"Yes. Then I went to the kitchen, picked up the tray

that Sally had left for me, took it to my room, and went to bed."

"Did you see Lily this morning?" Hannah asked.

"No. I didn't wake up until nine, and the desk clerk said she'd left by then. I'm not sure what time, but he's at the desk now, if you want to ask him."

Hannah nodded at Andrea, who'd jotted it down in her notebook. "Thank you for telling us all this, Rosa."

"You're welcome." Rosa began to frown again. "You don't think that . . ." She stopped and frowned even deeper. "You don't think that Lily killed Sonny, do you?"

Hannah thought about that for a moment and then she shook her head. "I don't know yet. . . . Do you think she could have?"

"No! She could never have done such a thing!" Rosa exclaimed.

"Why?" Andrea asked her. "She certainly had plenty of reasons to want him out of her life."

"Out of her life . . . maybe. But Lily would not have killed anyone. She loved Sonny. She knew he had faults, but she still loved him. And I can't believe that she could . . ." Rosa turned to Hannah. "You don't understand, Lily is a gentle person. She could never shoot anyone." Rosa glanced at her watch and frowned. "I have to go. I'm going to help Sally serve the evening buffet for the fishermen."

"Please keep your ears open for any talk about Sonny," Hannah told her. "Nobody knows he's dead, and all the fishermen will think is that he chose not to eat at the buffet."

Rosa gave a nod. "Is this the invisible waitress trick you told me about, Hannah?"

"That's right. It works, Rosa. People go right on talking when you fill their coffee cups or bring them food."

"I know. I tried it at one of Sally's luncheons. That's how I learned that Mrs. Dugan's youngest daughter is having another baby."

"I didn't know Fanny was having another baby!" Andrea said once they'd said their goodbyes and Rosa had left.

"You look shocked," Hannah said, staring at her sister. "Is there something wrong with Fanny having another baby?"

"No, it's not that," Andrea said. "It's just that Rosa gave me an idea for the bar tonight."

"What's that?"

"I'm going to be Dick and Sally's new barmaid. I'll deliver drinks and appetizers. That'll give me an excuse to go from table to table and I might overhear something that could help us in our investigation."

"That's a very good idea, Andrea! But aren't you too tired to work tonight, after all you've done today?"

"I'm too tired to work, but delivering drinks and appetizers isn't exactly working. And I'll be able to pick up a lot more information that way than I would just going over, sitting down, and trying to make conversation with people I don't know."

"That's true," Hannah agreed. "I just don't want you to wear yourself out, Andrea. We're trying out a couple new recipes tomorrow and I'm going to need you in the kitchen."

"No problem," Andrea insisted. "Besides, I'm younger than you are, Hannah, and I have more energy than you have. I read an article that said women over forty need a lot more sleep than younger women."

Hannah bristled slightly. "I'm not ready for the retirement home yet, Andrea!"

"I know *that*!" Andrea looked a bit sorry she'd brought up the difference in their ages. "Besides, I haven't done anything like this for a while. I might overhear a major clue."

"That's true," Hannah said. "It's a good idea, Andrea, as long as you don't mind doing it."

"I don't mind at all!" Andrea insisted. "It'll be fun playing the invisible waitress again!"

BLUEBERRY COFFEE CAKE

Preheat oven to 350 degrees F., rack in the middle position.

Hannah's 1ˢᵗ Note: Some coffee cake is more like sweet bread. This coffee cake is more like a cake. Coffee cake is a staple in Minnesota. It is what most people serve when they invite friends over for coffee in the morning. With guests, the cake type of coffee cake is served more often. When it's breakfast with the family, the sweet bread type is usually served, especially if the slices are toasted and buttered.

Ingredients for the Cake:

> 1 cup salted butter (*2 sticks, ½ pound*) softened to room temperature
> 1 and ¾ cups white (*granulated*) sugar
> 1 teaspoon salt
> 2 teaspoons vanilla extract
> 1 and ½ teaspoons baking powder
> 6 large eggs
> 3 cups all-purpose flour (*pack it down in the cup when you measure it*)

Ingredients for the Filling:

3 cups thawed and crushed frozen blueberries *(you can also use fresh blueberries, if they're in season)*

⅓ cup white *(granulated)* sugar

⅓ cup all-purpose flour *(pack it down in
the cup when you measure it)*

Ingredients for the Peek-a-Boo Crumb Topping:

½ cup brown sugar *(pack it down in the
cup when you measure it)*

⅓ cup all-purpose flour *(pack it down in
the cup when you measure it)*

¼ cup salted butter *(½ stick, ⅛ pound)*
softened to room temperature

Spray the inside of a 9-inch by 13-inch rectangular cake pan with Pam or another nonstick cooking spray.

**Hannah's 2ⁿᵈ Note: This recipe is very easy
to make with an electric mixer. It's also possible
to do it by hand if you wish.**

To Make the Cake Dough:

Cut the softened butter into chunks and place them in the mixer bowl.

Place the white (*granulated*) sugar on top of the butter.

Turn the mixer on LOW speed for 30 seconds. Then turn the mixer up to MEDIUM speed and mix until the butter and sugar are fluffy and of a uniform color.

Turn the mixer down to LOW speed again and add the salt and the vanilla extract and baking powder. Mix until everything is well incorporated.

Add the eggs one at a time, mixing thoroughly after each addition.

Shut off the mixer and add one cup of the all-purpose flour.

Turn the mixer back on LOW speed and mix the cup of flour in thoroughly.

Turn off the mixer and sprinkle in the second cup of all-purpose flour.

Turn the mixer on LOW speed again and mix in that second cup of all-purpose flour.

Turn off the mixer and sprinkle in the third cup of flour.

Turn the mixer back on LOW speed again and mix in the flour thoroughly.

Shut off the mixer, scrape down the sides of the bowl, take the bowl out of the mixer, and use a mixing spoon to spoon one-half of the cake batter into your prepared cake pan.

Spread the cake batter out with a rubber spatula as evenly as you can.

Leave the rest of the cake batter in the mixing bowl and take out another bowl to prepare the coffee cake filling.

To Make the Fruit Filling:

If you haven't already done so, measure out your blueberries and crush them in the bottom of the bowl.

Stir in the sugar. Stir it in thoroughly.

Measure out the all-purpose flour and then sprinkle it on top of the sugar and blueberry mixture in your bowl.

Mix the flour in thoroughly.

Place spoonfuls of the blueberry filling all over the top of your cake dough. Make extra sure you get a spoonful in all four corners of the pan.

Carefully spread the blueberry filling out from spoonful to spoonful so that the filling covers the entire surface of the cake batter.

Give the rest of the cake batter a final stir by hand.

Drop spoonfuls of the remaining cake batter on top of the blueberry filling and spread it out as best you can.

Hannah's 3rd Note: Don't worry if the cake batter on top doesn't completely cover the blueberry filling. It doesn't have to. You will put the crumb topping right over the top of your coffee cake.

To Make the Peek-a-Boo Crumb Topping:

Mix the brown sugar and the all-purpose flour together in a small bowl.

Add the softened butter and cut it in until it's crumbly. *(You can also do this in a food processor with chilled butter and the steel blade.)*

Use your impeccably clean fingers to sprinkle the crumb topping over the top of the cake pan. Do this as evenly as possible and don't worry because the topping doesn't cover the top of the pan completely. The blueberries are supposed to show through so everyone will know what's inside.

Bake your Blueberry Coffee Cake at 350 degrees F. for 45 to 55 minutes or until the edges of your cake are nice and golden brown.

Take your coffee cake out of the oven with potholders and set it on a cold stovetop burner or a wire rack to cool.

This coffee cake can be served warm or cold, depending on when your guests are coming.

To serve, use a knife to cut your coffee cake into squares right in the cake pan. Then remove

the squares to small plates with a wide metal spatula. Be sure to serve your Blueberry Coffee Cake with plenty of strong freshly brewed coffee or icy-cold glasses of milk.

Yield: At least 12 squares of delicious, fruit-filled coffee cake that both adults and kids will enjoy.

Hannah's 4th Note: Several people have told me that they made this coffee cake the easy way by simply opening a can of fruit pie filling and using that, straight out of the can, for the coffee cake filling. I told them that Edna Fergusson, the queen of shortcuts, would be proud of them. Lisa told me that Aunt Nancy is going to try to make this coffee cake with a mincemeat filling at Thanksgiving. I'm not quite that adventuresome, but I have made it with lemon pie filling and it was scrumptious.

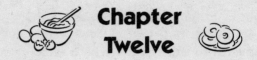

Chapter Twelve

"Hi, Sally!" An attractive young woman walked into the bar and hurried over to Sally, who was standing by Hannah at a table.

"I didn't expect to see you today!" Sally said, looking surprised. "I thought you left this morning. Oh my gosh, where are my manners? Lily, this is Hannah Swensen, she's been helping bake this week. And Hannah? This is Lily Wallace, Wally's daughter."

Lily turned to Hannah. "How nice to meet you, Hannah." Then she turned back to Sally. "I *did* leave this morning. I drove straight up to help my dad with the new store, but he already had everything under control. I came back here to see if I could help the situation with Sonny. Dad said he'd been acting up again, and I saw *that* with my own two eyes."

Sally shot Hannah a panicked glance, and then she drew a deep breath. "Lily is engaged to our fishing star, Sonny Bowman. Will you be staying the night, Lily?"

"I thought I would if you have a single room.

There's no way I'm staying in Sonny's suite. He had one too many visitors in there last night!" Lily stopped and looked around the bar. "And there she is right now. At least she's not with Sonny!"

Sally shot Hannah another desperate glance, and Hannah shoved back her chair. It was clear that Sally was out of her depth when it came to making conversation with Lily. "Please come with me, Lily," Hannah said, extending her hand to Lily. "There's some people I'd like you to meet."

Sally's sigh of relief was almost audible as Hannah ushered Lily over to Mike and Lonnie's table; it was time for Mike to take over.

"Lily?" she said, tapping Mike on the shoulder. "This is Mike Kingston and one of his deputies, Lonnie Murphy." She turned to Mike. "And guys? This is Lily Wallace, Wally's daughter and Sonny Bowman's fiancée. Lily was here at the Inn last night."

"Glad to meet you," Lily said, smiling politely but looking a bit puzzled about why Hannah had brought her to Mike and Lonnie's table.

"Hello, Lily," Mike said, and both men stood up. Mike pulled out Lily's chair, and Lonnie pulled out Hannah's.

"Please join us," Mike said. "We have something we need to discuss with you, Lily."

"Of course," Lily agreed, taking her chair. "Is it about the fishing tournament? Dad told me that you two were a big help in keeping his tournament running smoothly." She frowned slightly. "Dad filled me in on a couple of things, and I'm sorry that Sonny caused you some problems last night."

"That's okay," Mike said, smiling at her. "We took care of it."

"Dad was sure you would, but he called me and told me to drive up here and try to talk some sense into Sonny."

"And did you succeed?" Lonnie asked her.

"Not exactly!"

Hannah heard the edge in Lily's voice and she glanced at Mike. Something was going on here that she didn't understand.

Lily gave a little sigh. "I should have just stayed up at the store. Sonny was in no shape to talk to me."

"Hello, Lily," Dick greeted her as he arrived at their table with a tray. "White wine for you?"

"Thanks, Dick, but not tonight," Lily replied quickly. "I'll have a big glass of iced tea if you have it."

"I do and I'll get it, but I brought this for you first." Dick set the basket of crackers down in the center of the table and placed one of the miniature martini glasses that Sally had ordered in front of Lily. "I brought you one of the drinks I created for the fishing tournament."

Lily glanced at the martini glass that Dick had set in front of her. She reached out to touch one of the olives on either side of the rim and began to smile. "Oh, Dick! How clever! It has Walleye eyes!"

"That's right. And it's a dirty vodka martini made with olive juice so it looks a bit like lake water."

"Yes, it does." Lily lifted the glass and took a sip. "And it's delicious!"

"And very small," Dick added. "A full-size Walleye Martini might been a bit much for some of the contestants, but Sally managed to find these small miniature glasses."

"Perfect!" Lily declared, putting down the glass and taking a Goldfish cracker from the basket. "Bait fish?"

"Yes, but this is a no live bait tournament."

Lily gave a little laugh. "Has anyone tried to put one of these crackers on the hook?"

"No, we just got them tonight. Hannah's sister brought them from our grocery store in town."

"Well, they're a great addition to the atmosphere," Lily said, taking a handful. "Plus, they're delicious. I love Goldfish crackers."

Hannah glanced at Mike and realized that he was frowning slightly. Dick must have realized it, too, because he backed away from the table. "I'll get your iced tea," he said, giving a little wave and turning to go. "I'll talk to you later, Lily."

Mike glanced at Hannah and realized that she didn't have a drink. "Do you want a drink, Hannah?"

"No, thanks, Mike. I have a glass of wine already. I must have left it on Michelle's table."

"And here it is, Hannah," Andrea said, arriving at the table and setting Hannah's glass of wine down in front of her. "Michelle noticed that you were sitting down here and asked me to bring it to you."

"Andrea?" Mike asked, gesturing toward one of the empty chairs at their table.

"No, but thanks, Mike," Andrea said quickly. "One of Dick's waitresses is on break so I'm taking her place."

"So Michelle's at the table all alone?" Hannah asked.

"No, one of the other teachers just walked in and she's sitting with Michelle. I heard her tell Michelle that her husband is a contestant in the tournament."

Hannah knew she was stuck here, watching Mike and Lonnie interrogate Lily. She mentally reminded herself that Mike and Lonnie were running their own investigation and that she had no right to interfere.

Mike looked at her and smiled. Perhaps she was

wrong, but Hannah thought she knew what that smile meant. It was almost as if he'd said, *You brought her here and she's ours now. The ball's in our court and we've got this handled without any help from you.*

Hannah gave a little nod as she picked up her wineglass and took a sip. She wished that she could cue Mike and Lonnie in on what Rosa had told her, but there had been no opportunity to do that before Lily had entered the bar, spotted Sally, and come over to say hello.

"You said you were here last night?" Mike said, smiling at Lily.

"That's right. I had some things I had to take care of before I could leave, so I didn't get here until late. The bar was already closed and no one was around except the night clerk at the desk. I was about to ask for a key to my fiancé's room when I saw Rosa. She took me upstairs and let me into Sonny's suite."

"Did you run into anyone else besides Rosa?" Lonnie asked.

"No. I think all the fishermen had gone to bed by then," Lily replied. "There was no one else around."

Hannah felt a little jolt of surprise. Lonnie was taking the lead and usually Mike controlled the whole interview. It was uncharacteristic, but perhaps the two detectives had worked it all out beforehand.

"Do you have any idea what time that was?" Lonnie followed up, and Hannah noticed that he had his small notebook and pen in his lap. She glanced at Mike, but Mike seemed to be perfectly comfortable with Lonnie's line of questioning.

"I think it was after midnight, but I'm not really sure. I drove here from the Brainerd store and I know I left close to ten. I was helping them with their inventory and doing product coding. Our grand opening is tomorrow and we wanted everything in shape for that."

"Did you call your fiancé to tell him that you were coming?" Lonnie asked her, and again Hannah was a bit disconcerted. Lonnie was definitely taking the lead and Mike didn't seem to mind that at all.

"I called, but Sonny didn't answer his cell phone," Lily replied, glancing at Mike.

"How about Sonny?" Mike asked her. "Had he gone to bed yet?"

"You bet he had!" Lily said, and she gave an exasperated sigh. "And true to form, he was *not* alone!"

"Did you recognize the person who was with your fiancé?" Lonnie asked.

"Not until I saw her again tonight." Lily looked over at the table where the blonde had been sitting. "I guess she must have recognized me, too, because she's gone now."

"What did you do when you found the other woman in Sonny's room?" Lonnie asked.

Lily looked a bit embarrassed. "I'm not exactly proud of what I did, but I was so mad at Sonny, I'm afraid I took it out on her."

"How did you take it out on her?" Lonnie questioned.

"I grabbed her by the arm and threw her out in the hallway. She was naked and I didn't bother to pick up her clothes and throw them out after her. I just locked the door and stood there shaking. I was so furious at Sonny, I could have killed him!"

Hannah did her best not to wince visibly. She really wished that Lily hadn't said it quite that way.

"What did Sonny say when you threw the other woman out?" Lonnie asked.

"Absolutely nothing. He was dead drunk, and he didn't even wake up."

"Did you try to wake him?" Mike asked, and Hannah was glad he'd asked the obvious question.

"No. When Sonny's drunk, you could set off fireworks in his room and he'd sleep through it. And I knew, from experience, that if he'd actually been awake enough to listen to me, he would have forgotten everything I said, anyway."

"So did you sleep there in your fiancé's suite?"

"Yes. It was a two-bedroom suite so I just went in the other bedroom, got into bed, and tried to go to sleep."

"And did you sleep?" Mike asked her.

"I think I must have slept for a while," Lily told them. "It was just such a . . . a disappointment! It's not like this hasn't happened before. It has. Sonny's a handsome man, and women throw themselves at him. Unfortunately, he doesn't seem to be able to resist them. He swears he loves me, but he can't resist playing the game with other women."

"You must have been furious," Mike said.

Lily said, "It wasn't the sort of night that I wanted, but it wasn't unexpected, either."

"Some men like to flirt and that's as far as it goes," Mike said. "Other men like to flirt and they don't know when they should stop. I think Sonny was one of the latter group."

Hannah watched as Lily's face paled. *"Was?"* she repeated. "You said Sonny *was* and that's past tense! I heard you!"

Mike sighed. "You're right, Lily. I didn't mean to blurt it out like that, but I have to tell you that Sonny's dead."

"When?" Lily choked the word out, and Hannah immediately reached out to put an arm around her shoulder. She wasn't sure why Mike had chosen to tell Lily this way, but perhaps it had just slipped out.

"Lily and I have to leave now," Hannah announced, tightening her arm around Lily's shoulders and helping her to her feet. "We'll be in the kitchen, and I'm going to get her something to eat. Come there if you have to ask her more questions."

"Good. Thank you, Hannah," Mike said, looking very grateful. Then he turned to Lily. "I'm sorry, Lily. I didn't mean to tell you in quite that way. It just slipped out."

Lily gave a little nod. "It's okay. I know what I told you made me a suspect. I can't blame you for that. I'll answer any other questions you and your partner have, if you'll just give me a little time to . . . to digest all this and . . . and grieve."

Mike threw Hannah a sympathetic look. "Of course we will. I'm sorry, Lily. I apologize again for springing all this on you this way. If I could take it back, I would."

"Apology accepted," Lily said, reaching out to touch Mike's shoulder. "I'll be with Hannah if you need me."

Hannah stopped at their table and leaned down to talk to Michelle privately. "Tell Andrea that I'm going to be busy for a while," she said. "I'll meet her later, back at our room." Then she turned to Lily. "Come on, Lily. I'll take you back to the kitchen now."

Hannah glanced behind her as they exited the bar. No one was looking at them curiously. That was good. She just hoped that she could get Lily calmed down before Mike and Lonnie decided to come to the kitchen to question her further.

"Do you think I'll have to answer more questions?" Lily asked, as they walked down the long hallway that led to the kitchen.

"I don't know," Hannah answered truthfully. "In a way, I hope not. You look like you're on your last legs."

Lily smiled. "I *am* tired. And you were right, I'm hungry."

"What sounds good?" Hannah asked her, leading her into the kitchen and pulling out a chair at the table.

"I don't know. Anything, I guess."

Hannah stepped inside the walk-in cooler and made a quick survey of the contents. "I can always fix you a sandwich. There's plenty of cold cuts and cheese. And there's always soup. That'll only take a few minutes to heat. I can even bake you something if you know what you'd like."

"I . . . I don't," Lily admitted. "One minute, I'm practically starved and the next minute, I'm not sure I could eat anything."

"You're probably in shock," Hannah told her. "Sugar might help. I mixed up some cookie dough for tomorrow and . . ." She stopped and turned to face Lily. "Do you like chocolate?"

"I *love* chocolate! It's my favorite thing!"

"How about peanut butter?"

Lily gave a little laugh. "That's my other favorite thing. They used to make jars of peanut butter with swirls of chocolate fudge sauce inside. That was my favorite sandwich when I went to college."

"I remember that. There was another one with peanut butter and swirls of grape jelly. Do you remember that?"

"Yes, I do. It was good, but the one with chocolate was my hands-down favorite."

"How about some Chocolate Peanut Butter Whippersnapper Cookies?" Hannah asked.

"That sounds perfect! What are Whippersnapper Cookies? I've never heard of them."

"They're cookies with Cool Whip in them and they're really simple to make. My sister, Andrea, makes dozens of different kinds."

"Andrea?" Lily looked slightly puzzled. "Didn't you say your sister's name was Michelle?"

"It is. Michelle was sitting at the table with me, when you walked in. Andrea is the sister who delivered my wine and is relieving some of Dick's barmaids when they go on break." Hannah picked up the bowl of Chocolate Peanut Butter Whippersnapper Cookie dough that she had mixed up early and brought it to the work table. "This won't take long," she said, walking over to the industrial oven to set it to the proper temperature. "I might as well make the whole batch while I'm at it. That way, you can take some up to your room too."

"Good!" Lily said quickly with a smile.

"I am sorry that you had to learn about everything so . . . so suddenly."

"So am I, but it doesn't change what happened. I don't blame Mike. He seems like a very nice man and so does his partner. It's just that . . . that it was such a shock!"

"Of course it was. Try to lean back and relax now. You've been through a lot today." Hannah sniffed the air and gave a little smile. "Can you smell the cookies baking?"

"I can! They smell wonderful, Hannah! How many minutes do they have left to go?"

Hannah glanced at the clock. "Not long now, but they'll have to cool for about five minutes. If you try to eat them right after they come out of the oven, you'll burn your mouth."

"I know. I did that once with chocolate chip cookies. I didn't realize that the chocolate would stay hot for longer than the rest of the cookie does."

"Just close your eyes and think about how good they're going to taste," Hannah told her, noticing that Lily had relaxed a bit. "Shut your eyes and concentrate on the wonderful scent of cookies baking. Perfume will never be able to compete with the scent of chocolate cookies in the oven."

"That's really true," Lily said, and Hannah noticed that her eyes were closed. "It's the best scent in the world. It reminds me of when I was little and my mother baked every morning. I really miss those days. I used to wake up to the most wonderful scents in the world!"

CHOCOLATE PEANUT BUTTER WHIPPERSNAPPER COOKIES

DO NOT preheat oven—this cookie dough must chill before baking.

Ingredients:

1 large egg, beaten *(just whip it up in a glass with a fork)*

2 cups Cool Whip, thawed *(measure this—Andrea said her tub of Cool Whip contained a little over 3 cups)*

1 cup mini chocolate chips *(Andrea used a 6-ounce package of Nestlé Mini Morsels)*

1 cup peanut butter chips

1 package *(approximately 18 ounces)* chocolate cake mix, the size you can bake in a 9-inch by 13-inch cake pan *(Andrea used Betty Crocker Chocolate Fudge)*

½ cup powdered *(confectioners)* sugar in a separate small bowl *(you don't have to sift it unless it's got big lumps)*

First of all, chill 2 teaspoons from your silverware drawer by sticking them in the freezer.

You want them really ice cold. This will make it a lot easier to form the cookies after the dough has chilled.

If you haven't done this already, whisk the egg until it is fluffy and of a uniform color.

Transfer the egg to a large mixing bowl.

Measure the Cool Whip and stir it in.

Measure and stir in the mini chocolate chips.

Measure and stir in the peanut butter chips.

Sprinkle the cake mix over the top and fold it in, stirring only until everything is combined. The object here is to keep as much air in the batter as possible.

Cover the bowl with plastic wrap, and stick it in the refrigerator for an hour.

Hannah's Note: Andrea said this dough is very sticky. It's much easier to work with if you chill it.

When your cookie dough has chilled for an hour, preheat your oven to 350 degrees F., rack in the middle position.

Take your dough out of the refrigerator, your spoons out of the freezer, and scoop the dough one teaspoon at a time into the bowl of powdered sugar. Roll the dough around with your fingers to form powdered sugar–coated cookie dough balls.

Place the powdered sugar-coated cookie dough balls on a greased cookie sheet, 12 balls to each cookie sheet. *(Andrea used parchment paper sprayed with nonstick cooking spray on top of a cookie sheet.)*

Bake the cookies at 350 degrees F., for 10 minutes.

Take the baked cookies out of the oven and place them on a cold stovetop burner or wire rack.

Let the cookies cool on the cookie sheet for no more than 2 minutes, and then move them to a wire rack to cool completely. *(This is easy if you line your cookie sheets with parchment paper—then all you have to do is grab the corner and pull it onto the wire rack.)*

Yield: 3 to 4 dozen yummy cookies, depending on cookie size.

Chapter Thirteen

"I have to talk to you, Hannah," Mike said, walking into the kitchen. "Where is Lily?"

"Sleeping. Sally found a room for her, and Doc gave her something to help her sleep. Come in, Mike. Would you like some coffee and a cookie?"

"I don't know, Hannah. I don't know what I need. A new head might help."

Mike sounded so depressed, Hannah went over to give him a comforting hug. "Are you upset because of the way you told Lily about Sonny?"

"Yes, but that's just part of it. There's more, Hannah. There's something really wrong."

For the first time in her life, Hannah wished she'd taken more psychology classes. She poured a cup of coffee for Mike, set a plate of cookies in front of him, and sat down. "Tell me about it," she invited.

"There's an important question I have to ask you first," Mike said, and Hannah noticed that he hadn't even reached for a cookie.

"What is it?"

"Did you mention to Lily that I didn't want anyone to know that her fiancé was dead?"

"Yes, I did. I asked her not to tell anyone, not even her father, until you said it was okay."

"Does Lily know that he was *murdered*?"

Hannah thought about that for a moment. "I think she probably guessed as much. She didn't come out and ask me, so I'm not sure, but she did agree not to mention anything to anyone about Sonny's death until you give her the okay."

"Good! Thank you, Hannah." Mike looked relieved as he reached for a cookie. "I was all set to question Lily tonight when you brought her over to our table. You know that, don't you?"

"Yes, that's why I brought her there. I didn't want her to talk to anyone else until she'd talked to you."

"That's what I thought. And I was all ready to question her, but then I looked at her and . . . I'm not really sure what happened, but I realized that I was going to blow it if I tried to take the lead in interviewing her."

Hannah felt a moment's vindication. Her instinct had been right, after all. "Why was that, Mike?"

"I . . . This will probably sound crazy, Hannah. I've taken the lead in every interview I've ever done with a partner, but this time was different. This time I just couldn't seem to get a handle on her."

"A handle on Lily?"

"Yes. I knew she was a suspect. Family members always are. And I knew I had to ask her the right questions."

Hannah gave a little nod. She wasn't sure what else to do. "And . . . ?" she prompted.

"I had to back off, Hannah. I thought I'd be too

tough on her and I knew that wasn't fair. So I sat back and let Lonnie take the lead."

"Did you tell Lonnie that you were going to do that?"

"No, I just hoped he'd pick up on it. We've worked together a long time, Hannah. I figured he'd know that something was wrong, and he'd ask the questions that I should have asked."

"And did he?"

"Yes. He took over and his questions were probing and insightful. He did exactly what I should have done . . . if I'd been able to do it."

Hannah winced as she realized that Mike had admitted that he hadn't been able to question Lily.

"Why *couldn't* you question Lily?" Hannah asked. "Do you know?"

"I'm not sure, but I think I do." Mike took a big drink of his coffee, but Hannah noticed that the friend she'd previously referred to as *The Cookie Monster* put his cookie back down on the plate.

"Tell me why," Hannah said, locking eyes with him. "Give me the reason why you couldn't question Lily."

"I've always been able to sympathize with the victim," Mike said with a sigh. "This time, I just couldn't do it, Hannah. As the chief investigator I am charged with the duty of finding who killed Sonny. And . . . this is very hard to say, Hannah. And this time, my heart's just not in it." Mike stopped speaking and took another sip of his coffee.

Hannah got up and refilled Mike's coffee cup. She needed a moment to mull over his startling admission. "Mike, you haven't even tasted a cookie yet! And it's Andrea's new recipe. They are chocolate and peanut butter."

Mike let out a huge sigh. "Good idea, Hannah. I am

feeling really down and maybe the chocolate will help. Right now all I want to do is give this case to Lonnie and walk away."

Hannah felt like groaning. She had absolutely no idea what to say to Mike. Only one question occurred to her, so she asked it.

"Are you sure that you want to bow out, Mike?"

Mike reached for his cookie again, held it for a moment, and put it back down. "No, I'm not sure of anything right now."

"Okay, then you need to take some time to think about this."

"Some time, yes, but not much. We only have two teams of detectives, Hannah. There's Lonnie and me and there's Rick and the new guy. Rick's been working with the new guy, but he's not quite up to speed yet."

"Do you think you might be able to work on this case if Lonnie takes over the lead like he did for you tonight?"

Mike thought about that for a long moment. "Maybe. I'm not completely sure, Hannah, but maybe."

"Then that's what you should do for now," Hannah said, trying to sound more positive than she felt. "I can tell that you're tired, Mike. Get some sleep and maybe you'll feel better in the morning."

"I thought you'd *never* get back here," Andrea said as Hannah came into their room. "Were you with Lily all this time?"

"No. I'm sorry if I worried you, Andrea, but I didn't have time to call you on your cell."

"It's okay. I wasn't worried. I was just . . ." Andrea stopped speaking and gave a little laugh. "I was just a little jealous that I was left out of the action."

Hannah laughed. "There wasn't *that* much action. It was just that when I got ready to leave the kitchen, somebody else came in."

"Who came in?"

"Mike. He was hungry and he needed something to eat, so I fed him. I started out with cookies and I had some soup left."

"So you baked cookies?" Andrea looked surprised. "I thought we were doing that tomorrow morn . . ." She stopped speaking as she glanced at the clock. "I mean, *this* morning."

Hannah shook her head. "We don't have to get up early this morning, Andrea. I needed to decompress, so I finished baking everything we mixed up. The cookies are all done and the only thing that's left for tomorrow is to make the caramel sauce for the Caramel Pecan Rolls and bake them."

"You baked my Chocolate Peanut Butter Whippersnappers?" Andrea asked, and Hannah realized that she sounded a bit territorial.

"Just the one batch and they're all gone. I gave Lily a dozen and I gave Mike some to take with him. I know it's extra work for you, but you can mix up a couple more batches in the morning, after all?"

"Of course I can! What did Lily and Mike think of them?"

"Lily went absolutely crazy over them! She told me that chocolate and peanut butter were her two favorite things and she scarfed down a whole bunch before Sally came to take her to her room."

"Sally was there?"

"Yes. I packed up another dozen for Lily, and Sally asked if she could take another dozen for Dick and for her. Before I knew it, they were all gone!"

Andrea's expression changed to one of pleasure. "So did they like them too?"

"I don't know about Dick, but Lily loved them and so did Mike and Sally. They're a huge hit, Andrea."

"Oh, good! So they passed the taste test?"

"They passed three taste tests . . . actually four if you count the five or six that I ate while I was baking the rest of the cookies and cakes."

"So what time do we have to go down to work tomorrow?" Andrea asked, glancing at the clock again.

"The breakfast buffet is at eight, so six should be just fine. Almost everything's done, Andrea."

"And you did it all yourself." Andrea looked slightly disappointed. "You should have called me, Hannah. I've been up here for over an hour and I could have come down to help you."

"I figured you might need a little more rest than usual," Hannah said, choosing the first excuse she could think of. "After all, you delivered cocktails to the tables all night at the bar, plus you kept your eyes and ears open for any clues you might pick up. That's hard work, Andrea."

"It wasn't that difficult," Andrea said, waving off Hannah's compliment. "I had a good time talking to people and listening to what they were saying."

"Did you pick up anything interesting?" Hannah asked, pulling her pajamas out from under her pillow.

"Yes, but I'll wait to tell you until you get ready for bed. How about you? You said that Mike came into the kitchen. Did he tell you anything interesting?"

Hannah knew she was treading on thin ice. She didn't want to lie to her sister, but what Mike had told her about his personal problems was confidential. "I didn't learn anything worth relating," she said, fudging as best she could. "I think he just needed to talk to someone, and I was handy."

"Personal stuff?" Andrea asked, looking interested.

"Yes, but nothing that's relevant to catching the killer."

"So Mike just needed to talk?"

"I think so, at least until he tasted your newest Whippersnapper cookie. Then he just needed more cookies."

Andrea laughed and went over to the dresser to pour herself a glass of water from the tray that Rosa had put there. "Go ahead and get ready for bed," Andrea said, waving Hannah off toward the bathroom. "I'm going to put this on my side of the bed table and then I can tell you what I learned tonight."

Hannah took a quick shower so she wouldn't have to shower early in the morning. She knew she'd be tired and she wasn't sure she could sleep. The personal crisis that Mike was having and the things that he'd told her were buzzing around in her mind. In a way, she hoped that Andrea didn't want to talk any longer. She was very tired and she wasn't sure she could talk about Mike, or Lily, or Sonny's murder for much longer tonight.

It seemed to take forever to dry off from her shower and get into her night clothes. Hannah's feet were dragging as she walked to the bathroom door and opened it. The bedside lamp was on, and she glanced over at Andrea's bed. Luck was with her tonight. Andrea was curled up in a ball, fast asleep.

Chapter Fourteen

When Hannah opened her eyes in the morning, their breakfast tray was sitting on the dresser and Andrea was not in her bed. Hannah sat up, blinked a couple of times, and took a look around the room. It was a nice double room, but there weren't any alcoves or places to hide. Then she heard the shower running and she gave a little smile. Andrea was in the bathroom, getting ready for the day ahead.

Even though she felt like turning over and going back to sleep, Hannah made herself sit up on the side of the bed. The urge for morning coffee was stronger than the lure of the blankets, and soft pillows couldn't compete with the inviting scent of breakfast coffee. She got to her feet, slipped into her robe, and padded across the room to the breakfast tray on the dresser. She had just taken her first sip of the aromatic brew when Andrea emerged from the bathroom.

"Oh, good, you're up," Andrea said, coming over to pour a cup for herself. "I figured that if I took the lid off the pot, you'd have to wake up and have some."

"You figured right," Hannah said, smiling at her sister. "The scent of hot coffee is what woke me up. I didn't realize it at the time, but I sat up, saw the tray, and knew I had to get up and get a cup."

"I thought if I tried to wake you up, you'd get mad at me the way you used to do when we were kids. I didn't want that, so I decided to try another way."

"Well, it worked. And I'm not at all mad at you," Hannah declared, taking another sip of her coffee. "Room service is a wonderful thing, isn't it, Andrea?"

"I'll say!" Andrea agreed, biting into one of the doughnuts that Rosa had brought them for their breakfast treat.

"I'll be awake in a couple of minutes and we can go to work," Hannah said, draining her coffee cup and getting up to pour herself more. "I'm almost awake and I showered last night, so all I have to do is climb into some clothes and put on my shoes."

"Take your time," Andrea told her. "I'm going to run down to the kitchen in a minute to mix up more Chocolate Peanut Butter Whippersnapper Cookies. I'm really glad that Lily, and Mike, and Sally liked them last night."

"Don't forget me." Hannah added herself to the list. "I liked them, too. They're going to be a huge hit with the fishermen, Andrea."

"Good!" Andrea looked very pleased. "Is Lily going to come down to the breakfast buffet?"

"I'm not sure. Mike called Wally last night and he was supposed to drive in this afternoon. I'm not sure if he'll get here in time for happy hour. I heard Mike tell him that Sonny was dead."

"Did Mike say that Sonny was murdered?" Andrea asked.

"Mike said he's keeping that fact under wraps for

now and if we're lucky, Sonny's killer will say something incriminating."

"Very smart. I hope it works, Hannah. It kind of creeps me out to know that we're serving the buffets to a killer."

When Andrea left for the kitchen, Hannah stayed in the room for a while. She washed her face, brushed her teeth, did what she could to tame her unruly red curls, and dressed in the clothes she'd chosen for the day. Then she sat at the desk, had another cup of Sally's excellent coffee, and, a bit reluctantly, left the room to walk to the kitchen.

"I'm here," she announced, pushing open the door. "It smells absolutely wonderful in here!"

"That's Andrea's cookies," Sally told her. "I can't believe you worked for hours last night, finishing the baking, Hannah."

"I needed to calm down and baking always helps," Hannah told her, walking over to look at the recipe that was on the surface of the stainless steel work station.

"Apricot, Coconut, and Milk Chocolate Bar Cookies?" Hannah asked, looking down at the recipe. "Is this recipe yours, Sally?"

"No, it's Andrea's," Sally replied, smiling at Andrea. "She brought it in this morning and asked me what I thought of it. I told her we'd try them for the lunch buffet."

Hannah turned to look at Andrea, who was blushing slightly. "I hope you don't mind, Hannah, but I adapted your recipe for Multiple Choice Bar Cookies and came up with this one. I haven't tried it yet, so I don't know if it works, but Sally says she wants to try it."

Hannah just stared at her sister for a moment and then she began to smile. "I think that's fantastic!" she said.

"But . . ." Andrea looked slightly guilty. "It's your recipe and I messed with it."

"So what? There are only a finite number of recipes, Andrea. New recipes come from taking what you learned from the recipes that work and adapting them to make new recipes."

"But . . . isn't that almost like cheating?"

"Not really," Hannah said with a smile. "Baking involves chemistry, Andrea."

"But I flunked chemistry!" Andrea said, sitting down at the table. "I don't know anything about chemistry. I couldn't even memorize the whole periodic table of the elements!"

"Don't feel alone," Sally said. "How about you, Hannah?"

"I made it, but not by much. I memorized some of it, but only enough to get by. And only the elements I thought I needed for the final test. The point I'm trying to make is that there are these basic recipes that you almost have to follow if you want a certain outcome. There's one for soft cookies, one for crisp cookies, one for pies, and right on down the list. It's really a matter of knowing how many dry ingredients to use, how many wet ingredients to use, and what kind of leavening you need if you need any at all."

"I know about leavening," Andrea said quickly. "That's what makes something rise."

Sally nodded. "You're right, Andrea."

"Yes, but that's all I know."

"That's okay," Hannah agreed. "The type of leavening depends on which outcome you want. If you want something light and airy, you have to have a certain blend of ingredients. And if you want something moist and heavy, you need an entirely different blend of ingredients."

Andrea looked confused. "But how do you know which ones to use?"

"I'm out of my depth," Sally said, getting up from her chair. "You two sisters carry on. I'm the cook, not the baker. I'm going to go check on my other kitchen staff to make sure the prep work is getting done."

"See you later," Hannah said, picking up her coffee cup and taking another sip. "You won't know what kind of leavening to use without studying it, Andrea. It's complicated, unless you're like our Great-Grandma Elsa. I think she probably learned to bake before she even learned to walk, and when she read the ingredients in a recipe, she just figured it out."

Andrea smiled. "I was younger, but I remember her, Hannah. She used to make wonderful cookies!"

"And pies, and cakes, and everything in-between. I have all her recipes, and sometimes I'll look for one I remember and adapt that one to the ingredients that I want to use. It sounds to me like that's what you did with the Apricot, Coconut, and Milk Chocolate Bar Cookie recipe, Andrea."

"You mean because I adapted it from one of your recipes?"

"Exactly. And I don't really remember, but I may have adapted my recipe from one that Great-Grandma Elsa used."

"That's . . . I'm not sure of the word, but it's almost like we're keeping Great-Grandma's memory alive."

"That's a lovely thought, Andrea, and I wouldn't be a bit surprised if you were right. She's probably looking down at both of us right now and saying something like . . ."

"I liked my recipe better," Andrea interrupted Hannah's thought. "She used to get mad when somebody took one of her recipes and changed it around."

"I remember, but she also was good about sharing her recipes." Hannah reached down for her shoes and began to put them on. "Did you learn anything important from the contestants in the bar last night?"

"You bet I did!" Andrea declared, and she looked very excited. "I learned that Joe Dietz and his son-in-law, Mark, are here for the fishing tournament."

"Really! I thought Joe's daughter and her husband were stationed in Germany."

"They are, but Mark had to come back to the States for two weeks of training."

"And Darla and the kids aren't here?"

Andrea shook her head. "Darla didn't want to pull the kids out of school, so they stayed on the base. Mark's only here for one more week, but he heard about the fishing competition and talked Joe into signing up as a contestant."

"That makes sense. Joe loves to fish."

"I know. Since he retired, he goes fishing practically every day in the summer. Mark signed as Joe's second and they're using Joe's boat."

"I feel a little sorry for Darla. I bet she would have liked to come to see her parents."

"That's what Joe told me, but she wanted the kids to finish the year at the base school, and Joe and his wife are going to Germany to visit them for Octoberfest, the way they do every year."

"So Joe's son-in-law fishes?" Hannah asked, wondering why Andrea had told her all this.

"Yes, and Mark, he's the son-in-law, knew Sonny when they were in college."

"Really?" Hannah asked, and then she was silent. She'd let Andrea tell her why this was important.

"That's why I mentioned it. Joe said that Mark and

Darla met while they were in college, but she was dating Sonny at the time."

Hannah felt a bit like shouting *Aha!* But she didn't. Andrea would get to the crux of the story in her own time.

"Joe told me that Darla was engaged to Sonny at the time, and Mark was dating Darla's college roommate. They used to double-date and Mark noticed that Sonny flirted with every pretty girl who crossed his path."

"Did Darla realize that Sonny was flirting with other girls?" Hannah asked.

"Yes, and she didn't like it at all, especially since they'd moved in together in a one-bedroom apartment just off-campus. She complained to Sonny about it and he told her that he was just being friendly."

"And she believed him?"

"Yes, until she came home early one afternoon and found him in bed with another girl."

"Poor Darla!" Hannah commiserated, remembering her first brush with an unfaithful boyfriend. "What did she do?"

"Darla kicked him to the curb, and joined the Air Force."

"Without finishing school?"

"That's right. The Air Force sent her to another college to finish her degree and then they assigned her to a base in Germany."

"But how did Mark get back in the picture?" Hannah asked.

"Pure luck. It turns out that Mark joined the Air Force too. And he got stationed to the same base in Germany." Andrea gave a little smile. "Joe said it was meant to be."

"I guess it was!"

"Darla and Mark met again there, fell in love, and ended up marrying on their first leave back here."

"And you think that Mark may still carry a grudge against Sonny for the grief he caused Darla?" Hannah asked the important question.

"I asked Joe that. He says he doesn't think so, but I'm not that sure."

"I'm not that sure, either. It's certainly a possibility."

The two sisters were silent for a moment and then Andrea asked, "Do you think we should check it out?"

"Oh, yes!" Hannah said, no doubt in her mind. "We should definitely check it out just as soon as we can."

Andrea looked slightly doubtful. "Then it's not too far-fetched?"

"It's far-fetched but that doesn't mean it can't be a motive for murder," Hannah said. "Anything that's possible is suspect. Thanks for telling me about it, Andrea. It's a lead I didn't have before."

Andrea began to smile. "Thank you, Hannah. But . . . do you really think it's possible that Joe or Mark is Sonny's killer?"

"Of course it's possible. Anything is possible at this point. Do you know anything about Mark's military career?"

"He's a pilot. That's all I know. I do know something about Joe's career, though. Bill asked Joe about that once, and Joe showed him the medals he'd won when he was a sharpshooter. Bill tried to recruit Joe for the sheriff's department, but Joe didn't think there was enough call for his bomb technician and sharpshooter skills. He told Bill that if push ever came to shove, he'd be happy to help with any emergency, but he had his military retirement and he just wanted to relax and enjoy his wife and family for the rest of his life."

"I can understand that," Hannah said, getting up from the table. "Okay, Andrea. We'll check all this out later. In the meantime, let's try out your Apricot, Coconut, and Milk Chocolate Bar Cookie recipe and see how we like it."

"Are you sure?" Andrea asked, looking excited about the prospect but a bit nervous, too.

"I'm sure. We'll mix up the whole recipe, but we'll make a test pan to see if it works."

"What if it doesn't?" Andrea asked her.

"Then we'll see if we can figure out why. And if we can't, we'll toss it out and try something else. Do you have a copy of it that I can read through quickly?"

"Yes." Andrea rushed to the notebook she'd brought with her, turned to one of the pages, and handed it to Hannah. "It's right here," she said.

Hannah glanced down at the recipe, checking it against the recipe that she remembered. The amounts of dry and wet ingredients were the same and everything looked fine to her.

"What do you think?"

"There's only one thing," Hannah told her. "Your recipe calls for chopped dried apricots. How were you planning to chop them?"

"Um . . . in a food processor?" Andrea said, but it was more of a question than an answer.

"That'll work just fine, but you'll have to put something else in the food processor to keep the apricots from sticking together and forming a ball when you chop them."

"Oh!" Andrea looked surprised and then she nodded. "You're right. I tried to chop up marshmallows in a food processor once and I got . . . well . . . it was really a mess!"

"Let's figure this out together, Andrea. What did

you use for the crust on this recipe?" Hannah handed the notebook back to Andrea.

"I used crushed Lorna Doone cookies. But . . . they don't ball up when you crush them in a food processor, do they?"

"No. They're a dry ingredient. Think about it, Andrea. What dry ingredient could you add to the apricots so they'd chop up and not form a sticky ball?"

"Flour? That's a dry ingredient."

"Yes, it is. But there's no flour in your recipe."

Andrea looked down at the notebook again. "What about . . . the Lorna Doone cookies? When I crush them up for the recipe, could I just crush up some extra cookies and put them in with the dried apricots when I'm ready to chop them?"

"Bravo!" Hannah said, clapping her hands. "That's perfect, Andrea. When you chop up the cookies, just make sure you have some extra left over and use the extra underneath and on top of the apricots when you are ready to chop them. It won't add a new ingredient or change the taste of the recipe. But it will keep the apricots from sticking together."

Andrea looked very proud of herself. "How about the coconut? It'll be okay when I chop it, won't it?"

"Yes, as long as you don't chop it too fine. Is there anything else you're worried about?"

Andrea glanced down at the recipe again. "I don't think so."

"Let's make your recipe and see if it works," Hannah suggested. "It should, but you never know, for sure, until you test it."

"Right." Andrea gave a little nod. "Shall I get the ingredients?"

"No."

"No?" Andrea looked completely puzzled. "Why not?"

"Because it's your recipe. This time I'll get the ingredients and you can be in charge of mixing everything up and putting it into the pans."

"But . . . are you sure that—"

"I'm sure," Hannah said quickly, interrupting her younger sister. "It's going to work just fine, Andrea, and you can do this one on your own. There's only one thing you have to promise to do for me."

"What's that?"

"I get to taste the first one," Hannah said, walking over to give Andrea a big hug.

APRICOT, COCONUT, AND MILK CHOCOLATE BAR COOKIES

Preheat oven to 350 degrees F., rack in the middle position.

Ingredients:

½ cup salted butter, melted *(1 stick, 4 ounces, ¼ pound)*

1 and ¾ cups Lorna Doone cookie crumbs *(measure AFTER crushing) (buy 2 packages—you'll have some left over, but the kids will love them as an after-school snack)*

1 can *(14 ounces)* sweetened, condensed milk *(NOT evaporated milk)*

½ cup dried apricot pieces *(measure AFTER chopping)*

2 cups milk chocolate chips *(I used Nestlé—an 11-ounce or a 12-ounce package will do fine.)*

1 cup shredded coconut flakes *(pack it down when you measure it)*

Directions:

Prepare your pan. Use a 9-inch by 13-inch cake pan to make these yummy bar cookies.

Melt ½ cup of salted butter *(1 stick, 4 ounces)* in the microwave or on the stovetop. Pour the melted butter into the bottom of the cake pan. Tip the pan so that the melted butter covers the bottom of the pan and approximately an inch up the sides of the pan.

Crush 1 package of the Lorna Doone cookies in a food processor with the steel blade attached. Measure the cookie crumbs and if you have one and three-quarters cups of cookie crumbs, you have enough for this recipe.

Take out one-quarter cup of cookie crumbs and set them aside in a small bowl on the counter.

Scatter the one and one-half cups of cookie crumbs that remain, over the bottom of the cake pan as evenly as you can.

Open the can of sweetened, condensed milk and pour it, as evenly as you can, over the cookie crumbs in the bottom of the pan.

Remember that quarter-cup of cookie crumbs you saved? Take one Tablespoon of the cookie crumbs and sprinkle them over the bottom of the bowl of the food processor.

Place approximately 15 dried apricot halves on top of the cookie crumbs in the bottom of the food processor.

Sprinkle another Tablespoon of the cookie crumbs over the top of the apricots.

Chop the dried apricots with the steel blade, using an on-and-off motion until the pieces of apricot are in small pieces.

Take the chopped apricots out of the food processor and measure them. If you have ½ cup of chopped apricot pieces, you have enough.

If you don't have enough chopped, dried apricots, sprinkle another Tablespoon of cookie crumbs over the bottom of your now empty food processor bowl.

Place more apricot halves over the crumbs in the food processor. *(If your first batch of apricot halves made approximately a half-cup of pieces, then that is perfect. If you have too many, that's okay. These bar cookies will work anyway.)*

Sprinkle the remaining cookie crumbs over the dried apricot halves.

Chop the second batch of dried apricots (*only if needed*) with the steel blade in an on-and-off motion until the apricots are in small pieces.

Measure out enough chopped apricot pieces to equal approximately ½ cup in all. Scatter them over top of the sweetened, condensed milk in your pan.

Measure out 2 cups of milk chocolate chips. Scatter the chips over the chopped apricots as evenly as you can.

Measure out 1 cup of shredded coconut flakes. Don't forget to press them down in the measuring cup.

Scatter the coconut over the top of the milk chocolate chips in your baking pan.

Use a wide, flat metal spatula to press everything down in the cake pan. If you don't have a wide, flat metal spatula, moisten your incredibly clean palms and use your hands to press everything down.

Bake your Apricot, Coconut, and Milk Chocolate Bar Cookies at 350 degrees F. for 30 (*thirty*) minutes.

Take your bar cookies out of the oven and place them on a cold stovetop burner or a wire rack to cool.

Wait until your bar cookies are cool before cutting them into brownie-sized pieces.

Yield: 20 to 30 deliciously sinful bar cookies, depending on the size you cut the bars.

Serve these bar cookies with strong black coffee, or icy cold glasses of milk.

# Chapter
Fifteen

Of course Andrea's bar cookies worked just fine, as Hannah knew they would. They'd finished the day's baking and were sitting down with a cup of coffee after cleaning the kitchen when Sally came in.

"Oh, good," Sally said. "You're taking a coffee break. Can we join you? There's someone I want both of you to meet."

"Of course," Hannah said quickly, and Andrea gave a nod of agreement. "We just put on a fresh pot of coffee and you can taste Andrea's new bar cookie."

Sally beckoned to the woman who'd followed her in. "Come in, Janette. I want you to meet my friends, Hannah Swensen and Andrea Todd. They've been kind enough to fill in for my pastry chef this week."

"How nice of you both," the woman said, taking the chair that Sally pulled out for her. "Sally explained what a pickle she was in, and how you two stepped right in to help her."

"This is Lily's mother, Janette," Sally introduced her. "Mike told Lily that he was going to make an announcement about Sonny this morning, and said it was okay to invite her mother."

Janette, a well-groomed older woman, nodded. "I drove here the moment I got Lily's call this morning. What a horrid thing to happen to my poor daughter!"

"Did your husband mention that he asked Lily to come here and take control of the situation with Sonny?" Hannah asked.

"No. I haven't spoken to Wally about it." Janette sighed and glanced at Sally. "You didn't tell them?"

"No. I didn't think it was my place to mention it," Sally replied. "Go ahead, Janette."

"Wally and I are separated," Janette said, frowning slightly. "We've been married for years and we didn't want to divorce, but we just don't do well spending all our time together. We still love each other and we're together on the weekends, but we lead separate lives during the week."

"And that works?" Andrea asked, and Hannah noticed that she looked utterly amazed.

"Yes, it's worked for the past several years. You see, I had a terrible addiction problem. I was depressed, and lonely, and used pills to fill the void in my life."

"The void?" Hannah asked, hoping that Janette would go on.

"That's right. It was just that Wally was so busy with the business, he didn't have much time left over for me. Part of that was my fault. I wanted him to be successful for me, and for Lily. My father was a very successful man and, as I remember, he worked all the time. And that meant he didn't see much of Mother and me. It seemed to work for our family, and I thought it would work for Wally and me, too."

"Hold on a minute, Janette," Hannah said, getting up to cut a pan of Andrea's bar cookies. "What you're telling us is fascinating, but I think you need some nourishment with your coffee."

Sally laughed. "I warned you, Janette. Hannah will feed you if you even look like you're hungry. She's always the first to offer coffee and cookies."

"These are Andrea's new cookie," Hannah said, walking over to the table with a plate of bar cookies she'd just cut. "Try one, Janette. They came out of the oven just before you got here, but they're cool enough to eat now."

Janette reached out to get a cookie and took a bite. "Oh my!" she said, beginning to smile. "These are incredible!"

"They certainly are!" Sally said, swallowing her first bite and giving Andrea the high sign. "You did it, Andrea! Your new bar cookies will be a huge success with the fishermen!"

Hannah waited until Sally and Janette had eaten two of Andrea's bar cookies each and then she poured more coffee for them all. "Tell us more about your marriage, Janette."

Janette drew a deep breath. "All right. Shortly after Wally and I were married, my father died and left me the boat works. Wally had always been fascinated by boats, and I convinced him to take charge of the business. A few years later on, we decided to open a chain of sporting goods stores to showcase our new boats. After that, I learned that I was pregnant with Lily. I didn't realize that the business would take Wally away from home so much." Janette paused to take a sip of her coffee. "Unfortunately there were always business-related things to take Wally away from home. I was lonely and our marriage suffered because of it."

"It's that way with a lot of upwardly mobile couples, Janette," Sally told her.

"I know. I told myself that it would be the same way if Wally had been a long-distance truck driver. Then he would have been gone for a week or two at a time. But . . . I just couldn't take it and I started to rely on pills to help me cope with being pregnant and alone."

Hannah and Andrea exchanged glances. Neither one of them knew quite what to say to this startling admission.

"Luckily, Janette had Rosa," Sally said, reaching over to pat Janette's shoulder. "Rosa was the glue that held Janette and Wally's family together."

"And Rosa was Lily's second mom," Janette added. "After I had Lily, I realized that I was still taking too many pills and I needed professional help. I got it. I spent months in rehabilitation and finally I was successful. But during that time, Lily was without a mother at home and with a father who was only there on the weekends. All I can say is, thank God for Rosa! She helped all three of us have something closer to a normal life."

"Rosa was your live-in nanny?" Andrea asked, giving Janette a sympathetic look.

"Yes. Rosa was perfect. She was my surrogate when it came to Lily's elementary school, and she went there at least once a week to deliver cookies the way the other room mothers did. And Lily loved Rosa. She still does."

"But you beat your addiction," Sally said. "Everything worked out for the best, Janette."

"Yes, it did. Lily was happy having Rosa as her second mom, and . . ." Janette gave a little laugh. "Rosa even attended P.T.A. meetings and teachers conferences for me. You have no idea how indebted I am to Rosa."

"How long did Rosa work for you?" Hannah asked.

"Until Lily was a junior in high school. Then Rosa moved to Lake Eden, and she went to work for Sally once Sally and Dick opened this place."

"And we're very grateful for her!" Sally said quickly.

"Anyway . . . once I'd successfully beaten my addiction, I went to work for our business. I'm a certified public accountant and I spend most of my work days going over the books. That means I travel, and I was at the St. Cloud store when Lily and Wally were opening the new Brainerd store."

"How about your husband?" Andrea asked. "Did he tell you that he was sending Lily here to the Inn?"

Janette shook her head. "No, Wally never called me. He knew I never approved of her engagement to Sonny, but Lily has a mind of her own. She'd decided that she wanted to marry him, and that was that. I never felt that Sonny was right for her, but there's not much you can do when your daughter is head over heels in love with the wrong person."

"Did you know that Sonny had a drinking problem?" Hannah asked her.

"No. If I had, I might have worked much harder to talk Lily out of the engagement. Sonny never drank in front of me, and I really had no idea that it was this bad."

"I'm surprised that Lily didn't call you to tell you what was happening," Hannah said. "If I was engaged and had trouble with the man I wanted to marry, I know I'd call my mother for advice."

"I wish Lily *had* called me!" Janette sighed deeply. "I suspect that Lily probably didn't want to raise that subject with me. There's another factor, too. Lily didn't confide that much in me. She was always her daddy's girl."

"But she loves you, doesn't she?" Andrea asked.

"I know she does. We're just not all that close. She knew that I didn't approve of Sonny, and I may have made a big error by not pretending to like him. It's just that I was convinced he was wrong for her. Lily wasn't that . . ." Janette stopped, obviously searching for the best word to use. "She wasn't that *worldly*. Lily trusted everyone and, unfortunately, that included Sonny."

"Did you ever talk to Lily about her fiancé?" Andrea asked.

"No. I did my best to be nice to him, but I'm sure Lily knew I didn't like him. It did make holidays and parties difficult. I did my best, but Lily must have realized my basic dislike for him. The worst time was when they went on vacation with us. Wally and I have a cabin up in the North Woods that borders a beautiful lake. Of course we took two of our boats with us. We always do. Lily and Sonny had one, and Wally and I had the other. Sonny knew absolutely nothing about boating, and it was clear that he wasn't interested in learning. He just sat there and let Lily do everything without lifting a finger to help her."

"He must have learned a lot very quickly to be on the fishing show," Sally said.

"Not at all! That's why Joey's on the show. He does all the actual work while Sonny provides the handsome face that attracts female viewers. Lily was right about that. She told her father that Sonny would provide a female audience, and he did. But my daughter's fiancé was a womanizer. I checked up on him, and he'd been engaged four times before he proposed to Lily!"

"Did you ever tell Lily about this?" Andrea asked.

"No. What good would it have done? Lily was crazy about Sonny. She wouldn't have believed me."

"So Sonny had Lily completely fooled about his personality?" Hannah asked.

"That's a nice way to put it," Janette said, giving a humorless smile. "Lily was completely under Sonny's spell, and I know that she wouldn't have believed anything bad about him. My hands were tied when it came to talking to her about Sonny. I had to be very careful that I didn't say anything bad about him and alienate her. It's true that I didn't want her to marry him, but I couldn't come right out and tell her that. I simply kept hoping and hoping that she'd see his faults for herself."

Hannah gave a little sigh. "And that never happened?"

"No, at least, not that I know about. Lily was always so bright and creative. She saw through people almost immediately. But there was something about Sonny that blindsided her."

"It sounds as if you were walking a tightrope between trying to guide your daughter and fearing you'd alienate her," Andrea said.

"That's right! And that's exactly the way I felt." Janette looked grateful that someone seemed to understand. "I probably shouldn't say this, and I know that Lily would be horrified to hear it, but . . . I'm not sorry that Sonny is dead!"

Chapter
Sixteen

Sally glanced at the clock on the kitchen wall, and turned to Janette. "We have to go, Janette. I promised to take you in to see Mike."

"I know he's going to want to ask me all sorts of questions."

"Take some bar cookies with you, Janette," Andrea invited, getting up to prepare and package some of her cookies for Lily's mother.

"You'd better prepare a box for Mike, too," Hannah warned her sister. "That way, Mike won't eat all of Janette's cookies."

"You're right," Andrea said, hurrying to prepare another box of cookies. "If I were you, Janette, I wouldn't let Mike see that you have two packages. He might eat them all!"

"I'll take yours up to your room," Sally said. "That way, Mike won't be tempted!"

Hannah waited until Sally and Janette had left and then she turned to Andrea. "Well?"

"Well, what?"

"Well, what did you think of what Janette told us."

"I thought it was . . . sad. I think she really loves Lily and she wants the best for her. And she told us, straight out, that she didn't think that Sonny was the best for her daughter."

"That's all true." Hannah was silent. She wanted Andrea to think about what they'd heard.

"She came right out and told us that she didn't think the fact that Sonny was gone was a bad thing for Lily." Andrea stopped and began to frown. "You don't think that . . ."

"Everyone's a suspect until they have an alibi," Hannah told her.

"But Janette said she was at the St. Cloud store, going over their books."

"I know. Are you going to take her at her word?"

"Well . . . maybe not. Do you think we should check with someone at the store?"

"I think we should," Hannah replied. "You're better at that than I am. You make the call to them."

"Really?" Andrea looked surprised and then a big smile spread over her face. "You'd trust me to do that?"

"Absolutely. Just let me know what happens. In the meantime, let's mix up another batch of your Apricot, Coconut, and Milk Chocolate Bar Cookies for the lunch buffet."

"Okay, but I already baked two batches."

"I know you did. They're wonderful, Andrea! And I think they're going to be a huge hit. Your two batches will be gone in a flash, and they're going to want more."

"Really?" Andrea looked very pleased. "I hope you're right, Hannah. Otherwise we're going to have another couple of batches left over."

"Not necessarily," Hannah told her with a laugh. "You're forgetting about Mike. The minute he tastes them, he's going to want even more for himself."

Once Andrea and Hannah had baked another batch of Apricot, Coconut, and Milk Chocolate Bar Cookies, they cleaned up the kitchen and left. Sally had gone to see Mike and Lonnie with Janette, and there was nothing else to do until they served the lunch buffet for the fishermen after the noon weigh-in.

"You can leave early if you want to, Andrea," Hannah told her sister. "I can handle the lunch buffet."

Andrea shook her head. "Grandma McCann is taking Tracey and Bethie out to her farm right after she picks up Bethie from preschool. They're going to plant a little flower garden."

Hannah began to smile. "That's really nice. I know how much Tracey loves flowers."

"Yes, and I'm hopeless when it comes to planting anything," Andrea admitted. "I can't even grow nasturtiums and they're the easiest flower in the world to grow." Andrea led the way to the elevator and held the door for Hannah. "Do you want to take a nap?"

Hannah considered that for a moment, and then she shook her head. "No. I probably should be tired, but I'd rather do something else before the fishermen come in."

"What do you want to do?"

"I'd like to . . . go out on the lake. The weather's nice and it's relaxing to be on the water. It's too bad we don't have a boat."

"I bet we can borrow a boat. Let's ask Dick if there's an extra boat we can use. I know how to handle an outboard motor."

"So do I, and I'm okay in a rowboat, too. We could

even take one of the Inn's canoes if you promise that you won't stand up and wave at someone."

Andrea rolled her eyes at the ceiling as they got into the elevator. "I'm never going to live that down, am I?"

Hannah laughed. "No, you're not. You dumped both of us in the lake when you saw Bill's boat ahead of us."

"I didn't mean to. And we managed to right the canoe and bail out all the water," Andrea pointed out.

"And we also managed to get absolutely soaked."

"True," Andrea conceded. "Maybe a rowboat is a better idea, but let's ask Dick anyway. He's probably cleaning and restocking the bar."

"Okay. Let's pick up our jackets and go back down," Hannah suggested, getting off the elevator when it stopped at the second floor and leading the way to their room.

It didn't take long to get into warmer clothing and grab their jackets. In less than five minutes both sisters were ready for an outing on Eden Lake. They rode the elevator back down to the ground floor, walked down the long hallway, and went straight to Dick's bar.

"He's here," Andrea said, stating the obvious.

"Hello, ladies!" Dick called out, as they entered the bar. "You know that I'm closed . . . right?"

"We know," Hannah said, walking up to the bar and taking a seat on a barstool. "We just came by to ask you if you had a boat that we could borrow. Andrea and I would like to go out on the lake for a while before the lunch buffet."

"You can use mine," Dick told them. "Do you know how to operate an inboard motor?"

"I do," Hannah spoke up.

"So do I," Andrea added. "I went with Bill when he took his new boat out on the lake, and he let me drive."

"Nice man!" Dick said, sounding as if he meant it. "I'm not sure I'd let Sally take my boat out."

"We can take a rowboat," Hannah offered. "You don't have to give us your best boat, Dick."

"I'm not *giving* it to you. I'm just letting you use it."

Hannah laughed. "You got me, Dick! I'm usually more careful about my word choice."

Dick laughed. "Chalk one up for me. I'll walk you down to the boat and see you off."

In what seemed like no time at all, Hannah and Andrea were out on the lake, the dock fading into the background behind them.

"I'm glad you're driving," Andrea said, settling back in the comfortable captain's chair beside her sister.

"Actually . . . so am I," Hannah replied, looking over at her with a grin. "I feel much drier when I'm behind the wheel!"

"Look over there, Hannah!" Andrea sounded excited as she pointed toward the small island. "Isn't that Joe?"

Hannah squinted slightly in the bright sun. "Yes, it looks like Joe. And that must be his son-in-law with him."

"Mark," Andrea reminded her. "Shall we go over and interview them now?"

"Yes, as long as they're not fishing. And it looks like they're just sitting there talking and eating the Caramel Pecan Rolls they took with them from the breakfast buffet."

"Do you want to question them now?" Andrea asked.

"Only if the opportunity presents itself. Let's just go talk to them and see what happens."

"But they don't know about Sonny's murder yet, do they?"

"No, and that's one of the reasons I want to talk to them now. We can't tell anybody until they make the announcement about Sonny."

"Okay, Hannah. Let's see what happens when we talk to them. You know Joe Dietz, don't you?"

"Yes." Hannah hid a little smile. Evidently, Andrea didn't know that their mother had dated Joe. "I'll take the lead. You jump in whenever you feel the time is right."

Hannah drove the boat up to the small island where Joe and Mark were sitting. They'd found a place in the shade of the one tree that had grown on the island, and Hannah pulled right up next to them. "Hi, guys," she said by way of greeting.

"Hello, Hannah!" Joe said, and he looked happy to see her. "We were just sitting here wishing that we'd taken more of your Caramel Pecan Rolls."

"Well, you're in luck," Hannah told him, handing over the bag of rolls that she'd brought with her. "I just happen to come supplied with exactly what you want."

"Hannah's a mind reader," Joe said as Hannah handed him the bag. "Have you met my son-in-law Mark before?"

"No, but Andrea told me that you were here for the fishing contest, Mark." Hannah gave him a friendly smile. "It's good to meet you."

Joe turned to Mark. "This is Hannah Swensen and her sister Andrea. They bake all the rolls and cookies for the buffets."

"They're great, ladies," Mark complimented them. "I saw you behind the buffet tables, but I haven't met you formally."

"Hannah, I didn't realize you had your own boat," Joe said.

"I don't," Hannah told him. "We borrowed Dick's boat so that we could go out on the lake."

"To find me?" Joe asked, looking a bit puzzled.

"No, just to enjoy the morning until we have to go back for the lunch buffet." Hannah paused and drew a deep breath. "I did want to talk to you in private about Sonny, though."

Joe gave a little nod. "Because of what I told Andrea last night?"

"That's part of it." Hannah turned to Mark. "Joe told Andrea that Sonny was once engaged to your wife."

"That's right. It was a college romance and it didn't last long. From what Darla tells me, Sonny was a real playboy back then."

Hannah smiled. "That's right. And if you'd been in the bar two nights ago, you would have seen him in action."

"I heard about that," Mark said. "Joe said he was trying to pick up on all the women there."

"And that includes Hannah and Andrea's mother!" Joe told him, a wide grin spreading over his face. "But Delores came through big-time. She stepped on Sonny's foot and Mike, Lonnie, and Doc were able to get him on a stretcher and take him up to his room."

"I could kick myself for missing the whole thing!" Mark said, shaking his head. "I was on the phone with Darla. I would have loved to tell her about that, but maybe it's a good thing I didn't."

"Why?" Andrea asked him.

"Because she's still a little upset over the way he broke their engagement," Mark explained. "I think Darla would like to believe that Sonny regrets it now."

Mark shook his head. "Of course Sonny doesn't regret it. I found that out the first day of the fishing contest."

Hannah leaned forward. This was getting interesting. "How did you do that?" she asked Mark.

"I got a chance to talk to Sonny alone and I asked him if he happened to remember my wife, Darla. I said she told me that they had gone to college together and she asked me to say hello from her."

"Did Sonny remember your wife?" Hannah asked.

Mark shook his head. "No. I even showed him a photo of her when she was in college, but he said he'd met so many people back then, he just couldn't remember having met her."

"And they were *engaged*?" Andrea sounded shocked.

"That's right. It's one of the reasons she left college and went into the Air Force. She told me that she was going to wait until she graduated to join the military, but she just didn't want to be on the same campus with him."

"I can understand that!" Hannah said, thinking back to her own failed engagement in college.

"So can I," Andrea added. "What did you do, Mark? Did you tell your wife that Sonny didn't remember her?"

"Of course not!" Mark looked horrified at the prospect. "Darla doesn't need to know that the man she wanted to marry thought so little of her that he forgot all about her the minute he found someone new." He turned to Andrea. "That's why I wasn't in the bar when you talked to Joe. I was on the phone to Germany, calling my wife at the base."

"It sounds like Sonny was a big disappointment for Darla," Hannah said. "I wouldn't blame you a bit if you didn't like Sonny."

"I don't particularly like him, but I do owe him a vote of thanks. Darla joined the Air Force because of Sonny, and I'd never have met her at the base in Germany if she'd ended up marrying him."

Hannah began to smile. "That's a very good way to look at it. And I think you're exactly right for not telling her. That might have hurt her feelings."

"That's exactly what I told him," Joe said, patting Mark on the shoulder. "Darla was head over heels over Sonny at one time. It would be a real slap in the face for her to realize that she'd meant that little to him."

Hannah glanced at her watch. "It was nice meeting you, Mark. And Joe . . . it's always good to see you. We'd better get back to put out the food for the lunch buffet. There's a really good Wild Rice Soup that I hope you try. It's one of my favorite recipes."

"Then I'll be sure to try it," Joe promised.

Andrea frowned slightly, and Hannah knew exactly what she was thinking. "I have something to tell you two," Hannah said, taking a deep breath. "I'm not supposed to tell anyone, but . . . considering the circumstances, I don't want either of you to be blindsided by the news that you're going to get."

"Murder?" Joe asked, giving her an assessing look.

"Yes."

"Sonny?" Joe glanced at Andrea and then back at Hannah.

"Yes."

"When?" This time it was Mark who asked the question.

"Yesterday morning. Mike isn't going to tell anyone until this afternoon."

"And that's why you came over to talk to me last night," Joe said to Andrea.

"That's right. I'm sorry, Joe. I didn't think you did it or anything. I was just trying to collect information."

Joe turned to smile at Mark. "That's what these two sisters do. Hannah solves crimes, and Andrea helps her. And sometimes Michelle, their younger sister, gets into the act, too."

"Then you're detectives?" Mark asked.

"No." Hannah shook her head. "We're not officially anything. It's just that we love Lake Eden and the people here. It's our hometown, and if something like this happens, we want to help figure out who did it."

"You don't think I killed Sonny, do you?" Mark looked slightly worried at the prospect.

"No, we don't," Hannah answered quickly. "And neither did Andrea when she told me about talking to Joe at the bar. It was just that we had to check it out to make sure, that's all."

"So neither one of us is a suspect?" Joe followed up.

"Not anymore," Andrea answered him, and then she turned to Hannah. "Isn't that right, Hannah?"

"That's right," Hannah assured them.

"But why did you suspect us in the first place?" Joe asked.

"I knew you were a sharpshooter in the military," Andrea said. "Bill told me that he tried to recruit you for the sheriff's department."

"You mean Sonny was . . . shot?"

"I shouldn't have said anything," Andrea admitted, glancing at Hannah.

"Yes, Sonny was shot." Hannah rescued her sister, who looked guilty for even mentioning it. "Please don't repeat what we told you. I don't know if Mike is going to tell everyone exactly how Sonny was murdered."

"We won't say a word," Joe promised them. "Isn't that right, Mark?"

"That's right. But we're in the clear, right?"

Hannah nodded. "I have a list of suspects, and you are definitely going to get crossed off the list the minute I get back to my room at the Inn."

"Well . . ." Joe gave her a little smile. "That's a relief! Now that you told us, Mark and I might be able to enjoy the Wild Rice Soup at the lunch buffet after all!"

WILD RICE SOUP

This soup can be made in a 4- or 5-quart slow cooker.

WARNING: This recipe contains many dry ingredients in boxes or packaged in envelopes. Some of these ingredients may have tiny packets of silica gel inside to keep these dry ingredients from becoming moist and sticking together. The best way to find these small packets is to measure out the dry ingredients and place them in a small bowl to check for the small packets BEFORE you put them in your crockpot.

Ingredients:

> 2 cans *(14.5 ounces net weight)* beef broth *(I used 2 cans of Swanson)*
> 1 cup of instant mashed potato flakes
> 1 envelope of dry Lipton Onion Soup
> 1 pint *(2 cups)* Half & Half *(that's light cream)*
> 8 ounces dry wild rice *(I used 2 packets of Uncle Ben's Long Grain & Wild Rice—the name was changed to Ben's Ready Rice Long Grain & Wild on the newer packaging, and there was no mention of anybody's "Uncle")*

1 10-ounce can Campbell's condensed
  cheddar cheese soup
½ pound ham cut into cubes OR 1 package Hormel Real Crumbled Bacon
  (4.3 ounces net weight)

Hannah's 1st Note: This recipe is from Edna
Fergusson, Lake Eden's School District head
cook. Edna is the queen of shortcuts and this
recipe proves it!

Hannah's 2nd Note: Everything can simply be
thrown in the crock of the slow cooker, stirred,
and set to cook on the LOW setting.

Prepare your pans.

If you're using a slow cooker, spray the inside of
the crock with Pam or another nonstick cooking
spray. If you're making this soup on the stovetop,
find a pot large enough to hold 4 quarts of soup.

Directions:

Open the cans of beef broth and pour them
into the crock.

Open the package of instant mashed potato
flakes and place them in the crock on top of the
beef broth.

Open the package of dry Lipton Onion Soup Mix and sprinkle the top of the dried mashed potato flakes in the crock.

Pour in the pint of Half & Half.

Open the packages of the Long Grain and Wild Rice mixture and place them in the crock.

Open the can of cheese soup and place the contents inside the crock.

Put in the ham or the real crumbled bacon now.

Stir everything together to combine, and put the lid on the crock.

Turn the slow cooker on LOW heat (*make sure that the slow cooker is plugged in*).

Your soup is ready to serve in three to four hours.

Yield: 8 to 10 servings of hot, creamy, and satisfying Wild Rice Soup.

Hannah's Final Note: Actually, wild rice is an aquatic grain and not really a rice at all, but it is a staple in Minnesota and a real favorite because of its smoky, nut-like flavor.

ONION SOUP

A Crockpot Recipe for a 4- to 5-quart crockpot.

You will only use your oven to toast the French bread that tops the bowls of soup.

Ingredients:

> 3 Tablespoons salted butter
> 4 cups chopped sweet white onions
> 1 clove garlic, minced, or 1 teaspoon
>   jarred minced garlic
> 3 14.5-ounce cans beef broth
> 4 cubes beef bouillon
> 1 cup water
> 1 and ½ teaspoons Worcestershire sauce
> ⅛ teaspoon ground black pepper (*freshly ground is best*)
> 2 ounces cognac or brandy (*optional*)
> 1 French bread baguette (*enough for 8 to 10 1-inch thick slices*)
> 1 cup finely grated Gruyere or Swiss cheese

Hannah's 1st Note: I love onion soup, but one of the things I've always hated about it is that sometimes the onion pieces were so long

236

that they would drip on my clothes if I wasn't extremely careful. I always wished that restaurants would provide bibs like they sometimes do for lobster, but then Michelle and I came up with another solution. This is the main reason we decided to use chopped onions in this recipe, rather than using a mandolin. The second reason we chose to use chopped onions was purely for convenience. Florence sells bags of chopped onions down at her Red Owl grocery, and this recipe is simple to put together if the onions are already chopped.

Directions:

Get out a large skillet.

Put the salted butter inside and turn the stovetop burner on MEDIUM-LOW. Swish the butter around until it covers the bottom of the pan.

Add the onions and garlic and sauté for 20 minutes on MEDIUM-LOW until tender.

Spray the interior of the crockpot with Pam or another nonstick cooking spray.

Transfer the sautéed onions and garlic into the bottom of your crockpot.

Add the 3 cans of beef broth and stir them in.

Add the 4 beef bouillon cubes and stir them in.

Add the cup of water and stir that in.

Add the Worcestershire sauce and black pepper and stir them in.

Cover the crock pot and cook your soup on LOW heat for 5 to 8 hours. *(If you're in a hurry, you can cook this on HIGH heat for 2 and ½ to 3 hours.)*

Before serving your French Onion Soup, preheat the oven to 400 degrees F., rack in the middle position.

Turn off the crockpot and add the 2 ounces of cognac or brandy to your soup and stir it in thoroughly. Re-cover the crock and set it on a towel on the kitchen counter.

Slice the French bread into 1-inch-thick slices and butter both sides. Then place them on the cookie sheet.

When the oven comes up to temperature, put the cookie sheet in the oven for 2 minutes or until the top has toasted. Then take it out, place

it on a cool stovetop burner, and flip the bread over to the uncooked side.

Place the cookie sheet back in the oven and bake for another 2 minutes or until the top is nice and golden brown.

Take the cookie sheet out of the oven, place it on the stovetop burner again, and sprinkle on the grated Gruyere or Swiss cheese.

Return the cookie sheet to the oven until the cheese has melted, while you fill your soup bowls with onion soup from the crockpot.

Take the toasted cheese bread from the oven and place one slice, cheese side up, on top of each bowl of your onion soup. Your guests will love this soup. It rivals anything that's served in fancy French restaurants.

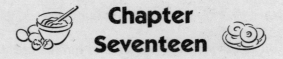

Chapter
Seventeen

"I wish I knew how to drive a boat like this," Andrea said as they headed back to the Lake Eden Inn. "This is a lot newer than Bill's boat and has a lot more bells and whistles. And it looks like it's fun to drive."

"It is. Why don't you try it, Andrea? It's just like driving a car, and there's no one else even close to us on the lake."

Andrea began to smile. "Are you *sure*?" she asked.

"I'm sure. If you get into trouble, I'll be right next to you. I'm sure you can keep this one afloat."

"I'd really like to try," Andrea said. "Are you sure it'll be okay with Dick?"

"I'm sure. He let me drive it without even asking if I'd ever driven a boat like his."

"He's probably got really good insurance," Andrea said, and Hannah noticed that there was a grin at the corners of her sister's mouth.

"He probably does," Hannah agreed and then she laughed out loud. "Don't worry, Andrea. We're a long way from the dock and there's absolutely nothing to hit out here. Even if you have trouble steering, you can't mess up too badly."

"Oh, no? Remember the first time Dad took me out in the car for a driving lesson?"

Hannah burst into laughter. "He was more ready for you than he was for me. I did exactly the same thing when we came to a corner. I didn't realize that I had to slow down so I took it too fast, and almost went into the ditch."

"He never told me that!" Andrea said, laughing along with Hannah. "Do you think he forgot about it?"

"I doubt it. Maybe he just wanted to see if excessive speed on corners ran in our family."

"Do you mean Michelle did the same thing?"

"That's what Dad said when he called me right after Michelle's first driving lesson."

"I wonder if Mother—"

"She did," Hannah interrupted her. "I asked her about it. Her parents never let her drive their car and they didn't teach driver's education in the schools back then. Dad had to teach her how to drive after they got married."

"We're almost in, Hannah," Andrea said as the dock appeared in the distance. "I'm not sure I know how to park this boat."

"You mean . . . how to dock it?"

"Yes. What do you do? Just shut off the motor?"

"It's a little more complicated than that. I'll do it, Andrea. You can watch."

"Oh, good!" Andrea looked very relieved as they switched seats. "I really wouldn't want to have to tell Dick that I broke his boat."

Once Hannah had docked Dick's boat, the two sisters hurried up to the Inn. They entered the lobby and Hannah glanced over at the desk clerk. "Isn't that Sally's night desk clerk, Andrea?"

"I think so. He looks like the same person."

"Great! Come with me. I want to ask him if he was here the morning that Sonny was killed."

"Good idea! Are you hoping he saw something?"

"Saw or heard something," Hannah amended the thought. "He must be working double shifts now that the college is on semester break."

"Hi, Craig," Hannah said, reading his name tag to get his name.

"Hello, Miss Swensen. Good to see you again." The desk clerk gave her a friendly smile. "And this is your sister, right?"

"That's right, but I'm not Miss Swensen anymore. Now I'm Mrs. Todd."

"The sheriff's wife. Sally told me that."

"Were you here the night that Sonny Bowman got so drunk they had to carry him up to his room?" Hannah asked.

"You bet I was! I held the elevator door open for Doc so they could get the stretcher inside. I've never seen anyone quite that wasted, not even at the frat house parties."

"You live at the frat house?" Andrea asked.

"Not right now. They're painting the inside of the place and Sally found a room for me here. That way I don't have to drive back and forth and I can work double shifts when she needs me."

"I bet Sally's taking full advantage of that," Hannah said, and then she smiled.

"She is and that suits me just fine. Sally pays really well and I do little odd jobs for her during the day. She doesn't charge me for the room and she feeds me all sorts of great food. If I have to pull an all-nighter, she even brings me rolls and coffee the minute they're ready in the morning."

"Were you here when Lily came in late that night?"

"I was here, and so was Rosa. I think Lily called Rosa to tell her that she was coming."

"You're probably right," Hannah agreed.

"I met Lily before the fishing competition started," Craig told them. "She came here with Wally the week before the contestants came in."

"How about Sonny?" Andrea asked. "Did he come here, too?"

Craig shook his head. "Not him. I asked, and Lily told me he was busy shooting another fishing show at a different lake."

"How about Lily's mother?" Hannah asked. "Did she come along with her husband and daughter?"

Craig shook his head. "I just met her for the first time this morning. Sally introduced me."

Hannah knew it was time to get down to the questions she really wanted to ask before someone else came in and needed something from the desk clerk. "Were you working when Sonny and Joey went out on the boat two mornings ago?"

"Yes. Actually, I think Sonny was still drunk from the night before. I thought, for sure, that Doc would have given him something to sober him up, but he was still acting like he'd had more than a couple."

"I'm glad you noticed," Hannah told him. "What was Sonny doing to make you think that he was still drunk?"

"He was wearing his dark glasses, and it was before the sun had come up. And he was walking really carefully, the way drunks do when they're trying to convince people that they're not drunk."

"Sonny was probably wearing dark glasses to hide his bloodshot eyes," Andrea commented.

Craig nodded. "That's sure possible. Either that, or he had such a bad headache, the lights in the lobby hurt his eyes."

"Did you talk to Sonny at all?" Andrea asked.

"I didn't get the chance because Joey came rushing in and they went outside together."

"Where did they go? Do you know?"

"No, but I heard a boat start and I figured they were getting out on the lake really early for some reason. And then Sally came in with my coffee and rolls and she manned the desk while I went in and had my breakfast."

"Were you able to get some sleep after your breakfast?" Hannah asked him.

"Eventually, but not right away. I heard the phone ring when I was drinking my second cup of coffee and when I came back out, Sally told me that the morning guy was coming in late and she asked me if I could stay until he got here."

"After you got back to the desk, did you hear any other boats start up outside?"

"No, not until Joe Dietz and Mark left. They were the first ones to come out from the breakfast buffet. They told me they wanted to get out to the lake early so they could pick a good spot before it got crowded."

"How long did you have to work before the day desk clerk came in?" Hannah asked.

"Not that long. An hour, maybe. I knew it was already daylight because I could see the dock from the side window and I saw Sonny bring Joey back. When Joey came in here he smelled like a distillery and his clothes were soaked!"

"Did you ask him what happened?" Andrea asked him.

"Oh, yeah! Joey was hopping mad about it! He told me that Sonny had been drinking again in the boat and he'd spilled booze all over him. Joey said all he wanted to do was go upstairs, get out of his clothes, and take a shower."

"Do you think that Joey was drinking, too?" Hannah asked.

"Joey doesn't drink anything except beer. Sally told me that. And Dick told her that Joey can make one beer last him the whole night."

"Did Joey tell you any more about what had happened in the boat?"

"No, he just asked me to come with him to the elevator and press the button. He said he was going to get on and stand in the middle without touching anything."

"And you did that?"

"Yes. And when the elevator came back down, I went out with some disinfectant and wiped down all the surfaces."

"Did you hear any other boats go out while you were wiping down the elevator?" Hannah asked.

Craig shook his head. "No. A couple of the contestants came down early to take tables for the breakfast buffet, but nobody went out through the lobby to the dock."

Hannah took a moment to digest this information. "Do you happen to know when Joe Dietz and Mark came downstairs?"

"I do!" Craig looked pleased that he could actually answer one of her questions with certainty. "It was a few hours after Joey went up in the elevator and Sonny went back out on the lake with his boat."

"You heard Sonny go back out on the lake?"

"No, but either Joey or Sonny had turned on the running lights when they docked. They were still on when I went out to wipe down the elevator, but it was completely dark when I came back."

"So either Sonny turned off the running lights, or the boat was gone?" Andrea asked, drawing the obvious conclusion.

"Yes. And when it was light enough outside to see, I checked and Sonny's boat was gone."

"Did you happen to notice when Joe Dietz and Mark's boat left the dock?" Hannah asked.

"As a matter of fact, I did. Joe's motor boat has an outboard and it's old. You can hear it for miles when it's calm on the lake. I didn't hear it until the day clerk arrived and I got ready to go up to my room."

"And that was what time?"

Craig looked thoughtful. "It must have been close to ten a.m. Sally and you two were just closing the buffet and packing up things to take back to the kitchen. That would have been right around ten, wouldn't it?"

Hannah nodded. "Yes. And Joe and Mark's boat left shortly before that?"

"That's right, along with George Coulter."

"George Coulter?" Hannah repeated the name. "I don't think I've met him."

"Maybe not, but you've seen him in the bar. He's the contestant who's married to the blonde that Sonny was trying to dance with. He's a nice guy, Hannah. Joe and Mark stopped by here with George, and they told me that they were taking George out with them in the boat because there was something wrong with George's boat and the mechanic couldn't get to it until late afternoon."

"So George went out with both Joe and Mark all day?" Hannah asked, just to make sure.

"That's right."

"Thank you, Craig," Hannah said with a smile. "You've been very helpful."

"So you two are trying to solve the murder case?" Craig asked them.

Hannah just stared at him for a minute. "What makes you say that?"

"Because you don't get involved until it's murder, and you're obviously involved, because you're asking me questions."

"Did someone tell you that it was murder?" Andrea asked, looking a bit shocked at Craig's admission.

"No, but it wasn't hard to figure out. The day guy called me at noon and told me that Mike and Lonnie wanted to ask me some questions. And he asked me if I knew what was going on, because some guys in uniforms went upstairs to one of the rooms. And then he told me that the paramedics came in, went straight through to the dock to load somebody into their ambulance, and that person was wrapped in a sheet."

Just then, a group of wives came into the lobby and approached the desk. Hannah knew their private time with Craig had just expired, and she gave him a parting smile. "Looks like you have business," she said, glancing at the group behind her. "Thanks for answering our questions, Craig. We'll see you later."

Hannah noticed that Andrea was frowning as they left the lobby and started down the long hallway to join Sally in the kitchen. She waited a few moments, but Andrea didn't say anything.

"What?" Hannah asked her.

"Why did you ask Craig about Joe Dietz and Mark?"

"That's simple. It was because I wanted to know."

"But why? They already told you exactly what happened on the morning that Sonny was murdered."

"I know."

"So why did you ask Craig all those questions? Didn't you believe Joe and Mark?"

Hannah gave a little nod. "I believe them. I asked because I was just substantiating what they told me."

"But that means you *didn't* believe them!"

"No, not really. I was just double-checking, that's all."

"Oh," Andrea said, and she took a moment to digest that. "Do you always do that?"

"Yes, if I can. Everybody's a suspect until you clear them, Andrea. You know that."

"I do, but . . . you told them you were going to go back and cross their names off your suspect list."

"And I will . . . just as soon as I get back to the room after the lunch buffet."

Andrea thought about that as they passed the entrance to the dining room and Dick's bar. They turned the corner to head for the kitchen and she sighed heavily.

"So," she said, giving Hannah a probing look. "What you're telling me is that you don't really trust anything that anyone tells you. Is that right?"

Hannah winced slightly. "In a way, but . . ." She stopped to think for a moment before she continued. "I *do* trust people. It's just that I trust with reservations. It helps to get some kind of confirmation, like someone who can verify it. And I got that for Joe and Mark by talking to Craig. I'll cross them off my suspect list when I get back to the room, just like I said I would."

"But you wouldn't have if Craig had told you some-

thing that contradicted what Joe and Mark told you . . .
is that right?"

"Right," Hannah agreed.

"So you're always suspicious, all the time, when
you're doing detective work."

Hannah stopped in her tracks and thought about that
for a moment. "I think you're right, Andrea," she said
with a sigh. "It's something you learn when you ask
people questions. You always take what they tell you
with a grain of salt until you find another source to
substantiate it."

The two sisters walked in silence for a few moments, and then Andrea sighed. "I'm glad Bill's not a
real detective!" she said. "I'd be very upset if he didn't
trust what I'd told him."

Hannah smiled. "I don't blame you a bit for that.
You're not a suspect in a murder, Andrea. If you were,
then he might look at what you told him differently."

"But . . . Hannah!" Andrea looked completely dis-
mayed. "That's not love! When you're in love, you
have to trust your wife, or your husband. It's . . . it's
practically required!"

"Of course it is," Hannah said, thinking back to how
she'd trusted Ross, and how devastating it had been
when she'd found out that he'd lied to her. "But detectives can't have blind trust," she said, slipping her arm
around Andrea's shoulder. "And maybe that's why so
many of us are single or divorced. It's a profession that
could be very hard on a marriage, Andrea. Their incli-
nation may be to trust what people tell them, but because of the line of work they're in, they can't."

"Now that I think about it, I think you're right. And
I'm really glad that Bill's the sheriff, and he doesn't
have to be a detective."

Chapter Eighteen

"Hannah, I need to talk to you." Mike came up behind her as she was filling the Double Pineapple Cookie tray. "Will you meet me in Dick's bar this afternoon?"

"Of course," Hannah said immediately, wondering what Mike wanted. Had he found out that they'd interviewed Joe and Mark, and did he want a rundown of the results?

"These are great cookies, Hannah!" Lonnie said, coming up behind Mike.

"Tell Andrea. She's the one who made them," Hannah said with a smile.

"Well, it's a good one! Do you think she could teach Michelle to make them?"

Hannah almost burst out laughing, but she managed to control herself. Michelle was a veteran baker, while Andrea was still learning. "I'm sure Andrea would be happy to give Michelle the recipe," Hannah sidestepped. "As a matter of fact, I think she'd be very complimented if you'd ask her for it."

"Lily and Janette are here," Andrea said, carrying

the container of meatballs in mushroom sauce that Hannah had asked her to get. "Do you want me to put more in the serving dish?"

"That would be good," Hannah said, smiling at her sister. "And you'd better check the dish of pasta, too. By the way, Lonnie just left and he loves your pineapple cookies. He wanted to know if I thought that you could teach Michelle to make them."

"What?!" Andrea looked completely stunned. "Lonnie wanted *me* to teach Michelle to bake cookies?"

"That's what he said."

"Oh, that's funny! Michelle's been baking for years and she bakes a lot of things that are a million times more complicated than those cookies."

"I know that, but it's still a real compliment to know that Lonnie liked your cookies."

Andrea thought about that for a few seconds, and then she smiled. "You're right. I'm going to go tell him I'm glad he likes my cookies. And I'll say that I'll be glad to give Michelle the recipe." She gave a little chuckle. "You, and Michelle, and I are going to have a real laugh over this, aren't we?"

Hannah was smiling as Andrea hurried off. It was obvious that Andrea was delighted with Lonnie's compliment. Hannah'd just dished up a serving of lasagna for one of the fishermen when Lily and Janette came up to the table. "Would you like to have lunch?" Hannah asked, gesturing toward the stack of plates and silverware.

"It looks wonderful, but I don't think I could eat anything," Lily responded. "Mike's going to tell everyone about what happened to Sonny right after they finish eating and . . . well . . . I'm just not hungry."

"I can understand that," Hannah said, and then she turned to Janette. "How about you, Janette?"

"No, thank you. I feel the same way Lily does. I just want to get through this so we can go back up to our rooms and relax."

"How about your dad?" Hannah asked Lily. "Is he here yet?"

"No, he's not coming until tonight. He's going to drive here right after they do the big drawing at the new store."

"We have to go, Lily." Janette took her daughter's arm. "Mike's gesturing for us to join him. We just came over here to say hello."

Hannah felt a stab of compassion as she watched the two women walk away. She imagined that Mike's announcement would not be easy for either of them to hear. As she waited on several competitors, dishing up what they wanted on their plates, Hannah wondered what reaction they'd have when they heard Sonny was dead. No doubt there would be shock, and perhaps a few tears from some of the women. And there were bound to be questions about what had happened to Sonny. Normally, when the daily postlunch fishing announcements were made, Hannah and Andrea had already packed up leftover food and were headed back to the kitchen. Today would be different. She intended to stick around and judge people's reactions.

When the bell sounded for the ending of the buffet, both Hannah and Andrea worked feverishly to pack up the leftovers. Since lunch had been a big success with the competitors, there wasn't a lot left over to pack. Once the dishes were stacked on the cart and the food was wrapped and secured, one of Sally's kitchen workers came by to push the loaded cart back to the kitchen.

"Where shall we sit?" Andrea asked Hannah.

"You're staying?"

"Yes, I want to watch people when they hear about Sonny. Maybe we can learn something that way."

Hannah gave a little nod. Andrea was beginning to think like a detective. "We won't be able to see the contestants unless we stand backstage and peek out."

"That's true, but we can do that, can't we?"

"Of course we can. It's like a stage back there and they don't open the curtains until there's a live performance of some kind. Follow me and I'll show you where we can stand."

Hannah led them out of the buffet room and into the hallway. She opened a door and motioned for Andrea to follow her through into the dim interior. "Backstage," she said in a voice as soft as a whisper. "As long as we're quiet, no one will know we're here."

Quietly, Hannah moved two chairs over to the curtain. There was a slight split between the start of the curtain and the wall behind it. "Sit here," she said, indicating one of the chairs. "I'll go sit on the other side. I watched Sally from back here when she sang with the Cinnamon Roll Five last year."

"I wish I'd known. I would have come back here with you," Andrea said.

Once Andrea and Hannah had taken their chairs and learned exactly which vantage point to use to see the buffet room, Lonnie climbed up the steps to the podium that sat on the apron of the stage.

As if by magic, all conversation ceased as Lonnie cleared his throat. "Okay, sit down and relax, everyone," he said. "I have several important announcements to make."

There was a slight sound, and Hannah turned to see Mike standing behind her. He held his finger to his lips, pulled up a chair beside her, and then found a slit in the curtain where he could see.

Hannah motioned to Andrea, and her sister nodded. Mike wanted both of them to be quiet and listen as Lonnie began to speak.

"My first announcement concerns Sonny Bowman," Lonnie told them. "Joey will be taking Sonny's place from now on. Wally just called here from his Brainerd store and he's going to arrive tonight in time for happy hour in Dick's bar to answer any other questions you might have."

"Where's Sonny?" someone at one of the tables asked, and Hannah recognized the blonde's husband, George Coulter.

"Sonny was taken to Doc Knight's hospital yesterday afternoon and he won't be back for this tournament. Wally wanted me to tell you that he's coming here to answer any questions you might have."

"Is it serious?" someone asked.

"Yes, but I'm not authorized to answer any more questions about Mr. Bowman's condition. I just wanted you to know that Joey and Wally will be running the tournament from now on."

There was silence for a moment and then someone asked, "Will Joey be doing the weigh-ins?"

"Yes, and the protocol will remain the same. And here's a little bit of good news . . ." Lonnie stopped speaking as several people clapped. "I'm going to let Joey tell you himself. It's pretty amazing, if you ask me. And after you hear what Joey has to say, you'll be *really* glad you're a contestant!"

There was applause as Lonnie climbed down the steps and Joey took the place behind the podium. "Lonnie's right! Two people in this room are going to be very, very lucky winners because Wally has added two more prizes!"

There were several whistles of approval and Joey laughed. "I'll tell you this . . . I wish *I'd* signed up!"

"We don't!" someone shouted out. "You're an expert and you're not allowed to compete."

"Thank you, Captain Obvious," Joey responded with a big smile. "I know I'm not Sonny, but I do know a lot about fishing for Walleye."

"You probably know more than Sonny ever did," one of the wives responded.

"Thank you for the vote of confidence," Joey said, smiling at her. "The other bit of information I have for you is the news that Stan Jordan won the weigh-in last night. Sorry that I didn't get the chance to tell you at dinner. And I want all of you to know that Barry Withers has offered to operate the rescue boat that'll go out after the noon weigh-in and the evening weigh-in to release the fish."

"Thanks, Barry!" someone shouted, and everyone began to applaud. Hannah smiled at the proud look on Barry's face. She knew that Barry was on vacation from the University of Minnesota, where he was enrolled in the pre-med program. Since the Withers family didn't have that much money, Barry had applied for every scholarship he could find, and the U of M was paying for his tuition.

"That's about all I have except for the biggest news, and I saved that for last."

"That figures," Joe Dietz said, and everyone laughed.

"Thanks, Joe. And thanks to Joe's son-in-law Mark, for helping me with the weigh-in last night."

"What's the big news?" someone shouted out.

"Tell us, Joey," someone else shouted.

"I will. It's just that it's such big news, I want all of you to put down your water, or whatever you're drinking, so you don't spill when I tell you."

There was a chorus of laughs, but Hannah could see that everyone did exactly what Joey wanted them to do.

"Thanks," Joey said. "I talked to Wally right before the lunch buffet opened and he told me something that knocked my socks off."

"What is it?!" one of the fishermen said, and then there was complete silence. Everyone was waiting for Joey to tell them about the prize.

"Instead of just one custom fishing boat for the winner, Wally wants to award another custom boat for second place. Isn't that fantastic?"

There was stunned silence for the space of several seconds, and then the entire audience of contestants broke into applause.

"What about the other prize," someone yelled from the back of the room.

"I'm glad you asked," Joey said. "You all know Wally's sitting on a lot of cash . . . right?"

"What do you mean?" someone else asked.

"You'll find out exactly what I mean when you come to happy hour tonight. Wally will be there and we're having a drawing. The lucky winner will receive all the cash Wally has in his wallet!"

Someone in the back yelled, "Woo hoo!" and there was a burst of applause.

"How about the second person in the boat, the contestant's helper?" one of the wives asked.

"The helpers will get tickets for the drawing, too. And if one of them wins, they'll be awarded the cash."

There was a burst of applause from the wives and helpers.

"Thank you," Joey responded with a smile. "And there's something else I should tell you. Wally was so grateful to Barry Withers for offering to drive the fish release boat after each weigh-in, he's going to foot the bill for the remainder of Barry's pre-med program."

Barry looked completely awestruck. "I never expected . . ." Barry stopped speaking and just shook his head. "That's . . . that's incredible!"

"And it's the reason why the people in Minnesota love Wally Wallace," Joey said. "Now . . . let's all pick up our afternoon snack bags. I took a quick peek at mine, and I noticed that Sally, Hannah, and Andrea had baked us some of my favorite things. We have Double Pineapple Cookies, Hot Fudge and Vanilla Bar Cookies, and there's even a couple of Chocolate, Fruit, and Nut Cupcakes. There's even a little thermos of Dick's famous lemonade."

"With or without Dick's special ingredient?" one of the contestants asked.

"I didn't ask Dick, but I think it's probably without something from behind the bar," Joey answered. "And I'm pretty sure Doc told Dick to make it nonalcoholic. Doc said all of you had a perfect record for HRIs so far and that made him very happy."

"What are HRIs?" one of the wives asked, and Joey laughed. "I asked Doc about that, and he told me the initials stood for hook-related injuries." There was a burst of general laughter and then everyone was quiet again. "Okay," Joey said. "I think we've covered everything. Now . . . let's all get out on the water and catch the biggest lunker in Eden Lake!"

DOUBLE PINEAPPLE COOKIES

DO NOT preheat oven—dough must chill before baking.

Ingredients:

⅓ cup well-drained crushed pineapple

6 ounces *(1 and ½ sticks)* salted butter

½ cup white *(granulated)* sugar

½ cup brown sugar *(pack it down in the cup when you measure it)*

1 teaspoon salt

1 teaspoon vanilla extract

½ teaspoon pineapple extract

½ teaspoon baking soda

1 teaspoon baking powder

2 large eggs, beaten *(just whip them up in a glass with a fork)*

2 cups all-purpose flour *(pack it down in the cup when you measure it)*

2 cups white chocolate or vanilla baking chips

Hannah's 1st Note: You can mix up these cookies by hand, but it's easiest with an electric mixer.

258

Prepare your cookie sheets by spraying them with Pam or another nonstick cooking spray. Alternatively, you can line your cookie sheets with parchment paper.

Set a strainer over a small bowl in the sink. Then open the can of crushed pineapple and drain it in the strainer, reserving the pineapple juice in the bowl for later.

Melt the butter in a microwave-safe bowl on HIGH for 1 minute *(60 seconds)*.

Let the melted butter sit in the microwave for an additional minute. If it's not completely melted, microwave it in 20-second increments with 20-second standing times until it is melted.

Set the melted butter on the kitchen counter to let it cool a bit.

Put the white sugar in the bowl of an electric mixer.

Sprinkle the brown sugar on top of the white sugar.

Add the teaspoon of salt and the vanilla and pineapple extracts.

Turn the mixer on LOW and mix until the sugars and salt are well blended.

With the mixer still running on LOW speed, add the baking soda and the baking powder. Mix thoroughly.

Drizzle in the melted butter, continuing to mix on LOW speed.

Shut off the mixer and scrape down the inside of the mixing bowl.

Use several thicknesses of paper towels to pat down the crushed pineapple in the strainer. Then measure out ⅓ cup of the pineapple and add it to your mixing bowl.

Turn the mixer back on LOW speed again and mix in the pineapple.

If you haven't done so already, break the 2 eggs into a glass and beat them with a fork from your silverware drawer.

Add the beaten eggs to your bowl and mix them in.

Measure out the flour and add it to your mixing bowl in half-cup increments, mixing on LOW speed after each addition.

Turn off the mixer, scrape down the sides of the bowl again.

Take the mixing bowl out of the mixer and set it on the kitchen counter.

Give your Double Pineapple Cookie dough a stir by hand.

Open the bag of white chocolate or vanilla baking chips and sprinkle them into your mixing bowl.

Mix in the chips by hand.

Press a piece of plastic wrap over the top of the cookie dough and tuck it in at the sides.

Refrigerate your cookie dough for at least 45 minutes. *(Overnight is fine too.)*

Make sure you cover that small bowl you used to reserve the pineapple juice and refrigerate it along with your cookie dough. You can either use it to make the Pineapple Frosting

Drizzle on the following page or add it to the kids' orange juice in the morning. If there's any crushed pineapple left over, it makes a very nice addition to a bowl of vanilla ice cream.

When you're ready to bake your cookies, preheat your oven to 375 degrees F., rack in the middle position. Leave your cookie dough in the refrigerator until your oven has come up to baking temperature.

Take your cookie dough out of the refrigerator and use a spoon or a 2-teaspoon scooper to transfer balls of dough to your prepared cookie sheets, 12 cookies to a standard-size cookie sheet.

Bake your Double Pineapple Cookies at 375 degrees F. for 10 to 14 minutes. (Mine took 12 minutes.)

When your cookies are done, take them out of the oven and place them on cold stovetop burners or wire racks. Let them cool on the cookie sheets for at least 3 minutes, and then remove them to cool completely on wire racks.

When your cookies are cool, decorate the tops with Pineapple Frosting Drizzle. (Recipe follows)

Yield: 3 to 4 dozen soft, chewy cookies, depending on cookie size.

Hannah's 2nd Note: These cookies are good just the way they are, but everyone seems to think that the frosting drizzle adds a lot.

PINEAPPLE FROSTING DRIZZLE

Ingredients:

¾ cup powdered sugar (*pack it down in the cup when you measure it*)
1 teaspoon pineapple extract
2 to 3 Tablespoons pineapple juice

Mix everything together and beat until smooth and of the right consistency to drizzle on the top of your cookies. You can either drizzle it off the tip of a spoon, or put the frosting drizzle in a squeeze bottle like the ones they used to use in diners to hold ketchup.

HOT FUDGE AND VANILLA BAR COOKIES

Preheat oven to 325 degrees F., rack in the middle position.

2 cups *(4 sticks, 16 ounces, 1 pound)* salted butter, softened to room temperature

1 cup white *(granulated)* sugar

1 and ½ cups powdered *(confectioners)* sugar

2 Tablespoons vanilla extract

4 cups all-purpose flour *(pack it down in the cup when you measure it)*

The Hot Fudge Filling:

12.25-ounce jar hot fudge ice cream topping *(I used Smucker's)*

12-ounce bag *(approximately 2 cups)* white chocolate or vanilla baking chips

1 Tablespoon sea or Kosher salt *(the coarse-ground kind)*

Before you begin to make the crust and filling, spray a 9-inch by 13-inch cake pan with Pam or another nonstick baking spray.

Hannah's 1ˢᵗ Note: This crust and filling is a lot easier to make with an electric mixer. You can do it by hand, but it will take some muscle.

Combine the butter, white sugar, and powdered sugar in a large bowl or in the bowl of an electric mixer. Beat at MEDIUM speed until the mixture is light and creamy.

Add the vanilla extract. Mix it in until it is thoroughly combined.

Add the flour in half-cup increments, beating at LOW speed after each addition. Beat until everything is combined.

Hannah's 2ⁿᵈ Note: When you've mixed in the flour, the resulting sweet dough will be soft. Don't worry. That's the way it's supposed to be.

Measure out a heaping cup of sweet dough and place it in a sealable plastic bag. Seal the bag and put it in the refrigerator.

With impeccably clean hands, press the rest of the sweet dough into the bottom of your prepared cake pan. This will form the bottom of the crust. Press it all the way out to the edges of the pan and a half-inch up the sides, as evenly

as you can. Don't worry if your sweet dough is a bit uneven. It won't matter to any of your guests.

Bake your bottom crust at 325 degrees F., for approximately 20 minutes or until the edges are beginning to turn a pale golden brown color.

When the crust has turned pale golden brown, remove the pan from the oven, but DON'T SHUT OFF THE OVEN! Set the pan with your baked crust on a cold stovetop burner or a wire rack to cool. It should cool approximately 15 minutes.

After your crust has cooled approximately 15 minutes, take the lid off the jar of hot fudge ice cream topping and put it in the microwave.

Heat the hot fudge topping for 15 to 20 seconds on HIGH.

Let the jar cool in the microwave for 1 minute. Then use potholders to take the jar out of the microwave.

Pour the hot fudge ice cream topping over the baked bottom crust in the pan as evenly as you can.

Open the bag of white chocolate or vanilla baking chips and sprinkle them over the baked crust as evenly as you can.

Here comes the salt! Sprinkle the Tablespoon of sea salt or Kosher salt over the hot fudge in the pan.

Take the remaining sweet dough out of the refrigerator and unwrap it. It has been refrigerated for 35 minutes or more and it should be thoroughly chilled.

With your impeccably clean fingers, crumble the dough over the hot fudge and chip layer as evenly as you can. Leave a little space between the crumbles, so the hot fudge sauce can bubble up through the crumbles.

Hannah's 3rd Note: If the hot fudge topping bubbles up through the top of your bar cookies, it will look very pretty.

Return the pan to the oven and bake your bar cookies for 25 to 30 minutes, or until the crumbles on top are a light golden brown.

Hannah's 4th Note: Your pan of Hot Fudge and Vanilla Bar Cookies will smell so delicious,

you'll be tempted to cut it into squares and eat one immediately. Resist that urge! The bubbly hot fudge topping will burn your mouth.

After 5 minutes of cooling time, use potholders to carry the pan to a wire rack to cool completely.

Hannah's 5th Note: When I bake these bar cookies at home in the winter, I place a wire rack out on the little table on my condo balcony and carry the pan out there. The Hot Fudge and Vanilla Bar Cookies cool quite fast when exposed to a Minnesota winter.

When your Hot Fudge and Vanilla Bar Cookies are completely cool, cut them into brownie-size pieces, place them on a pretty plate, and serve them to your guests.

Yield: A cake pan full of yummy brownie-size treats that everyone will love. Serve with icy-cold glasses of milk, mugs of hot chocolate, or cups of strong, hot coffee.

Hannah's 6th Note: Mike says these are his favorite bar cookies. Of course, Mike has *never* met a bar cookie that wasn't his favorite!

CHOCOLATE, FRUIT, AND NUT CUPCAKES

Preheat oven to 350 degrees F., rack in the middle position.

Ingredients:

1 cup regular raisins
1 ounce rum (*I used Bacardi*)
4 large eggs
½ cup vegetable oil
½ cup heavy cream (*whipping cream*)
8-ounce (*by weight*) tub of sour cream (*I used Knudsen*)
1 Tablespoon chocolate syrup (*I used Hershey's*)
1 box of chocolate cake mix, the kind that makes a 9-inch by 13-inch cake or a 2-layer cake (*I used Pillsbury*)
5.1-ounce package of DRY instant chocolate pudding and pie filling (*I used Jell-O*)
1 cup salted cashews chopped into small pieces (*measure AFTER chopping*)
12-ounce (*by weight*) bag of chocolate mini chips (*11-ounce package will do, too—I used Nestlé*)

Hannah's Note: If you don't want to use an alcoholic beverage in this recipe, you can use 1 teaspoon of rum extract. That will give you the rum flavor without the alcoholic content.

Prepare your cupcake pans. You will need 2 twelve-cup pans lined with double cupcake papers.

Directions:

Start by plumping the raisins. Do this by measuring 1 cup of raisins out in a 2-cup microwavable bowl. *(I used a 2-cup Pyrex measuring cup.)*

Pour the rum *(or the extract)* over the raisins and then pour enough water in the cup or bowl to cover the raisins completely.

Place the bowl or cup with the raisins and liquid in the microwave and microwave it on HIGH for 1 minute.

Let the raisins and liquid sit in the microwave for an additional minute. Then stir and remove the bowl or cup from the microwave, and set it on a towel on your kitchen counter to cool.

Crack the eggs into the bowl of an electric mixer. Mix them up on LOW speed until they're a uniform color.

Pour in the half-cup of vegetable oil and mix it in with the eggs on LOW speed.

Add the half-cup of heavy cream. Mix that in at LOW speed.

Scoop out the container of sour cream and put it into a small bowl. Add the Tablespoon of chocolate syrup and stir it in.

Add the sour cream and chocolate syrup mixture to your mixer bowl. Mix that in on LOW speed.

When everything is well combined, open the box of dry cake mix and sprinkle it on top of the liquid ingredients in the bowl of the mixer. Mix that in on LOW speed.

Open the package of DRY instant chocolate pudding and sprinkle in the contents. Mix it in on LOW speed.

Shut off the mixer, scrape down the sides of the bowl, remove it from the mixer, and set it on the counter.

If you haven't done so already, chop the salted cashews in a food processor with a steel blade or cut them into small pieces with a sharp knife. Measure out 1 cup and add the chopped cashews to your mixing bowl.

Stir the raisins in the bowl or cup on your counter. If they're plumped and most of the liquid has been absorbed, drain off the excess liquid and add the plumped raisins to your mixing bowl.

Stir in the raisins and mix until everything in your bowl is well combined.

Sprinkle the mini chocolate chips in your bowl and stir them in by hand with a rubber spatula.

Use a mixing spoon or a scooper to fill the cupcake papers three-quarters full. The cupcakes will rise to the tops of the papers when you bake them in the oven.

Bake your Chocolate, Fruit, and Nut Cupcakes at 350 degrees F. for 20 to 25 minutes, or until a cake tester, wooden skewer, or long toothpick inserted a half-inch from the center of the cupcake comes out clean.

When they are done, take your cupcakes out of the oven and set the cupcake pans on cold stovetop burners or wire racks.

DO NOT remove the cupcakes from the pans. If you remove them from the pans while they are too warm, they may lose their shape.

Let the cupcakes cool in the pans until they reach room temperature. Then remove them from the pans and refrigerate them for at least 30 minutes before you frost them.

(Recipe and instructions follow.)

Yield: 18 to 24 rich chocolate cupcakes that everyone will love. After you frost them, serve them with icy cold glasses of milk or strong hot coffee.

CHOCOLATE FUDGE FROSTING

Ingredients:

2 cups semisweet *(regular)* chocolate
   chips *(a 12-ounce package)*
¼ teaspoon salt *(it brings out the flavor
   of the chocolate)*
14-ounce can of sweetened condensed milk
1 ounce *(2 Tablespoons)* salted butter

**Hannah's 1st Note: If you use a double boiler
for this frosting, it's foolproof. You can also make
it in a heavy saucepan over low to medium heat
on the stovetop, but you'll have to stir it constantly with a wooden spoon or a heat-resistant
spatula to keep it from scorching.**

Fill the bottom part of the double boiler with
water. Make sure the water doesn't touch the
underside of the top pan.

Put the chocolate chips and the salt in the top
of the double boiler, set it over the bottom, and
place the double boiler on the stovetop at medium heat. Stir occasionally until the chocolate
chips are melted.

Stir in the can of sweetened condensed milk
and cook approximately 2 minutes, stirring con-

stantly, until the frosting is shiny and of spreading consistency.

Shut off the heat, remove the top part of the double boiler to a cold burner, and add the butter and stir it in until it melts.

Your frosting is ready to use.

Hannah's 2nd Note: If you want to keep this frosting soft for several minutes, place the top part of the double boiler over the hot water again. This will enable you to use the frosting for ten minutes or so before it hardens.

If your frosting begins to harden and you're not yet ready to frost your cupcakes, simply heat the water in the bottom part of the double boiler again and place the top part over the re-heated water. Give it a couple of minutes and then stir the frosting again to re-soften it.

Once you have frosted your cupcakes, give the pan to your favorite person to scrape with a spoon and eat. Another alternative is to frost soda crackers, salt side down, or sugar cookies for snacking.

Hannah's 3rd Note: Once this frosting cools, it's just like fudge.

Chapter Nineteen

Hannah glanced over at the spot where Mike had been sitting, but he was gone. She folded up her chair, Andrea folded hers, and they put them back in the rack where they'd found them.

As they emerged from the dim interior of the backstage area, Andrea glanced at her watch. "I'd better go," she said.

"I thought that Tracey and Bethie were staying out at Grandma McCann's farm."

"They are, but I need to show a house this afternoon. It's my listing and if I let anyone else show it, I have to split the commission with them."

"Are you planning on getting new drapes for your bedrooms with the commission?"

Andrea's eyebrows shot up in surprise. "How did *you* know?" she asked.

"You've been talking about that for a while and I know you want to repaint the bedrooms in your house."

"So it was just a lucky guess on your part?"

"That's right. Go sell that house, Andrea. I'll see you later this afternoon when it's time to bake again."

Once Andrea had left, Hannah called Norman to tell him that she could go out on the lake with him in the afternoon. The phone rang several times, and then Norman answered.

"Hi, Hannah," he greeted her. "Sorry I missed you, but I'm on my way into town. I have to go to the clinic for a couple of hours this afternoon."

Hannah felt a stab of disappointment. She'd been looking forward to relaxing with Norman this afternoon. "What's up at the clinic?" she asked him.

"Doc Bennett booked an appointment for an implant and he's a little nervous about doing it. When he went to dental school, they didn't spend much time on the procedure, because it was experimental."

"So you're going to do the implant?"

"No, he is. I'm just going to be there in case he needs me."

"That's nice of you, Norman," Hannah complimented him. "Is it a very complicated procedure?"

"Not really, not if you know what you're doing. I'll just be there for backup and it shouldn't take more than a couple of hours. I'll be back in time for happy hour with the rest of the contestants. I'll see you later, Hannah."

Even though she knew it was silly, Hannah felt a sense of abandonment as she hung up on Norman. Mike was gone, Andrea had left, and now Norman was gone, too. She spent a few seconds wondering if she should go back to the kitchen to start another dessert, but she really didn't feel like baking something they probably wouldn't need anyway.

"Oh, well," she said with a sigh, walking down the hallway. Sally was upstairs by this time and there was absolutely no one she really needed to talk to. She glanced in as she passed Dick's bar, hoping that he was still there, but the lights were off and the bar was deserted.

She was about to turn on her heel and go back to the elevator when she saw Mike hurrying down the hall toward her.

"Wait a second, Hannah," he called out to her. "I need to talk to you."

At least someone needs me, Hannah thought, and then she smiled as she realized how pathetic that was.

"Hi, Mike," she said, waiting until he caught up to her.

"Where are you going, Hannah?"

Hannah gave a little shrug. "I wasn't really going anywhere. I was just wandering around, wondering what I should do."

"Lucky for me," Mike said, taking her arm. "Looks like I caught you at the perfect time. I need you, Hannah. Do you have your Murder Book with you?"

Hannah shook her head. "It's upstairs in the room."

"Then go up and get it. Dick told me that I can use the bar this afternoon for any interviews I have to do. You get your book and we'll go down there to talk about the case. I really need to compare notes with you, and I want your impression on a couple of things."

"Okay," Hannah said, surprised at how eager she was to talk to Mike.

"Good. Go get your Murder Book and I'll pour you a drink. White wine?"

Hannah shook her head. "Thanks, but no. If there's any lemonade, I'll take a glass of that."

"You got it," Mike said, pressing the elevator button and waiting until it arrived. "I'll go pour your lemonade, and I'll meet you in the bar."

Hannah unlocked the door to the room she shared

with Andrea and was surprised to see Rosa there, making her bed. "Hi, Rosa," she greeted Sally's head housekeeper.

"Hello, Hannah. I'll be through in less than ten minutes if you want to come back."

"No, that's okay," Hannah assured her. "I just came back to pick up my notebook. I'm going back downstairs again."

"Are you going to see Mike?" Rosa asked.

Hannah was more than slightly taken aback. "Actually, yes . . . I am. What makes you ask, Rosa?"

"I'm asking because it's almost two and Lily has an interview with Mike at two. Will you be there, Hannah?"

"I . . . I don't know." Hannah thought fast. "Would you like me to be there, Rosa?"

"Yes, please. I wanted to be there myself, and I asked Mike but he didn't want me there."

"Why did you want to be there?"

"Because Lily is my daughter."

Hannah was so surprised by this revelation, she opened her mouth and gasped. Then she quickly closed her mouth again. She knew she'd probably looked like a fish caught out of water and she was a bit embarrassed by her reaction. "Sorry, Rosa. You surprised me. Is Lily *really* your daughter?"

"If you're asking whether I'm her biological mother, the answer is no. Janette is Lily's biological mother, but I took care of Lily when she was a baby, and Janette had to go into treatment. Mr. Wally asked me to do this and I agreed because I love Lily. I didn't have any children of my own. I have worked all my life and I never married. I was Mr. Wally and Janette's housekeeper when Lily was born."

"I knew you took care of Lily. Janette mentioned that when Sally brought her to the kitchen."

"Yes. Because poor Janette got the disease you get after a baby is born."

"Are you talking about postpartum depression?"

"Yes! That's the name Mr. Wally called it. Janette had to go into the hospital, and she stayed there for a long time. Mr. Wally hired me to take care of Lily and he hired someone else to be the housekeeper."

Hannah took a moment to think about that. It put a new perspective on the Wallace family life. "So Janette was gone for the first few months of Lily's life?"

"She was gone for more than that. Janette didn't come home until Lily was six months old." Rosa stopped speaking and gave a deep sigh. "I did my best to teach her how to care for Lily. I really did. But Janette was still sick and she couldn't seem to understand what to do. I think it had something to do with the pills she was taking. They made her forget things like changing Lily's diaper and feeding her."

"What did you do when you realized that?" Hannah asked.

"I told Mr. Wally. I felt bad about it, but Janette just couldn't seem to take care of Lily. I don't think she wanted to take care of Lily. All she wanted to do was take more pills."

"What did Wally say when you told him?"

"He took Janette to a special doctor who said Janette needed a special treatment program and it could last for a while."

"And that's what happened?"

"Yes, and Mr. Wally asked me to stay and keep taking care of Lily."

"Was Janette upset that she had to go back for more treatment?"

"Oh, yes. She was very upset. Janette tried to stop taking the pills on her own, but it didn't work. And I know she wanted to take care of her baby. She just . . ." Rosa stopped speaking and sighed again. "She just couldn't get along without the pills."

"So Janette went back into treatment?"

"Yes. I told her not to worry, that I would stay to take care of Lily for as long as she wanted me to." Rosa stopped and clasped her hands together. "Perhaps I did wrong. I don't know. I did the best I could. Lily needed a mother and . . . and I think she thought that *I* was her mother."

"How long was Janette in treatment?"

"Over a year. Mr. Wally went to see her and so did I. I even took Lily with us once, but the doctors said that seeing her baby upset Janette too much."

"How old was Lily when Janette came back home from her treatment?"

"She came home every few months, but she always had to go back to the hospital again. I think it hurt her to see that Lily was growing up without her. She heard Lily call me Mama once, and that upset her so much she had to go back to the hospital that night. I did try to explain to Lily that I wasn't her mama, that Janette was, but she was too young to understand."

Hannah felt tears prickle behind her eyelids. Life must have been very confusing for baby Lily with Janette coming in and out of the house. Janette's good-byes when she had to leave Lily must have been tearful for everyone involved. "All these visits that ended badly must have been terribly hard on you, baby Lily, and Wally," she commented.

"Yes, and they were even harder on Janette," Rosa added. "She would cry when I packed her clothes and Mr. Wally carried her suitcase out to the car. But she knew she had to go back to the hospital."

"I'm sorry, Rosa. All this must have made you very sad."

"Oh, yes. It did. I would tell Janette not to worry, that I would take very good care of Lily. I promised Janette that I would treat Lily just like I would treat my own daughter if I had one."

"Did that make Janette feel any better?"

"I think so. She would smile and then she would hug me and tell me that I should be Lily's mother while she was gone."

There were tears in Rosa's eyes, and Hannah felt like crying, too. "How old was Lily when Janette managed to beat her addiction and come home for good?"

"Lily was just getting ready to go off to junior high when Janette came home to stay. It was a very happy day for all of us. That night, Janette told me that she would always regret that she hadn't been there to see Lily grow up. She said she wished she could do something to prove to Lily how much she loved her."

Hannah just shook her head. "What did you tell her, Rosa?"

"I said that Lily knew Janette loved her, but Janette began to cry and said that things could never be the same as if she'd been able to be home for her daughter. She said that someday she'd find something she could do to prove to Lily that she loved her."

Again, Hannah blinked back tears. "I'd better get going," she said, hurrying to the bedside table to snatch up her Murder Book. "I promised to meet Mike in Dick's bar." She headed for the door and then she stopped, remembering what Rosa had told her. "Don't worry about Lily, Rosa. When Mike interviews Lily, I will definitely be there."

Rosa looked a bit relieved, and she managed a shaky smile. "I wouldn't worry if Lonnie interviewed Lily. I know him and he is a . . . good person. But Mike is sometimes . . . I don't know the word, but he looks at everyone like he doesn't believe them and his mind is already made up."

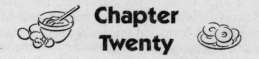

Chapter
Twenty

Hannah took a deep breath as she got off the elevator and walked down the hallway toward Dick's bar. There was no doubt in her mind that Rosa loved Lily. But did Rosa love Lily enough to kill, to try to keep her baby from marrying the wrong man? It was a definite possibility, and she had to explore the time line. The first thing to do was find out what hours Rosa had worked on the day that Sonny was killed. She'd check with the desk clerk to get that answer. And if Rosa had been able to go out on the lake that day, she had to find out when and how Rosa had managed to find Sonny and get out to the area where he'd been assassinated.

Hannah opened her notebook, took out a pen, and made a couple of quick notes about her conversation with Rosa. She chose words that would jog her memory so that she could write it up later.

The elevator gave a ding, and Hannah closed her Murder Book and slipped her pen back into her purse. It was time to go meet Mike and convince him that she had to be there when he and Lonnie interviewed Lily.

Even though it was only one floor, the elevator seemed to take forever to get down to the lobby. At last it reached ground level and the doors opened. Hannah stepped off, intending to stop at the desk in the lobby to ask the day clerk a couple of questions, but there were several people lined up there. Since she was already running late, she decided she'd catch the desk clerk later and headed straight for Dick's bar.

"Hi, Hannah," Mike greeted her as she came in. "Here's your lemonade. I was just about to call you to find out if you were coming down here."

"Sorry I'm late, but I ran into Rosa and we discussed a few things," she explained, sitting down in the chair Mike indicated and taking a big drink of her lemonade. "Thanks for pouring this, Mike. It's really good."

"I know. Dick makes the best lemonade. Did Michelle call you while you were upstairs?"

"No, why?"

"She wants all of us to meet her in the dining room tonight. It's Lonnie's birthday and she's having a little party for him."

Hannah was surprised. "I didn't know that it was Lonnie's birthday," she said.

"Yes, and since he's working out here with me, Michelle thought it would be nice for the family to get together here."

"You're invited, too, aren't you?"

"Of course. Michelle said we should all meet in the dining room at seven."

"Does Andrea know about it yet?"

Mike nodded. "Michelle called Andrea on her cell. She was on location, waiting for her client to arrive to see a house. Andrea said she'd call Norman and tell him about it."

"It sounds like fun," Hannah said, "but I didn't know that it was a birthday party, so I don't have a present for Lonnie."

"Michelle doesn't want presents. She says our company will be present enough for Lonnie."

"But I feel bad about not having anything. If I'd known sooner, I would have gotten him something."

"Michelle thought you'd say something like that, and she told me that if you wanted to do something, you should bake him some brownies."

"The same kind I baked for you?" Hannah asked, remembering the time she'd given Mike Jalapeno Brownies by way of retaliation because she was angry with him. But her plans had backfired because he'd tasted them and loved them.

"You'd better bake regular brownies," Mike told her. "I loved your Jalapeno Brownies, but they were too spicy for Lonnie. Lonnie loves chocolate."

"Then I'll bake my Double Fudge Brownies for him," Hannah said quickly. "Do you happen to know if Lonnie likes nuts?"

Mike took a moment to think about that. "I don't know about other nuts, but I know he's wild about Macadamia nuts. His dad and Bridget went to Hawaii for their last vacation, and they brought some back. Lonnie told me that they were the best nuts he'd ever had."

"I'll see if Sally has any, and if she does I'll throw them in."

"That'll be perfect," Mike told her. "Will you bake some for the rest of us, too?"

"That's no problem. Sally has an industrial oven and I can bake enough for everybody to have some."

"Great!" Mike looked pleased. "You said you talked to Rosa. Did she tell you anything interesting?"

"Not really," Hannah answered. "She did seem a bit worried about Lily and the fact that you were interviewing her again."

"Did she think I was too hard on Lily during the last interview?"

"I don't know for sure, but she wanted me to be there this time if that's all right with you."

"That's more than all right!" Mike looked a bit relieved. "I was just about to ask you if you'd sit in for me."

"For *you*?"

"Yeah. Lonnie's going to do this one alone. I've given him the lead on this investigation, and it's time he does some things without me."

"Oh," Hannah responded, mostly because she wasn't sure what else to say. "When is Lonnie's interview with Lily?"

"I'm not sure. Sally is clearing the conference room for them to use since the contestants will be coming from the nightly weigh-in and going to the bar for happy hour."

"That makes sense. Will you be in the bar?"

"No, I have to run out to the station to complete some paperwork. That's where Lonnie is now. We need to file all our notes before Bill gets back day after tomorrow."

Hannah frowned. "I thought you didn't have to submit your notes until after a case was closed."

"That's right . . . normally. But these are extenuating circumstances. And let me tell you, Hannah, I wish this case was closed right now!"

Hannah noticed the hard look on Mike's face. "Are you . . ." She stopped speaking to choose her words carefully. "Are you *uncertain* about this case?"

"Uncertain?" Mike gave a rueful laugh as he repeated the word she'd used. "I've got to get off this case, Hannah. I don't like what's happening."

"What *is* happening?" Hannah asked him.

"I'm not sure. It's just that I can't seem to get a handle on any of the suspects."

"Really?" Hannah was shocked. She'd never heard Mike talk like this before. "You once told me that after you'd interviewed all the suspects, you had a pretty good idea about who was guilty and who was innocent. Isn't that happening with this case?"

"No. It's different this time." Mike gave a little shrug. "I really don't care who's guilty and who's not. I just want to make somebody confess so the case is closed."

Hannah was puzzled. "But . . . you always said it was about having justice for the victim."

"I don't care enough this time to work effectively. And I've *always* worked effectively. I just want to intimidate someone into confessing so I don't have to think about this case any longer."

"I . . . I'm not sure what to say," Hannah admitted.

"It's like this, Hannah . . . I became a cop because I wanted to help people. I wanted to fight for justice for the victims, and make sure that whoever was guilty was punished. I always had empathy for people. I wanted to clear the suspects, to make sure they could go back to their lives. And I wanted to find the guilty person and make sure to lock him or her up to pay for their crime. You know me. And you know all that, don't you?"

"Yes, Mike. I *do* know that."

"I don't like this, Hannah. I feel like I'm losing my way. And even worse, I feel like I'm losing my . . . my humanity. And that's why I need your help on this case. I can't solve it on my own, Hannah. And I'm not sure that Lonnie can, either. Let's go over your notes, Hannah. Maybe it'll help."

Hannah's head was spinning as she went over her notes with Mike. She could tell that Mike's heart wasn't in it, even though he asked some good questions.

"Tell me something, Mike," she said, when they'd finished discussing the suspects.

"What do you want to know?"

"You always balked a little about my help on a case. And this time you're asking me to help you. Do you care who ends up solving Sonny's murder case?"

Mike took a full minute to think about that, and then he shook his head. "I don't think I do."

Hannah reached out to take his hand. "Is there anything I can do to help you?"

"I don't know. I've never, ever felt like this about a case before. I'm not sure what's happening to me. . . ."

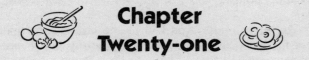

Chapter
Twenty-one

Hannah did her best to erase the worried expression from her face as she left the bar and walked down the hallway to the lobby. She'd assured Mike that, of course, she'd continue to work on the murder investigation, and solve the case if she could. But she wished there were something else she could do to help her friend. She loved Mike dearly, and it hurt her deeply to see him so troubled. Perhaps another law officer could help him, but she had no idea who . . .

"Stella!" she said aloud, as the answer came to her. She would call Stella at the Minneapolis Police Department to see if Stella could help.

Hannah was about to cross the lobby to the elevator when she noticed who was sitting behind the reservation desk. It was Craig, the night desk clerk.

"Craig!" she called out to greet him as she hurried over to talk to him. "What are you doing here this time of day?"

"I'm pulling a double shift again," Craig said with a smile.

"But . . . didn't you just get off work a few hours ago?"

"Yes, eight hours. And I went straight upstairs and went to sleep. Someone's bringing me my lunch in a few minutes and I don't have to do a thing except sit here, answer the phone, and answer any questions that the guests have for me."

"That sounds good," Hannah told him. "So it's working out well, now that you're staying here at the Inn?"

"It's perfect for me. I don't have to wash my clothes, shop for groceries, or commute back and forth. And since I'm not taking any classes right now, it works out great." Craig's smile grew even wider. "Not to mention the extra money. That's a big help for next year. If Sally keeps me on as night desk clerk and if I'm able to arrange all my classes in one block of time, I might be able to give up my apartment and live out here."

"That sounds great," Hannah said.

"It is great, especially the food. I don't have to shop for or cook anything. All I have to do is find out what they have in the kitchen and pick up the phone to order room service. It's a dream job, Hannah."

Hannah smiled. "And it sounds like Sally has found her dream employee."

"Thanks for the compliment, Hannah. Are you going upstairs to catch a nap now?"

Hannah considered that for a moment and then she shook her head. "No, I'm going to the kitchen. I have to bake brownies for Lonnie's birthday dinner tonight, and I might even start the cookies for tomorrow."

"So, do you need another cookie recipe?" Craig asked.

"I can always use cookie recipes. Do you have one?"

"Actually I do. My grandmother used to make me special cookies for my birthday."

"When is your birthday?"

"Not until two days after Christmas and that meant everyone combined my Christmas present with my birthday present. The only one who ever gave me a separate present for Christmas, and then a second present for my birthday, was Grandma."

"And she gave you cookies?"

"That's right. Grandma made special cookies from a recipe her mother had given her. They were made with potato chips, and I love potato chips!"

"Do you have the recipe with you?"

Craig nodded and reached inside the notebook he had out on the desk. "She wrote it out for me and I keep it in here. Do you want a copy?"

"I'd *love* a copy!" Hannah said quickly, flipping to a blank page in her Murder Book. "Is it okay if I stand here and copy it?"

"You don't have to do that! Why don't I make you a copy? We have a copy machine behind the desk that we use to make copies of credit cards and driver's licenses. It'll just take me a couple of seconds, and there's no one else behind you in line."

"That would be great!" Hannah said, watching as Craig reached into one of the pockets on the front of his notebook and took out a handwritten recipe card.

"Grandma's writing is pretty small, so I'll enlarge it for you."

Hannah stood in front of the desk and waited as Craig made a copy for her. She glanced at it and began to smile. "Your grandmother used cranberries and walnuts in the recipe?"

"That's right, but she told me that you could use any nut. I liked walnuts the most, so she used those."

"This looks like a great recipe," Hannah told him. "I think I'll make some this afternoon, and I'll save some for you."

"You're making some for me?" Craig was clearly surprised. "But . . . it's not my birthday."

"I know, but I want you to test them for me, and you can't do that if I don't give you some."

"Oh, boy!" Craig said, smiling widely. "I have Grandma's recipe book and they're all authentic recipes. I'll bring it out here next week when I go back to my apartment, and then you can read the recipe book and tell me which recipes you want me to copy for you."

"That would be wonderful," Hannah told him, carefully folding the recipe that he'd copied for her. "I'll be back in an hour or two, Craig. Will you still be here at the desk?"

"Yes, until six. Then I get a break for dinner."

"Then I'll see you in an hour or two. And thank you very much for the new recipe."

Hannah was smiling as she walked away from the desk. She loved trying new recipes, and this one promised to be interesting. Sally had all of the ingredients she needed for these cookies in the pantry of the kitchen. The only ingredient she might need to buy was Macadamia nuts for the brownies for Lonnie. She rounded the corner of the hallway and came very close to bumping into Rosa, who was coming from the opposite direction.

"Sorry, Rosa," she apologized. "I shouldn't have been reading over this recipe and walking at the same time."

Rosa gave a little laugh. "That's all right, Hannah. I wasn't reading anything, and I almost bumped into you, too."

Hannah thought fast. There were still a few questions she wanted to ask Rosa, but she really should get the brownies and cookies in the oven so she'd have time to take one of Dick and Sally's rowboats out on the lake to relax a bit before the interview with Lily. This day was turning out to have a shortage of hours in it, and Rosa's questions might have to wait unless . . .

"Would you like to go out on the lake with me later?" Hannah asked Sally's head housekeeper.

"The lake?" Rosa began to frown. "Thank you for asking me, Hannah, but . . . I don't go anywhere near the water."

It was a strange answer, and Hannah was puzzled. "Why not?"

"I am . . . do not know how to swim and . . . and the lake reminds me of my . . . my father."

"Your father?"

"Yes." Rosa looked so upset, Hannah was almost sorry she'd asked. "My father loved to fish and he took me along when I was a little girl. The wind came up, the boat tipped over, and . . . my father lifted me back in the boat, but he . . . he drowned."

"Oh, Rosa!" Hannah reached out to pat Rosa's shoulder. "What a terrible thing to happen!"

"Yes. I miss my father, Hannah. And I do not even walk on the dock. I don't go anywhere close to the lake. I can look at it through the window, but I never get any closer than that."

"Did it happen here at Eden Lake?"

Rosa shook her head. "No, but it is the same for all the lakes. They frighten me and I begin to cry."

"I'm sorry I made you sad by asking," Hannah apologized.

"No, it is all right, Hannah. It happened years ago, but I will always feel this way about lakes."

Hannah was thoughtful as she said goodbye to Rosa and walked on down the hallway. What Rosa had told her made one thing very clear. Rosa could not have taken a boat out on the lake to kill Sonny.

When Hannah got to the kitchen, she went straight to the pantry to gather up the ingredients for Lonnie's brownies and her new cookie recipe. The supplies in the pantry were neatly organized in groups, and as she inspected the nuts, she smiled when she spotted a large bag of roasted and salted Macadamia nuts, right next to the walnuts! She had been prepared to use a substitute for the Macadamia nuts, but Sally had saved her the trouble. Now she could use Lonnie's favorite nuts in his birthday brownies.

Once the ingredients were arranged in the order she needed them, Hannah propped open her Murder Book and crossed Rosa's name off her suspect list. Then, as she measured and added ingredients to her large mixing bowls, she thought about her three remaining suspects.

The first suspect who was still on Hannah's list was the suspect who always had a place on her list, the unidentified suspect with an unknown motive. Since she had no idea who that could be this time around, Hannah flipped the page to the next suspect. It was Lily, and Hannah read what she'd written about Lily.

Rosa had told Hannah the story of how Lily had found her fiancé in bed with the blonde and thrown her out in the hall without her clothes or her room key. It was obvious that Lily had been hopping mad, and that her fiancé had cheated on her was certainly enough to provide a motive for murder. There were other factors that also made Lily a prime suspect. Lily had been raised around fishing boats. She even towed her own boat behind her wherever she went. She had grown up working in her father's flagship sporting goods store, where she could have gained a working knowledge of firearms and how to use them. Lily was a perfect suspect.

Hannah added another ingredient to her mixing bowl and stirred it in. But was Lily the killer? Could she have followed her fiancé back to the far end of Eden Lake and cold-bloodedly murdered him? Could Lily have become so disillusioned that she'd execute the man she'd once promised to marry?

It was possible. Hannah knew that. A woman scorned could be very vindictive. She didn't want to believe that Lily, someone she liked, had actually murdered Sonny, but it was definitely possible.

The brownie batter was smelling so good, Hannah was tempted to dip her finger into the batter and try it. She barely managed to resist that urge, and hurried to prepare the pans for baking. She'd already set Sally's industrial oven for three hundred fifty degrees Fahrenheit, and it had come up to temperature.

Hannah divided the brownie batter between the pans as evenly as she could. Then she slipped them into the shelves in the oven, set the timer for the required baking time, and poured herself a cup of coffee before starting to mix up the cookies.

As she sipped the bracing brew, Hannah thought about Lily's life. It couldn't have been easy growing up without her mother. But how had it affected Lily? Did it cause her to lose her trust in the people she loved?

This kind of pseudo-psychological speculation was getting her nowhere, and Hannah knew it. She flipped to the third suspect in her book and read what she'd written about Lily's mother, Janette.

She'd written down the things that she learned when

Sally brought Janette to the kitchen. Andrea had written her results when she'd called the St. Cloud office of the sporting goods store. They'd told Andrea that Janette had worked for them on the day that Sonny was killed. That, in itself, should be enough to clear Janette, but Hannah decided to double-check. Rosa had mentioned that Janette often took the daily books home from various locations and worked on them in her home office. While it was undoubtedly true that Janette had worked for the St. Cloud store on the day that Sonny had been murdered, was Janette actually on location at the store itself?

A mouthwatering scent was beginning to come from the oven, and Hannah breathed it in and smiled. She could hardly wait to taste the brownies. She planned to frost them with her favorite fudge frosting once they cooled, but she could do that later. Right now she needed to mix up and bake the recipe Craig had given her. She mixed the cookie recipe while she was waiting for the brownies to come out of the oven. Once they had, she formed the cookies and filled the cookie sheets.

The cookie sheets went into the industrial oven. Then she sat down at the kitchen table to enjoy a rejuvenating cup of coffee. Once everything she'd made, baked, and frosted was finished and on the bakers rack, she was exhausted. Perhaps she should go out on the lake to recharge her batteries by getting some fresh air and sunshine.

POTATO CHIP AND CRANBERRY COOKIES

Preheat oven to 350 degrees F., rack in the middle position.

Ingredients:

1 and ½ cups salted, softened butter
(3 sticks, ¾ pound, 12 ounces)

1 and ½ cups white *(granulated)* sugar

2 egg yolks *(save the whites in a covered, refrigerated container and add them to scrambled eggs in the morning)*

2 teaspoons vanilla extract

2 and ½ cups all-purpose flour *(pack it down in the cup when you measure it)*

1 and ½ cups finely crushed salted potato chips *(measure AFTER crushing)*

1 and ½ cups finely chopped walnuts *(measure AFTER chopping)*

1 cup dried cranberries *(you can use the cherry flavored if you like)*

⅓ cup white *(granulated)* sugar for dipping

Approximately 5 dozen walnut or Maraschino cherry HALVES for decoration

Hannah's 1st Note: Use regular potato chips, the thin salty ones. Don't use baked chips, or rippled chips, or chips with the peels on, or kettle fried, or flavored, or anything that's supposed to be better for you than those wonderfully greasy, salty old-fashioned potato chips.

In a large mixing bowl, beat the butter, sugar, egg yolks, and vanilla until they're light and fluffy. *(You can do this by hand, but it's a lot easier with an electric mixer.)*

Add the flour in half-cup increments, mixing well after each addition.

Add the crushed potato chips, chopped walnuts, and dried cranberries. Mix until everything is well blended.

Form one-inch dough balls with your impeccably clean hands and place them on an UN-GREASED cookie sheet, 12 to a standard-size sheet.

Hannah's 2nd Note: Alternatively, you can line your cookie sheets with parchment paper.

Place the ⅓ cup white *(granulated)* sugar in a small bowl. *(You will use this for dipping the cookie dough balls.)*

Spray the flat bottom of a glass or the flat bottom of a metal spatula with Pam or other nonstick cooking spray.

Dip the cookie dough balls in the bowl with the sugar and roll them around until they're coated. Work with the balls one by one.

Hannah's 3rd Note: If you dip multiple balls in the sugar and try to roll them around, they may stick to each other.

Once you've placed your sugared dough balls on the cookie sheet, 12 to a standard-size sheet, dip the sprayed bottom of the glass or the metal spatula in the sugar to coat it. Then use the glass or the spatula to flatten the dough balls on the cookie sheet.

Hannah's 4th Note: You may have to dip the glass or the spatula in the sugar for each dough ball to keep it from sticking to the ball.

Bake your Potato Chip and Cranberry Cookies at 350 degrees F., for 10 to 12 minutes, or

until the cookies are starting to turn golden brown at the edges.

Take your cookies out of the oven and set the cookie sheets on cold stovetop burners or wire racks. Let them cool on the cookie sheet for 2 minutes and then remove them to wire racks to cool completely.

Yield: 5 to 6 dozen delicious cookies, depending on the size of your dough balls.

Serve these cookies with strong cups of coffee or icy cold glasses of milk. Everyone loves them down at The Cookie Jar, especially around Thanksgiving when everyone is in a cranberry mood.

Hannah's 5th Note: These cookies travel well and don't crumble as much as some other cookies. They are ideal for the kids to take to school with them.

Chapter Twenty-two

"Hello, Hannah!" Craig called out as she entered the lobby. "Did you bake my grandma's cookies yet?"

"I did, and they're cooling on the racks. I thought I'd go out on the lake for a little fresh air and then package some up for you when I come back."

"Perfect," Craig said, and then he turned to the person who had just entered the lobby. "Hello, Janette."

"Hello, Craig," Janette responded. "And hello, Hannah."

"Hello, Janette," Hannah said, smiling at the opportunity that had just landed in her lap. "I was just thinking about going out on the lake for a little fresh air. Would you like to go with me?"

"That sounds nice." Janette smiled at the thought. "Do you have a fishing boat?"

"No, but I'm sure Dick would let me borrow his again."

Janette shook her head. "There's no need for that. My boat is at the end of the dock. It's the newest Wally Boat. Would you like to go out on the lake with me?"

"That would be fun. I've been in Dick's boat and it was great. And my friend, Norman, rented a fishing boat from your husband's boat works. Your husband designs beautiful boats."

"Yes, he does. So did my father, and Wally learned about boat design from him. Come with me, Hannah. We'll take Wally's newest creation out for a spin to see if you like it."

"That sounds wonderful to me!" Hannah didn't hesitate to accept Janette's invitation. Of course she wanted to see the newest fishing boat that Wally had designed, but there was another even more important reason to go with Janette. It would give Hannah the perfect opportunity to ask Janette some probing questions in the privacy of her fishing boat. What could be better than that?

"I thought we'd go out to the water lily garden," Janette announced, once she'd gotten Hannah settled in the roomy seat next to her. "You'd better put on your seat belt, Hannah. The lake looks a little choppy this afternoon."

"Thanks for reminding me," Hannah said, reaching for her seat belt. "This one is a lot bigger than the one Norman rented."

"Was it a Wally Boat?" Janette asked, engaging the trolling motor and guiding the boat away from the dock.

"Yes, but it must have been an older one."

Janette gave a delighted laugh. "Of course it was! This is Wally's newest prototype. There aren't any boats exactly like this yet. They'll come off the assembly line sometime next month, but they won't be for sale until early next year."

"Then thank you for showing me what's coming next!" Hannah said, settling back to enjoy the ride out to the water lily garden. "I love it out there. The water lilies are beautiful."

"Yes, they are. And it's just in time for Lily's birthday later this month."

It took Hannah a moment to digest that fact. "That's wonderful. I wish I knew who planted it. I never knew that water lilies came in all those different colors."

"Neither did I. Wally hired the perfect aquatic specialist to design it."

"Your husband arranged for the water lily garden here on Eden Lake?"

"That's right. He chose ten of his favorite Minnesota fishing lakes and had them planted right after Lily was born. He told me he thought it would be a nice tribute for her, and I was so happy he'd thought of it."

"Your husband is a very nice man. I don't know if you noticed Barry Withers's face when he heard about his scholarship, but he was so grateful, he had tears in his eyes."

"Wally's always done nice things for people," Janette said. "I'm very glad my father talked me into marrying him."

"Didn't you want to marry Wally?"

"I hadn't really thought about it, before my father talked to me. I liked Wally. I used to do all my father's accounting work and I had coffee with Wally every time I went to the boat works. Wally was my father's foreman."

"You didn't think about Wally romantically?"

Janette shook her head. "It never occurred to me. I wasn't really interested in getting married even though I'd finished my college degree and I was certainly old enough. It was just . . ." She gave a little shrug. "It was just not on my list of things to do right then."

"Did you marry Wally because your father wanted you to?"

Janette took a moment to think about that. "You ask hard questions, Hannah. I probably did marry him because my father urged me to. Actually, I couldn't see any reason not to. Wally was perfect for me and he knew the family business. To tell you the truth, I think I married him mostly because there wasn't any good reason *not* to marry him."

Hannah was a bit confused. "So you didn't love Wally when you married him?"

"I'm not sure. I certainly liked him enough. I trusted my father when he said it would be good for me to marry Wally. It was almost like one of those arranged marriages. Sometimes they work out, and sometimes they don't."

"And yours worked out?"

"Heavens, yes! Wally and I have such similar interests. He loves the outdoors, and so do I. He hunts and fishes, and I enjoy hunting and fishing, too. We were actually a perfect match, even though I didn't realize it at the time."

"You love Wally now . . . don't you?" Hannah asked, knowing that she was treading on shaky ground.

Janette turned around and gave Hannah a questioning look. "Do you care?"

"Yes, but don't answer if it's too private a question. Sometimes things occur to me and I blurt them out without really meaning to."

Janette laughed. "So do I! I'll answer you, Hannah. Yes, I do love Wally, but . . . it's the quiet kind of love that's more like devotion. And now, let me ask you a personal question. Have you ever been in love?"

"Yes."

"Was it quiet? Or was it the kind of all-consuming, insane kind of love that drives people to stay with a lover when better sense would tell them to leave?"

Hannah knew she had to be honest. "It was the insane kind of love. And he left me."

"Then you're one of the lucky ones. Do you think you would have eventually left him?"

"I . . . don't know."

"Sometimes people just need a little push, a way to escape one of those crazy love relationships."

"Do you think Lily was in one of those relationships?"

"I know she was! You don't know how many times I told Lily that she should go for help, or . . . or at least take what they're calling a chill pill."

"A tranquilizer?"

"Something like that. They call them all sorts of things, but she needed something to deaden the effect that unhealthy emotion had on her. She was simply going crazy over Sonny's infidelities."

"It's heartbreaking to be in love with someone and know that person is cheating on you."

"Exactly right. You have to find a way to tamp down that craziness, or something dreadful will happen. I love Lily and she needed someone to help her. I tried, but she wouldn't listen to me. Lily thought she knew best, but she was so in love that it would have eventually killed her."

"But instead it killed Sonny and now Lily can recover?"

It took a moment, and then Janette's eyes narrowed. She stared at Hannah for several seconds, and then she reached into the pocket of her captain's chair and pulled out a gun. "You know . . . don't you, Hannah?!"

"What do you mean, Janette?" Hannah asked, stalling for time, even though she didn't know why. No one was coming to help her. Mike was busy writing his reports at the sheriff's station, Norman was at his dental clinic helping Doc Bennett do an implant, and Andrea was showing a house to a prospective buyer. The only person who knew where Janette had taken her was Craig, and he was probably upstairs in his room at the Inn, fast asleep.

"You know what I'm talking about, Hannah. You suspected all along that I killed Sonny, didn't you!"

"Actually . . . no, I didn't," Hannah told her. "I thought that perhaps Lily killed him."

"Lily?" Janette sounded perfectly astounded. "Lily is madly in love with Sonny. I told you that. She could never kill him. As a matter of fact, she planned to marry him next week! Right after she kicked that blonde bimbo out of their room, she called me to tell me her plans."

It was Hannah's turn to be astounded. "She wanted to marry him after that?"

"Oh, yes. He woke up right before she left that morning and they talked. He told her the only reason it had happened was because he missed her so much, and he was lonely."

"And Lily believed him?"

"Of course she did. Some women are silly that way. They always believe the men they love. Lily told me that she knew everything would be all right, as long as she married Sonny and went to every fishing tournament with him."

"But . . . how could she . . ." Hannah stopped speaking, remembering how she'd deluded herself into thinking that Ross had left her because *she'd* done something wrong.

"You're remembering your own experience, aren't you?" Janette asked.

"Yes."

"Tell me about it. I'm curious. I don't have to worry about Lily any longer. It'll take her a while to fall in love again, if she ever does. I'm just so glad that I could do something to help her. I love my daughter so much, and I've been searching for a way to prove it to her. Thank goodness I finally found it!"

Janette is insane, Hannah's mind told her. *Think of some way to keep her talking about herself. It could buy you some time.*

"You're right, Janette. I did have a very bad experience, but my feelings aren't important. I'm much more concerned about Lily."

"You are?" Janette was clearly surprised. "But you just met Lily, didn't you?"

"I did, but I liked her immediately. And thinking back about the way Sonny acted made me sad that Lily hadn't fallen in love with someone who was worthy of her."

"Exactly right!" Janette smiled. "What sort of man do you think would be right for my daughter?"

"I'm not sure, but I hope it would be someone like your husband. You seem very happy with him, Janette."

"I'm not sure happy is the right word. I'm content and that's good enough. Wally gives me everything I want. And he's taken care of me so well. He never blamed me for my addiction."

"I would hope not!" Hannah said, hoping that her voice had an inflection of truth. "It wasn't your fault, Janette. Many women suffer from postpartum depression after childbirth."

"That's what the doctors told me, but it didn't make it any easier. And I tried to stop taking the drugs, Hannah. I really did! It was just that I would get so depressed, and then the anxieties would plague me. I *had* to do something to keep myself from feeling that way."

"Of course you did," Hannah told her. "I've never experienced anything like that, but if I do, I'm sure I will feel exactly the same way."

"I was gone for so long," Janette said, sitting down in the captain's chair again. "I would beg to go home, but the doctors said I wasn't well enough yet, that I wasn't done with my treatment. They warned me that if I went home then, I'd get sick again and have to come back. I didn't want to go see my daughter, hold her in my arms, and then have to lose her all over again."

"It must have been heart-wrenching."

"It was! Every time, when I got back in the hospital, I'd vow to beat my addiction. I'd tell God that if I couldn't do it, He should take me right then and there, and not let me suffer."

"I'm sure that Lily missed you, every bit as much as you missed her," Hannah said, reaching down to make sure her cell phone was still recording their conversation. "But you did come home! And you're still home."

"Yes. Yes, I am. And I'm going to throw away the pills the minute I get back to the house. I don't want to go through this again, Hannah. I really don't. I want to be strong enough to get along without the drugs. I know I can do it this time, now that Sonny is dead and Lily is safe from living with a substance abuser."

"Do you think that Sonny was addicted to pills?" Hannah asked.

"No, but Sonny's addiction was just as dangerous. He couldn't stop drinking. Lily told me that. He promised her that if they got married he'd go into treatment, but he was weak-willed, Hannah. It never would have worked. He would have quit for a week or so and then he would have gone back to drinking again! I know how it works." Janette gave a resigned sigh. "I've been there."

"And you feel sure that treatment wouldn't have worked with Sonny?"

"That's right! He would have gone through treatment, come home, and fallen off the wagon so fast it would have taken a stopwatch to clock it! I couldn't let my daughter go through life the way that dear Wally did. Living with an addict is hell, Hannah. It's probably just as painful as *being* an addict. There was no way I could let Sonny put my sweet little girl through something like that!"

"So you killed Sonny to save Lily?"

"Exactly! I *had* to kill him before he hurt my daughter any more. You understand that, don't you?"

"I think I do understand," Hannah said.

"All right, then," Janette said, and she looked very determined. "Stand up, Hannah. I want you to look at the water lily garden. It's so lovely this time of year.

I'm going to kill you the same way I killed Sonny. I made him look at the water lily garden, too."

Janette stood up in front of her, and Hannah knew she had to use every trick in the book to keep Janette talking. A fishing boat was approaching them rapidly, and she needed to keep Janette from turning her head to spot it, so she said the first thing that popped into her mind. "Did Sonny think the water lily garden was beautiful?"

"What difference does *that* make?" Janette asked, and she sounded puzzled.

"I was just curious because I didn't think Sonny was the type of person to notice things like that."

"You're very observant, Hannah," Janette answered, "and you're right. Sonny didn't appreciate beautiful things like my daughter and he destroyed them." She paused for a moment and then she went on. "Look at the water lily garden, Hannah. I want your last sight to be of something beautiful."

"But you don't have to kill me, Janette." Hannah did her best to delay what seemed to be inevitable. "Everyone will understand that you *had* to kill Sonny to save your daughter."

"Maybe, but I don't want to take that chance. And you won't be able to tell anyone that I killed him, because the dead can't talk."

Hannah reached out for the side of the boat to brace herself. The fishing boat had accelerated and it was about to ram into them!

There was a loud crash as the fishing boat collided with them. Hannah was braced for the collision, but Janette was not. As she fought to keep her balance, Hannah reached out to grab the barrel of the gun and managed to wrench it out of Janette's hand. Janette was just beginning to recover when a fishing net smashed down over Janette's head and pulled her down to the floor of the boat.

"We're here!" a voice shouted as a patrol boat pulled up beside them. Lonnie held onto the side of Janette's boat and Mike leaped into it to cuff Janette.

Hannah sank back down in her seat. She was shaking, and she took several deep breaths to calm herself. She'd confronted another killer, and this time she'd come very close to losing her life. There was no doubt in Hannah's mind that if help hadn't arrived at exactly the right time, she would no longer be alive.

"Are you okay, Hannah?" Mike asked.

"I am now," Hannah replied. "How did you know where to find me?"

"Andrea came back from her showing and when she didn't find you in your room, she went looking for you," Mike explained. "She found your Murder Book in the kitchen with Janette Wallace's name at the top of your suspect page. After she called me, she talked to Craig, who told her you were going out to the water lily garden with Janette. He brought her out in a boat and left instructions for us to follow."

Hannah then looked over at her sister, who was still holding the handle of the fishing net and grinning broadly.

"I didn't forget!" Andrea told her. "I thought everything Dad told me to do for the little fish he caught was silly, but he taught me a useful skill after all!"

Hannah laughed. "Nice work, Andrea. This time you really netted a big one!"

Chapter
Twenty-four

That night they all had a double celebration. Of course they celebrated Lonnie's birthday, but they also celebrated closing Sonny's murder case. Janette was locked up in jail at the sheriff's station and everyone including Lonnie and Mike were at one of the big private tables in Sally's dining room.

Dinner had been excellent and they had toasted Lonnie with one of Dick's excellent champagnes. They were just leaning back in satisfaction when one of Sally's waiters had arrived with coffee for those who wanted it, and he took orders for after-dinner drinks for those who wanted them. Since Michelle had stipulated no presents, Hannah had decided to give Lonnie's brownies to Michelle to give to Lonnie later.

"It's almost time for Lonnie's special birthday dessert," Sally told them, arriving at their table. "It just came out of the oven and they're bringing it in two minutes. I hope you saved some room for dessert, Lonnie. It's something that has to be served right away so you can't take it home."

"I'm like Mike," Lonnie told her. "I can always find room for dessert. What is it, Sally?"

"It's Butterscotch Sundae Cake."

"Butterscotch?" Lonnie began to smile. "I *love* butterscotch!"

Sally smiled back. "I know. I called your mother to ask her your favorite flavors. She told me that butterscotch was number one on the list."

"It's number one on my list, too," Doc told Lonnie, and then he turned back to Sally. "What's a sundae cake? I've never heard of it before."

"You'll see because here it comes," Sally replied, gesturing toward the two waiters who'd just arrived with a dessert cart. "Ready?" she asked her waiters.

"Ready," one waiter replied, whisking the cover off a tray containing individual cakes in small aluminum pans.

Using potholders, Sally tipped one pan upside down over a dessert dish. She pressed down on the bottom of the pan and a cake popped out. She handed it to the second waiter, who used two forks to pull the bottom of the cake apart, and almost immediately the scent of hot butterscotch filled the air.

Lonnie began to smile, and his smile grew larger as the waiter put a scoop of vanilla ice cream in the center of the cake. "Oh, boy!" he said, accepting the dessert bowl. "I can hardly wait to taste this!"

"Don't wait," Sally told him. "It won't take long to unmold the rest of these and put on the ice cream. It's your birthday, Lonnie. You get to try yours first."

As Sally unmolded the cakes and the waiters pulled them apart and scooped on the ice cream, Lonnie took his first bite. "Incredible!" he said, looking positively rapturous.

It didn't take long for Sally and her waiters to serve the rest of the desserts, and soon identical smiles were on every face. Sally sent the two waiters back to the kitchen and they were replaced by another waiter, pushing another dessert cart with a large carafe of coffee for refills and the after-dinner drinks for those who'd ordered them.

"Just in case there's not enough dessert, I brought two other favorites of mine," Sally told them. "I'll sit down with you to have a cup of coffee and then I'll package up any of the other desserts you want to take home with you."

"What are the other desserts?" Michelle asked her.

"European Peach Cake and Apple School Pie."

"Is that Edna Fergusson's Apple School Pie?" Michelle asked.

"Yes, she gave me the recipe. It's great for buffets because you get more pieces than you would with a regular apple pie."

Lonnie turned to Sally. "Don't forget to package a slice of each one for me. I haven't had Apple School Pie since I graduated from high school."

"I'd like a slice of each one, too," Michelle said.

Hannah sat back and listened as Sally packed up the desserts and everyone gave their preferences. "Don't worry about the dessert cart, Sally," Hannah told her when Sally had finished packing the desserts. "When I leave, I'll wheel it back to the kitchen and put the leftovers in the walk-in cooler. That way Andrea and I can have some for breakfast when we come in early to bake."

The party broke up shortly after everyone had received their dessert care packages. Before Michelle left, Hannah pulled her aside. "What did you get Lonnie for his birthday? I'm dying to know."

"I'll tell you, but not until the work on your condo is finished. You'll find out then."

"Shall I stop by the bar and order drinks for us?" Norman asked when most of the crowd had left.

Hannah nodded. "Yes, but just lemonade for me. Carry the drinks to the lobby and I'll meet you there for a while."

When everyone was gone, Hannah went out with the dessert cart and wheeled it down the hallway to the kitchen. She had no sooner stashed the leftover desserts in the cooler when the kitchen door opened and Mike came in.

"Do you have a minute or two?" he asked. "I really need to talk to you, Hannah."

"Of course," Hannah agreed quickly. "What's on your mind, Mike?"

"I couldn't have solved that murder case, Hannah. And I'm not sure Lonnie could have, either. So I wanted to thank you for helping . . ." Mike stopped and shook his head. "*Helping* was the wrong word. I should have said thank you for solving the case by yourself, Hannah."

"You're welcome," Hannah said, realizing that he looked troubled. "Thank you for arriving when you did or I wouldn't be here tonight."

Mike gave a nod of acknowledgment. "I just came in to tell you that I plan to rethink my detective teams. I've talked to Rick about the new guy, and neither one of us think he's going to make it. He's really good at paperwork, though, and I think he'd be perfect as Bill's assistant."

"That makes sense. But if the new guy is Bill's assistant, Rick won't have a partner."

"Lonnie doesn't know it yet, but he's going to be

Rick's partner. A team of brothers would be good and they can take turns with the lead."

Hannah began to frown. "I agree that they'd make a good team since they get along so well, but who's going to partner with you?"

"Nobody."

Hannah was puzzled. "You mean . . . you're going to solve cases alone?"

"No. It'll take me a week or so to make sure that Lonnie and Rick will work well together and the new guy will be a good assistant for Bill. And then, if everything goes smoothly, I'm going to walk into Bill's office and tell him I quit."

BUTTERSCOTCH SUNDAE CAKES

Preheat oven to 500 *(that's five hundred)* degrees F., rack in the middle position.

Ingredients:

8 ounces salted butter *(2 sticks, ½ pound)*

8 ounces *(by weight)* butterscotch chips *(1 and ⅓ cups . . . I used Nestlé)*

4 egg yolks *(save the whites in a covered bowl in the refrigerator to add to scrambled eggs, or to make Forgotten Cookies)*

5 whole eggs

1 cup white *(granulated)* sugar

1 cup all-purpose flour *(pack it down when you measure it)*

Vanilla or chocolate ice cream to finish the dish

Before you start, select the pans you want to use from the following suggestions:

You can use large-size deep muffin cups to bake these cakes, but if your muffin pan is solid and the cups don't lift out, you'll have to remove each cake by using two soup spoons as pincers to pry them out. Each batch will make 9 cakes if you use large muffin tins.

A popover pan is also a possibility, especially the kind with removable cups, but you'll have to run a knife around the inside of each cup and tip it over to remove the cake. Each batch will make 6 cakes in large, deep popover cups.

You can also use individual soufflé cups, but again, you'll have to use two soup spoons or run a knife around the inside of the dish to remove the cakes from the soufflé cups. Each batch will make 8 small or 6 large soufflé dish cakes.

Hannah's 1st Note: I've found it's a lot easier to use the disposable foil pot pie tins you can buy at the grocery store. With those, you can just flip them over on the dessert plate or bowl, press down on the foil bottoms with a potholder, and the cakes will pop right out. (Yes, the pot pie tins are an extra expense, but removing the cakes will be much faster and the tins can be washed several times by hand or in the dishwasher before you'll have to throw them away.)

To Prepare Your Pans:

Grease and flour the insides of the pans you've chosen. As an alternative to that messy

procedure, you can spray them with nonstick BAKING spray *(the kind with flour added)*. If you decide to use the baking spray, spray the insides once, let them dry for a few minutes, and then spray them again before you fill them with the cake batter.

To Make the Cake Batter:

Place the salted butter and the butterscotch chips in a medium-size microwave-safe bowl.

Heat the contents on HIGH for 90 seconds.

Take the bowl out of the microwave *(use potholders or oven mitts)* and attempt to stir the contents smooth. *(Butterscotch chips sometimes maintain their shape even when they're melted.)* If you're able to stir the mixture smooth, set the bowl on the kitchen counter and let it cool. If the chips aren't melted yet, microwave them in 20-second intervals on HIGH until they are, and again, stir smooth.

When you're able to cup your hands around the bowl comfortably and you don't think the mixture is so hot it could cook the eggs, separate 4 eggs into yolks and whites. Refrigerate

the whites, and add the yolks to the bowl with the butter and chip mixture.

Stir the bowl thoroughly.

Next add the 5 whole eggs, one at a time, to your mixing bowl, stirring after each egg is added. Mix until everything is well combined.

Sprinkle in the white sugar and stir it in thoroughly.

Mix in the flour and stir until the batter is smooth and lump-free.

Transfer the batter to the pans you've selected, dividing it as evenly as you can between the pans.

Then get out a baking sheet with sides and line it with foil to serve as a drip pan, transfer the baking dishes to the drip pan, and check your oven to make sure it's risen to the proper temperature.

If your oven is ready, slide the baking dishes and drip pan into the oven and bake at 500 degrees F. for **EXACTLY** 7 minutes, no more and no less. Do this by setting a timer, and don't

open the oven door while your Butterscotch Sundae Cakes are baking.

Hannah's 2ⁿᵈ Note: The success of this recipe depends on high, even heat for a limited amount of time. Your goal is to bake the outside of the cakes and leave the inside filled with hot molten butterscotch.

When your timer rings, immediately take the cakes and drip pan out of the oven, and place it on a wire rack or cold stovetop burner.

Hannah's 3ʳᵈ Note: The center of each cake will jiggle a bit when you remove them from the oven, but don't worry. That's the way they're supposed to be.

Once the cakes are on the wire rack, give them 2 minutes to set up slightly. Then use potholders to upend them on dessert plates or bowls.

Use two forks to pull apart the tops to expose the sauce in the center.

Carry these cakes to the table and use a small ice-cream scoop to drop scoops of vanilla or chocolate ice cream in the center of the rich molten center.

Serve with plenty of strong hot coffee or icy glasses of milk and accept your guests' rave reviews.

Yield: 9 cakes in large muffin tins, 6 cakes in large removable popover tins, 8 cakes in small soufflé dishes, 6 cakes in large soufflé dishes, or 6 cakes in disposable foil pot pie tins.

If you have leftover cakes, they can be reheated in the microwave, but they won't be the same. They'll still be tasty, but the centers will turn into moist cake.

Hannah's 4th Note: If I want my dessert to be extra fancy, I make up some of the berry sauce I use on pancakes and create little designs around the edges of large dessert plates and set the cakes in the middle of the plate.

EUROPEAN PEACH CAKE

Preheat oven to 350 degrees F., rack in the middle position.

Ingredients:

4 cups frozen sliced peaches
3 eggs
1 cup vegetable oil
2 cups white *(granulated)* sugar
1 teaspoon vanilla extract
1 teaspoon baking soda
2 teaspoons cinnamon
½ teaspoon salt
2 cups all-purpose flour *(pack it down in the cup when you measure it)*

Directions:

Before you start assembling the cake, measure out 4 cups of frozen peach slices and put them in a large strainer to thaw. While you're waiting for your peach slices to thaw, prepare your cake pan.

Prepare your pan by spraying a 9-inch by 13-inch cake pan with Pam or another nonstick cooking spray.

When the peach slices are thawed, pat them dry with several thicknesses of paper towels.

Arrange the peach slices on the bottom of the prepared cake pan the way you'd do for a pie.

Hannah's Note: You can mix the cake batter by hand, or with an electric mixer. We use our electric mixer down at The Cookie Jar because we quadruple the recipe and make four European Peach Cakes at once.

In a medium-sized bowl, whisk the eggs with the oil until they're thick. Then add the sugar and beat it in.

Mix in the vanilla, baking soda, cinnamon, and salt. Mix thoroughly.

Add the flour in one-cup increments, mixing after each cup.

Scrape down the sides of the bowl. Then give the batter a final stir with a spoon.

Use a mixing spoon to drop the batter over the peaches in spoonfuls. *(**Don't worry if the batter doesn't completely cover the peach slices—the batter will spread out during baking.**)*

Bake at 350 degrees F. for 60 minutes. (*Mine took only 50 minutes.*)

Cool the cake in the pan on a cold stovetop burner or on a wire rack.

Frosting Ingredients:

8-ounce package softened cream cheese (*the brick kind, not the whipped*)

2 teaspoons vanilla extract

1 Tablespoon lemon juice (*freshly squeezed is best of course*)

4 Tablespoons (*½ stick, 2 ounces*) salted butter, melted

2 cups confectioners (*powdered*) sugar (*no need to sift unless it's got big lumps*)

If you forgot to take the cream cheese out of the refrigerator to soften naturally, unwrap it, place it in a microwave-safe bowl, and heat it for 20 seconds on HIGH. Check it to see if it's soft. If it's not, give it another 15 seconds or so, until it is.

Stir the vanilla extract into your cream cheese. Then add the lemon juice and the melted butter. Mix until it's smooth.

Beat in the powdered sugar in half-cup increments, checking the consistency after each addition. You don't want the frosting too runny, but you also want it thicker than a drizzle frosting.

When the mixture is the proper consistency, stop adding powdered sugar. *(I didn't add all of mine.)*

This frosting is very forgiving. If it's too runny, add more powdered sugar. If it's too stiff, add a little more lemon juice or vanilla.

Yield: At least 12 squares of delicious cake, depending on the size you cut the pieces.

APPLE SCHOOL PIE

Preheat oven to 350 degrees F., rack in the middle position.

Hannah's 1st Note: I adapted this pie from Edna Fergusson's recipe. Edna is the head cook for the Lake Eden School District and she makes this pie for school lunches. This recipe makes Apple School Pie in a 9-inch by 13-inch cake pan.

The Crust:

Either buy a package of your favorite 2-crust frozen pie crusts, or make your favorite 2-crust pie pastry recipe.

Ingredients for the Filling:

1 and ½ cups white *(granulated)* sugar

½ cup all-purpose flour *(pack it down in the cup when you measure it)*

¼ teaspoon ground nutmeg *(freshly ground is best, of course)*

1 teaspoon cinnamon *(if it's been sitting in your cupboard for years, buy some new cinnamon!)*

¼ teaspoon ground cardamom

½ teaspoon salt
4 cups cored, sliced, and peeled apples
   (*I used a combination of green Granny
   Smith and Fuji or Gala apples*)
2 teaspoons lemon juice

FOR LATER:

1 stick cold salted butter (*½ cup,
   4 ounces, ¼ pound*)

Ingredients for the French Crumble:

1 cup all-purpose flour (*pack it down in
   the cup when you measure it*)
½ cup cold salted butter (*1 stick,
   ¼ pound*)
½ cup brown sugar (*pack it down in the
   cup when you measure it*)

Directions for the Crust:

If you bought frozen pie pastry, thaw it according to the package directions. If you made your own pie pastry, it's all ready to go.

Prepare your crust by rolling it out in a sheet large enough to cover the bottom of your 9-inch

by 13-inch cake pan and extend up the sides. *(This piece of pie crust should be approximately 17 inches long and 15 inches wide.)*

Fit your pie crust in the pan and press it down so it's snug. Then set the pastry-lined cake pan aside and make your pie filling.

Directions for the Filling:

Mix the white sugar, flour, spices, and salt together in a bowl.

Prepare the apples by coring them, peeling them, and slicing them into a large bowl. Toss the apple slices with the lemon juice. *(Just dump on the lemon juice and use your impeccably clean fingers to toss the apple slices—it's easier.)*

Sprinkle the contents of the small bowl with the dry ingredients on top of the apples and toss them to coat the apple slices. *(Again, use your impeccably clean fingers.)*

Put the coated apple slices in the pan with the pie crust. You can arrange them symmetrically if you like, or just dump them in as best you can. There will probably be some leftover dry

ingredients at the bottom of the bowl. Just sprinkle those on top of the apple slices in the cake pan.

Here Comes the Butter:

Cut the cold butter into 4 pieces and then cut those pieces in half. Place the pieces on top of the apples just as if you were dotting the apples with butter.

Directions for the French Crumble:

Sprinkle the flour into the bowl of a food processor with the steel blade attached.

Cut the stick of cold butter into 8 pieces and add them to the bowl.

Sprinkle the brown sugar over the butter.

Process with the steel blade in an on-and-off motion until the resulting mixture is in uniform small pieces.

Remove the mixture from the food processor and place it in a bowl.

Sprinkle handfuls of the French Crumble over the sliced apples in the pan.

Bake your Apple School Pie at 350 degrees F. for 50 minutes, or until the French Crumble is golden brown on top.

Hannah's 2nd Note: To test for doneness, insert the tip of a sharp knife into the pie. If it pierces the apple slices, your pie is done.

When your pie is done, remove from the oven and place your baked Apple School Pie on a cold stovetop burner or a wire rack. Let it cool for 30 minutes to an hour before you cut it into squares.

Yield: At least 16 squares of mouthwatering pie that can be easily removed from the pan with a metal spatula and placed in dessert bowls (or in the dessert section of a school lunch tray).

Hannah's 3rd Note: If you serve this pie warm, you can top it with sweetened whipped cream or vanilla ice cream. It's delicious that way!

Index of Recipes

(By Order of Appearance)

Please turn the page for a special bonus recipe from *New York Times* bestselling author Joanne Fluke!

ANYTIME PARTY COOKIES

Preheat oven to 325 degrees F., rack in the middle position.

1 package (**16-ounce**) Kool-Aid powder
   (*Don't get the kind with sugar or sugar substitute added.*)
1 and ⅔ cups white (*granulated*) sugar
1 and ¼ cups softened, salted butter
   (*2 and ½ sticks, 10 ounces*)
2 large eggs, beaten (*just whip them up in a glass with a fork*)
½ teaspoon salt
1 teaspoon baking soda
3 cups all-purpose flour (*pack it down in the cup when you measure it*)
½ cup white (*granulated*) sugar in a bowl

Hannah's 1st Note: When Brandi, the Hannah fan who gave me this recipe, makes these cookies, she rolls them out on a floured board and uses cookie cutters. Rolled cookies take more time than other types of cookies, so I modified Brandi's recipe.

Combine the Kool-Aid with the one and two-thirds cups of granulated sugar.

Add the softened butter and mix until everything is nice and fluffy.

Add the beaten eggs and mix well.

Mix in the salt and the baking soda. Make sure they're well incorporated.

Add the flour in half-cup increments, mixing after each addition.

Spray cookie sheets with Pam or another nonstick cooking spray. Alternatively, you can line the cookie sheets with parchment paper.

Roll dough balls one inch in diameter with your impeccably clean hands. *(You could also use a 2-teaspoon scooper to do this.)*

Roll the cookie balls in the bowl of white sugar to coat them. Work with one dough ball at a time so they won't stick together.

Place the sugar-coated cookie dough balls on the cookie sheet, 12 to a standard-size sheet.

Bake the Anytime Party Cookies at 325 degrees F. for 10 to 12 minutes *(mine took 11 minutes)* or until they're just beginning to turn golden around the edges. Do not overbake.

Remove the cookies from the oven and set the cookie sheets on cold stovetop burners or wire racks. Cool the cookies for no more than a minute or two, and then use a metal spatula to move them to a wire rack to cool completely.

Yield: Approximately 6 dozen pretty and unusual cookies that kids and adults will adore, especially if you tell them that they're made with Kool-Aid.

Hannah's 2nd Note: Since Kool-Aid powder comes in many flavors and colors, you can make these for special occasions and holidays. For instance, if you're hosting a football party and the Minnesota Vikings are playing, make one batch with grape Kool-Aid and one batch with lemonade Kool-Aid so you can serve cookies with the home team colors. You can make green (lime Kool-Aid) cookies for St. Patrick's Day, orange cookies for Halloween, and red and green cookies for Christmas. Valentine cookies can be made with pink lemonade Kool-Aid, cherry Kool-Aid, or strawberry Kool-Aid.

Baking Conversion Chart

These conversions are approximate, but they'll work just fine for Hannah Swensen's recipes.

VOLUME

U.S.	*Metric*
½ teaspoon	2 milliliters
1 teaspoon	5 milliliters
1 Tablespoon	15 milliliters
¼ cup	50 milliliters

⅓ cup	75 milliliters
½ cup	125 milliliters
¾ cup	175 milliliters
1 cup	¼ liter

WEIGHT

U.S.	Metric
1 ounce	28 grams
1 pound	454 grams

OVEN TEMPERATURE

Degrees Fahrenheit	Degrees Centigrade	British (Regulo) Gas Mark
325 degrees F.	165 degrees C.	3
350 degrees F.	175 degrees C.	4
375 degrees F.	190 degrees C.	5

Note: Hannah's rectangular sheet cake pan, 9 inches by 13 inches, is approximately 23 centimeters by 32.5 centimeters.

Hi, it's Jo Fluke,

Thank you for buying the paperback edition of *Caramel Pecan Roll Murder*. This book is about my favorite pastime, fishing.

I used to go fishing with my dad, although I think he preferred to take one of his friends with him, since I always cringed every time he baited his hook with an angleworm. I also wanted Dad to take any fish that I happened to catch off the hook and let it go. You can imagine my surprise when I went fishing with a fishing expert and I caught the biggest fish! If you go to my website, joannefluke.com, you can see a much younger me and my trophy fish.

The next Hannah Swensen Mystery, *Pink Lemonade Cake Murder*, which I'm writing right now, centers around my favorite spectator sport, baseball. I'm also working on finding cookie recipes for cookies that Hannah will sell during the big baseball tournament that's being held in Lake Eden, Minnesota. Of course there's a murder, and this time it's Hannah's mother, Delores, who discovers the body and asks Hannah to help with the investigation.

Another project I'm working on is to make pink lemonade cookies and test them. The Cookie Jar is going to sell these cookies in the concession stand throughout the tournament. Since I'd prefer not to use artificial food coloring in my baked goods, I'm going to try to use grenadine to color the cookies pink. Grenadine is made from pomegranate juice, and it is quite dark red in color, so I hope I won't have to use much of it in the recipe to make these cookies pink.

Speaking of concessions, here's my real life "snack shack" story. When my son, John, was in Little League,

I was **banished** to the concession stand, which was in a small concrete bunker sitting *a long, long way away from home plate* at the ballpark. This banishment happened because I kept offering the umpire unsolicited advice on calling balls and strikes. This pattern repeated itself for as long as John played baseball. Strange to say, no one ever offered **me** an umpire job.

Thanks again for reading *Caramel Pecan Roll Murder*. If anyone has some family recipes you'd like to see in *Pink Lemonade Cake Murder*, you can contact us at my Facebook page (Joanne Fluke Author), or reach out to us at my website which is https://joannefluke.com.